Rank

D.R. GRAHAM

Harper*Impulse* an imprint of
HarperCollins*Publishers* Ltd
1 London Bridge Street
London SE1 9GF

www.harpercollins.co.uk

A Paperback Original 2015

First published in Great Britain in ebook format by Harper*Impulse* 2015

A catalogue record for this book is
available from the British Library

ISBN: 9780008142346

Automatically produced by Atomik ePublisher from Easypress

D.R. GRAHAM

My name is Danielle. I write both Young Adult and New Adult novels under the author name D.R. Graham. I am a child and family therapist and prior to going into private practice I worked as a social worker with at-risk youth. The novels I write deal with issues relevant to young and new adults in love, transition, or crisis. I am also an award winning columnist for the Richmond News. I currently live in Vancouver, British Columbia with my husband.

http://www.drgrahambooks.com/

https://www.facebook.com/drgrahambooks?fref=ts

@drgrahambooks

*For my Papa and every other cowboy
with heart and try.*

Chapter 1

Facial wounds bleed a lot. I was reminded of that the day my brother Cole had a bad wreck at a rodeo in Lethbridge, Alberta. In the finals on Sunday, Cole drew a rank bull that hadn't been ridden in fourteen outs. It was a nasty looking black and white Brahman that rammed its skull into the rail I was standing on.

After Cole eased down into the chute, I took a deep breath, pulled the bull rope, and slapped his back three times for good luck — just the way our dad used to. Cole secured his hat and tucked his chin before he nodded. The gate opened and the bull exploded into the arena with the same force as the adrenaline that shot through me.

A country song blared over the loud speakers, and the crowd cheered as the bull cranked out a succession of belly rolls and shivers. The bull turned into Cole's hand and side bucked before it whipped around and reared back. He spun twice more to the left, then jumped and kicked with a twist that should have knocked my brother off. When the eight-second buzzer went, Cole reached down with his free hand, jerked his riding hand out of his rope, dismounted, and landed on his feet. He didn't even lose his hat.

Once I was sure he was all right, I hollered, "Yeah! Now, that's how it's done."

The other guys working the chutes gave me high fives before

I leaned over the railing to slap palms with a bullfighter named Mutt. A score of ninety flashed up on the board, Cole tipped his hat to the crowd and then fanned the bull as it ran by him.

Mutt chuckled. "There he goes, stirring the pot again."

"Shit," I mumbled and checked over my shoulder. The last thing we needed was Cole disrespecting the stock contractor. I jumped down from the chute and jogged over to where Cole was making his way down the front row signing a bunch of programs and one particularly nice cleavage. Saving him from himself was getting to be a full time job.

"Okay, tone it down," I said as I pushed him under the grand-stand where it reeked of stale beer and popcorn.

"Why? I'm just giving them their money's worth."

"Yeah, well, Ron Miller looks like he's about to stroke out because you fanned one of his best bulls. Stop showboating."

He shrugged his shoulders dismissively. "I get sponsors by working the crowd, not by kissing a stock contractor's ass. I couldn't care less about Ron Miller."

"You should care because —"

We both stopped talking and watched the last rider leave the chute. He needed a ninety-two to beat Cole, which wasn't likely, but it was possible.

After the eight-second buzzer went, Cole mumbled, "Damn. That was a good ride." His cocky attitude faded and he chewed on the leather cuff of his glove as he stared at the scoreboard, waiting. Eventually, an eighty-seven flashed up on the screen. "Yeah, baby!" Cole shouted and thrust his arms victoriously into the air. "Looks like we're eating steaks tonight." He jumped on my back, hooting and hollering.

I pushed him off. Partly because he was acting like a fool, and partly because I was too tired to celebrate. "Just go get your buckle and the cheque so we can get the hell out of here."

"Aw, come on, Billy. I want to party and the girls here are half-decent. Let's stay a while." He shoved my chest. "I bet that new barrel racer you've been staring at all weekend wouldn't mind if you hung around tonight. What's her name again?"

Although I knew exactly who he meant, I wanted to sleep in my own bed for the first time in two weeks, not hang around while he got rowdy. "I don't know who you're talking about." I pulled my hat down at the front and spit tobacco juice on the dirt near his boot.

He laughed at my avoidance tactic. "Yes, you do. The blonde with the white horse and the tight ass."

I removed my hat and ran my fingers through my hair as I scanned the crowd, looking for her. "I'm tired. I just want to go home."

"You're too young to be tired. And if you don't rope that filly, I will."

"Don't," I warned.

He smiled at my reaction. "I knew you liked her. Let's stay."

"No. My credit card is maxed out. Meet me at the truck. We're going home."

"Come on, Billy. We can stay for a while," he begged as the rodeo queen approached us. Her hair was three feet wide, her make-up was three inches thick, and there were so many sequins on her outfit it was almost blinding.

She smiled in a flirty way and linked her arm around Cole's elbow. "Come on, darling. It's time for the presentation."

He winked at me, confident that he had convinced me to stay. Then he walked away with her.

"I'll leave without you," I shouted.

He waved jokingly without looking back. The cloud of perfume the rodeo queen likely wore to kill the stench of bullshit lingered — even after they were already at the champion's platform near the grandstand. Watching someone else take home the buckle and prize money was never something that sat well with me, not even when it was my own brother. When they announced Cole's name, I wandered out past the back pens. My phone rang as I reached

3

the lot where the participants all parked and camped. I wasn't in the mood to talk, but she would keep calling if I didn't answer.

"Hey, Ma."

"Is your brother still in one piece?"

"Yeah. He won. How did your doctor's appointment go?"

"Fine. Everything is about the same. How are you doing, hon?"

A combination of frustration and exhaustion shot out of my mouth when I exhaled. "I think it's time for me to stop touring and get back to making a regular paycheque."

"Cole won't take his medications or eat properly if you're not there with him. You know that."

"He's a big boy. I can't spend the rest of my life following around after him picking up his messes."

I knew she had hoped if I stayed on the tour for Cole's sake I would eventually start riding again. It didn't work. The more I hung around without competing, the more I hated it. I spit tobacco juice onto the grass.

"Are you chewing?"

"No, Ma'am."

"Don't lie to me."

"I ain't chewing." I paced around on the grass looking out at the horizon. She didn't say anything else, so I said, "Don't worry. I'll take care of him. We'll see you tonight."

She sighed. "Okay. Love you."

"Love you, too." I hung up and turned to drop the tailgate of my truck, because Cole knew I wouldn't leave without him, and I knew he was going to take forever milking the win.

Shae-Lynn Roberts, the youngest daughter of the best chuckwagon racer in the country, leaned against the side of the truck wearing jeans and a white tank top. She'd already brushed out the curls she wore for competition and had her hair pulled back into a ponytail.

"Hey Billy. How's your mom?"

"Good." I sat down on the tailgate and reached for a bottle of beer out of the cooler that I kept in the back.

"Is she still having falls?"

I glanced at her, not really wanting to get into it, but I knew she was asking because she actually cared, so I said, "Yeah. The doctor wants her to start using a wheelchair."

"A wheelchair. Really? I didn't realize she'd gotten that bad." Her eyebrows angled together in a genuinely sympathetic expression that made me uncomfortable.

I shot back some beer, then changed the subject to steer her away from the topic of my mom's health. "You took first place again."

"Yes, I did." She paused for a second, aware that I had purposefully avoided the other conversation. After some contemplation she must have decided to let me get away with it. "Did you see my run?"

"Yup. It was good. It could have been better though."

She propped her right hand on her hip and cocked her head to the side. "Really? What do you think I did wrong?"

"Harley dropped his shoulder at the first barrel."

"Oh, and you're an expert on barrel racing now?"

I chuckled. "You know how much rodeo I've watched in my life." I flicked the beer cap into the cooler. "You don't have to take my advice if you don't want to. I don't care."

Her expression changed again and she raised her eyebrow as if she thought I was being rude. "Aren't you going to offer me a drink?"

"You ain't old enough to drink."

She made a sweeping gesture with her arm to remind me where we were. "The drinking age in Alberta is eighteen."

I tipped the bottle back and drank almost half. She stared at me, still waiting for me to offer. "What?" I asked.

"What do you mean what? I turned eighteen last month. You and Cole ate some of the cake my mom made. Remember?"

I remembered the cake, but I didn't remember it was for her birthday. Even if I did know it was for her birthday, I would have sworn she was no more than sixteen. I didn't care enough to argue with her, though, so I reached into the cooler and handed her a beer.

"Thanks." She sat down beside me on the tailgate, eager to give it a go. I watched as she unsuccessfully tried to twist the cap off. She struggled with it for a while then, in frustration, handed it to me to do it for her.

"I thought barrel racers were supposed to be highly toned athletes." I grinned to tease her as I popped the cap off and gave the bottle back to her.

She made a mocking expression to let me know she didn't find my joke particularly funny. Then her gaze shifted to my mouth. She squished up her nose in disgust and asked, "How do you drink with tobacco in your mouth?"

"Practice," I said, then tipped the bottle back to prove it.

About as impressed with my tobacco chewing as my mom was, she said, "Nice," in a sarcastic tone. She stared at her beer bottle for a while as if she was building up the courage. After a quick breath she took a swig. It was obvious from the way her face twisted that she didn't like the taste. She tried another sip and gagged as if she wanted to spit it out.

I laughed. "You want me to finish that?"

She gladly handed it to me. "It tastes like piss."

"You have to drink enough to forget about how bad it tastes. Eventually, if you drink more, you start to forget about how bad everything else is too."

She shuddered and cringed, still disgusted.

My attention shifted to Tawnie Lang, the barrel racer with the white horse and the tight ass. She was exiting the grandstand with all the other spectators. As she passed by, she removed the sky blue hat that matched the colour of her eyes and ran her fingers through her long blonde hair. It was about then that I decided it wouldn't be so bad if we stayed one more night. I finished my beer and watched her walk towards her horse trailer.

"Oh my God. Stop drooling at the new girl," Shae-Lynn mumbled.

I turned my head to spit tobacco juice on the grass. "I wasn't drooling at nothing and she's not new. I remember her from the junior circuit."

"Oh." Shae-Lynn glanced over her shoulder in a casual way to check Tawnie out. "Where's she been since?"

I shrugged, wondering the same thing, then started on her beer. The cherry flavour of her lipgloss on the mouth of the bottle balanced out the horrible flavour of the tobacco that was getting washed down my throat.

Shae-Lynn faced me again and asked, "Why don't you ask her out?"

"Who says I want to?"

"It's obvious. You've been staring at her all weekend."

I looked over at Tawnie, then back at Shae-Lynn. "I don't date girls on the circuit."

"Wouldn't you make an exception for the right girl?"

I shrugged noncommittally. It wasn't likely. I couldn't imagine myself being interested in dating anyone, especially someone who didn't live in the same city as I did. Shae-Lynn stopped asking questions and we sat quietly for a long time. The colours of the sky changed and deepened as the sun got lower. I watched the spectators file out of the grandstand. Shae-Lynn seemed to be staring at her fingernails, thinking.

She sighed. "You sure don't talk all that much since what happened to your dad."

That change in topic came out of nowhere, and it caught me off guard since everyone else on the circuit acted as if they would rather cut out their tongue than talk to Cole or me about our dad. "I'm talking to you right now, ain't I?"

"Sort of. Not really." She swung her feet back and forth. "Do you think it might help if you talked about what happened?"

"Help what?"

"You."

"I don't need help," I said, but it came out less convincing than

7

I meant it to.

"You haven't ridden since it happened."

Uncomfortable with the fact that she could obviously see right through me, I spit on the grass and opened another beer to ignore her statement.

She watched me for a while, then said, "The sooner you get back on a bull, the better."

I exhaled and scratched the back of my neck. I'd been thinking about officially leaving rodeo, but hadn't even told Cole yet. Since she was hell bent on talking about my issues, I decided to practice telling her to test how Cole might react. "I'm thinking about retiring."

"What? Why? You're ranked number one." She nearly shrieked — confirmation that Cole was going to lose his shit when I told him.

"I don't want to still be doing this when I'm fifty years old. I'd rather get out now and finish university while I'm still young."

"You can do both. The season doesn't interfere with classes."

"I also have to work and take care of my mom."

She nodded as if she understood that part. She also frowned because she knew as well as I did that I was grasping for excuses. Unfortunately, instead of letting it go, she pressed on, "That's nice of you to take care of your mom, but you don't need to stop riding. You shouldn't quit because your dad's wreck spooked you."

Frustrated that she was forcing me to go to an emotional place I didn't want to visit, I threw the empties in the cooler. "I'm not spooked. I just don't want to waste my life touring around shit-hole towns with a bunch of hicks abusing my body and killing my liver just to end up dead in the ring one day."

"What happened to your dad was a fluke accident. The best way to get over the fear is to get back on."

"Listen, Shae-Lynn, I ain't scared. And I ain't interested in talking about it with you."

Not impressed with my harsh tone, she hopped off the tailgate

8

and glared at me. "You don't have to be an asshole about it. And how many times do I have to ask you to call me Shae? You know I don't like it when you add the Lynn."

"It's your name."

"It makes me sound hick."

I mimicked her sweeping arm gesture to present to her the grass parking lot in the middle of nowhere that was filled with campers and horse trailers. "I hate to break it to you, but this is about as hick as it gets."

"I'm not hick. Call me Shae." She took two strides, then turned and pointed at me as she walked backwards. "And, by the way, if you decide that you want Tawnie Lang to date you, you should probably know that chewing tobacco is repulsive and *ain't* isn't a word. Quitting the rodeo isn't going to make you any less hick, Billy Ray Ryan." She spun back around and stormed off towards her family's motorhome.

Tyson Wiese, my brother's best friend, stole a beer out of the cooler. He grinned at Shae-Lynn's feistiness as he watched her go. He had a shiner from knocking the bull's behind when he got thrown, so he squinted at me with one open eye. "I came over to get you. Cole just took a crazy bet."

"What?" Not again. "For how much?"

"Double or nothing on his prize money."

"God damn it. What's he planning on doing?"

Tyson chuckled as if he didn't quite believe it himself. "Ride Freight Train for eight."

Damn it. That's crazy. "When?"

"Right now. Before it gets dark."

I hopped off the tailgate and jogged to the chutes cursing Cole under my breath the entire way. The grandstand was empty and there were only a few people still lingering around the edge of the arena fence. The bull named Freight Train was already loaded into a chute and Cole was taping his riding glove around his wrist. I shoved his shoulder. "What do you think you're doing?"

"Ron Miller is going to pay me two thousand dollars to ride one bull."

"You mean you're going to pay Ron Miller two thousand dollars to get tossed off one bull. I already told Mom you won."

"I got this. Don't worry about it." He put his black mouthguard in, then smiled with the excessive confidence he always had right before he did something stupid.

"Freight Train is rank. He ain't never been ridden. He put four guys in the hospital."

Cole slapped my shoulder, undeterred. "You worry too much. Besides, I already shook the man's hand. Let's go make some money."

The only thing harder than getting Cole to do something he didn't want to do was stopping him from doing something he did want to do. It was usually easier to just let him do whatever he wanted and clean up the pieces afterwards. I gave up trying to argue sense into him, shook my head in frustration, and followed him. We both climbed the chute. It was already loaded with the black hairy mass of bovine muscle that was trying to shoulder its way through the metal rails. "Where are the bullfighters?" I asked.

"This is between me and the bull," Cole said, believing the delusion that he was invincible.

"Jesus, you're going to get killed."

Without even pausing to let it the danger sink in, Cole eased himself down onto Freight Train's back. "Just pull my rope."

"Cole, come on. This is crazy."

He looked at me with a wild expression in his eyes and smiled. "You'll be thanking me later."

"I doubt it." I relented and pushed my boot against Freight Train's shoulder to get him to move over. Then I pulled the rope as tight as I could. For some reason, what Shae-Lynn had said hadn't left my head. It was bugging me. "Hey, does it sound hick when I say *ain't*?"

Cole looked at me and laughed at the random question. "Yeah, you sound hick. What does that have to do with anything?"

"Nothing. I don't know. Never mind. Just don't get yourself killed."

When Cole finished weaving the loose end of the rope through his fingers, I slapped him three times on his back. He tucked his chin and nodded.

It was that fast — no time to think about it meant no time to change his mind. That was how Cole did everything. Tyson opened the gate to the chute, Ron pulled the flank strap, and Freight Train exploded straight up in the air. His back hoof just missed catching my face and instead, sprayed me with a sloppy mix of dirt and manure.

"Whoo!" Tyson hollered. "Hold on, Cole. Yeah, baby."

I glanced at the clock then back at my brother. It started out as a good ride. Then Freight Train sucked back and rolled his belly. Cole slid off balance. Since all he had to do was hold on, it didn't matter that it wasn't pretty.

When the buzzer rang at eight seconds, I exhaled and turned to smile smugly at Ron Miller. He threw down his hat in frustration, but his expression immediately changed. Without hesitating, he leapt over the fence into the arena. I spun around to see what he was doing.

Cole was hung up.

He was dangling by one arm and Freight Train was slamming him against the fence. I couldn't move. My mouth went dry and my knees felt as if they were going to give out on me. The image of my dad being hung up flashed. Then I blinked and saw Cole again.

Adrenaline flooded into my veins and snapped me out of my paralysis. I jumped into the arena and ran across the thick soft dirt to the other side, but Freight Train changed directions before I got there. Ron and Tyson headed him off and made him veer away from the fence. Cole was still hung up bad and his legs were getting trampled.

Three more cowboys jumped into the arena, but none of us

had experience bullfighting. Tyson was able to release the flank strap. All that did was stop Freight Train from kicking. He was still sprinting around and ramming Cole against the rails. Freight Train came straight at me, so I waved my arms to slow him down. He dropped his head and tried to horn me. I lunged to the left, but he got close enough to brush me. I wasn't wearing a protective vest, so he tore right through my shirt. When he circled around, I jumped on his shoulder and tried to free Cole's bull rope. It wasn't possible to get a good hold of it because the bull jerked in the other direction and took Cole with him, knocking me on my ass.

Before I had a chance to stand up, a palomino horse blew by me at full speed. It was Shae-Lynn riding bareback on her barrel horse, Harley. She raced around the arena to catch up with Freight Train. It took her a few attempts before she was able to manoeuvre her horse to nudge the bull off the rails and pull in alongside. She tried to lift Cole by his Kevlar vest, but she wasn't strong enough to carry his weight. Cole attempted to kick his leg up onto Harley. His arm hung like it was made of string, though, and he couldn't get enough momentum. When his legs dropped back down, they got stomped by Harley's hind hoof.

"Free the rope," I yelled.

Shae-Lynn leaned over and tugged at the rope, but Freight Train turned into Harley and the jolt almost threw her over the front. Tyson stepped into the sight of the bull to redirect him back. Shae-Lynn repositioned, then tugged at the rope one more time.

Cole fell to the ground.

"Get up," I shouted as I ran towards where he was lying in the dirt. "Get up!"

Freight Train spun around to face Cole. He snorted air out of his nostrils and hoofed the dirt getting ready to charge. Cole scrambled to his feet and hurried to the fence with his right arm flopping around. I ran between Cole and Freight Train. My plan was to distract him long enough to let Cole get to the fence — I distracted him all right — he forgot all about Cole and stampeded full speed at me before ramming his massive rock hard head into my ribcage.

He lifted his snout and launched me into the air.

After what seemed like eight seconds, gravity kicked in and the ground finally collided with my body, crushing all the air out of my lungs. My throat made a horrible sucking sound, but it didn't actually pull any oxygen into my chest. I couldn't move.

"Get up, Billy!" Cole shouted, frantic.

As I stared up at the darkening sky, waiting for my body to start working, I thought about how they were all going to mock me for getting freight trained by Freight Train. I was about to laugh at the irony when a huge hoof slammed down on my cheek.

The left side of my face shattered like a dropped teacup.

At first, everything was silent except for my pulse thudding through my ears. The side of my face felt warm and wet. When my hearing came back, I heard shouting. Then Shae-Lynn whimpered. "Oh my God. Billy." She knelt beside me and her hand wrapped around mine. "Call an ambulance," she shouted over her shoulder. "Somebody call an ambulance!" She started crying.

"Oh shit," Cole said. I couldn't see him. I could only hear the panic in his voice. "Shit. Shit. Shit. Ty, it's bad. He's hurt bad. It looks bad." He kept his distance because he couldn't handle the sight of blood. He never could handle it, but it got worse after we both witnessed our dad get killed. "How bad is it?"

Tyson crouched on my other side and took an objective look at my face. He scrunched his nose. "He's conscious, but his face is caved in."

"Oh my God. There's so much blood," Shae-Lynn whispered. "We have to get him to the hospital."

"Shae-Lynn," I tried to say, but it sounded like a gurgle because blood was pooled in the back of my throat. I turned my head and coughed out thick dark red liquid. Unfortunately, the coughing made the broken bones shift around. It hurt real bad. I stuck my fingers in my mouth and pulled out the tobacco along with three teeth. I squeezed her hand. "Make sure he takes his medication."

"I will. Don't even worry about anything."

"That —" I had to cough again. "— was dangerous."

"Yes, it was. You're an idiot."

I tried to smile, but moving my face made blood gush out. "Not me. You."

"Don't talk, Billy. Oh God. Cole, do something. He's bleeding to death."

"Where's the damn ambulance?" Cole yelled.

That was the last thing I remembered.

Chapter 2

Seven Months Later

I was in my room at my mom's house messing around on my guitar when Cole opened the door without knocking. He leaned his shoulder on the doorframe and grinned like he was up to something.

"What?"

"Is your bag packed?"

I shook my head, knowing he was going to launch into another round of high school peer pressure tactics to convince me to go on tour with him. "I told you, I'm not going. My vision is still messed up in my left eye."

He dismissed my excuse with a wave. "The doctor said you're fine to ride."

"I think I know if my eye is too messed up to ride better than she does."

His posture collapsed into phase two of his pressure tactic, which was whining. "Come on, Billy. Don't be a buzz kill. What are you going to do around here until September?"

"Work and take care of Mom," I said for likely the millionth time since I told him I was retiring.

"We can hire a nurse for Mom. You'll make more money on the circuit than what you make at the bar." Logic. Phase three.

"Hank Pollert needs a ranch hand. I told him I could help out during the week, so I'll be making two incomes."

"You don't want to be stuck here all summer doing that."

"You're going to be stuck here all summer doing that, too. Your shoulder is still too messed up to ride."

"What are you talking about?" He patted his arm roughly to prove its sturdiness. "It's as good as new."

"You haven't even been on a bull in seven months."

"I've been training."

"On saddle Broncs and mechanical barrels. It's not the same. You'll go one go on a bull and be done for the season."

"Come with me just this weekend. If I get tossed, you can come home. If I win, we go on tour."

Bargaining. That was an angle he hadn't tried before. He must have been getting desperate. Not interested, I strummed the strings of my guitar. "No thanks."

"You weren't really serious about quitting, were you?"

"I didn't quit. I retired."

"You can't retire. You're twenty years old."

"Well, I did."

"Fine. You can be retired from bull riding and still come with me as my manager."

"No."

"I got a surprise for you. Look out the window." He held the curtain back and pointed like a hyper kid.

When it became obvious that he wasn't going to leave unless I looked, I rested my guitar on the bed and walked over to the window. Attached to the back of his pickup was a silver camper.

"Do you like it? It's got a kitchen and a shower." He went on to list a bunch of top of the line features like a salesman.

"I don't care if it's got a porch and an attic. I'm not going." I sat on the edge of the bed and unfolded the paperwork from the University of Saskatchewan that I needed to fill out in order to reapply. "I have responsibilities. I can't dick around on the circuit anymore."

"I promise not to get killed."

The image of Dad getting stomped flashed through my mind and made my muscles flinch involuntarily. "Yeah, well, that could happen whether I go with you or not."

"Then what's the problem?"

I looked up and stared at him for a while. I hated being he reason for the disappointed look on his face, but I had to stand my ground. "I don't want to go."

"I need to do this, Billy. I can't end my career like that, and I need you there or I won't be able to get back up on a bull."

And, the guilt trip. Final phase. "Nobody cares if you quit."

"I do, and Dad would have."

I scoffed. "Look where that attitude got him."

Cole wandered across the room and stared out the window at the trailer for a while. Honouring Dad's memory was not an angle that was going to work on me and Cole obviously realized it because he sat on the edge of my desk and tried another approach. "Rodeo is all I know. It's the only place I feel like myself."

"I'm not stopping you from going. I just don't want to go."

"Who's going to make sure I take my medications?"

I shook my head, not buying his useless act.

"Who's going to remind me to fill out my forms?"

I propped the guitar back on my lap and practiced my picking, hoping he would eventually run out of arguments and go.

"Who's going to drag me out of bed and make me scrambled eggs every morning?"

"You can learn to do all that for yourself."

He pushed his hat back and propped his hands on his knees. He thought for a while then he said, "Mom will worry herself sick if you aren't there watching over me."

I sighed and rolled my eyes, wishing he would just give up and leave without me.

"Rodeo is all you know, too."

"Yeah, well that's the problem. I don't want to spend my whole life riding bulls and have nothing to show for it but a trunk full of buckles, arthritis, and an empty bank account. Besides, Mom needs my help around here."

"Come on, Billy. Just one more season. I need someone to slap my back for good luck. I can't do that myself."

Shit. I blinked hard then glared at him. Although it was nearly impossible to talk him into or out of things, with me, it was just a matter of finding the one thing that struck a chord. The back slap was that thing. The satisfied grin on his face made it clear that he knew he'd finally stumbled onto the bullseye.

"Please, Billy."

I rubbed my face and gave in. "Fine, one weekend, but if you wreck, I'm not going to help you."

"Deal." He clapped his hands.

"I must be crazy," I mumbled as I got up to pack my bag.

"We both know I'm the crazy one." He tackled me onto the bed and wrapped his arms around me in a headlock to rough-house. "Ooh, look at that. My baby brother is still stronger than me. Maybe we'll get you back on a bull yet."

I twisted out of his hold and pinned him across the throat. "I will always be stronger than you, but I'm never getting on a bull again."

"You lost your nerve?"

"No. One of us has to stay alive to take care of Mom. We both know it isn't going to be you."

"You got that right." He pushed his hands into my chest and launched me off him. "Stop horsing around and get your bag packed. That shiny new camper is pulling out of here in exactly eight seconds."

When we arrived at the rodeo, we parked in the participants' area and the smell of dust, diesel, and dung descended on us. Cole inhaled and smiled the same way he did when he took the first puff of a cigarette after quitting for a while. "Smells like home, don't it?" He swatted my shoulder and then headed over to the indoor arena to sign in.

I kicked at the dirt, raised my face up to the warm sunshine, and inhaled. It did kind of feel like home. I put my hat on and followed Cole to the arena. A girl with long strawberry red hair was practicing barrels on a palomino horse. I leaned my elbows on the rail and watched. Her turns were the tightest I'd ever seen and then she let it rip home.

"Damn," I said to Cole. "That girl is going to give Shae-Lynn a run for her money."

"That is Shae, you idiot."

I squinted and tried to make out her face. She looked different. It was definitely Harley, though. "Has her hair always been red?" I asked, confused why I hadn't noticed that before.

"I don't know," he replied, not actually caring. "I'll be right back."

I nodded to acknowledge I heard him, but I was more focused on Shae-Lynn walking Harley around to cool him down. I was pretty sure her hair used to be dirty blonde or light brown. I couldn't remember for some reason. When she noticed me, I tipped my hat. She smiled and waved, but then frowned and turned to walk him in the opposite direction.

"Hey, Cole," a girl behind me said.

I looked over my shoulder. Cole wasn't around. Tawnie was smiling at me. "Uh, Cole's signing in. I'm his brother, Billy."

"Oh, sorry. You look alike." She held out her hand to shake mine. "Nice to meet you. I'm Tawnie Lang." She bit the corner of her bottom lip and slid her hands in her back pockets, which made her top stretch across her chest and the fabric gape between the buttons. "Actually, who am I kidding? I knew you were Cole's brother. I was just looking for an excuse to come over and introduce myself."

"You don't need an excuse. Nice to meet you, Tawnie."

She smiled and relaxed. "Which event are you competing in

19

this weekend?"

"I'm not competing. I don't ride anymore."

She moved in next to me to lean her elbows on the rail. She smelled like wild lavender. Up close, she was even prettier. "Do you know anything about barrel racing?" she asked without actually looking at me.

"A little."

"Something hasn't been quite right with my timing on Willow lately. Will you watch my run and tell me how my form is?" She turned her head and looked right into my eyes in a sexy way that she likely knew had an effect on men. It had been so long since the last time I saw her, I had forgotten how strong the attraction was.

I couldn't quite remember the question, but I knew whatever it was, I was okay with it. "Sure."

She touched my arm flirtatiously before she climbed the fence and walked over to where her horse was tethered. Shae-Lynn looked over at me one more time before exiting the arena with Harley following behind. Tawnie warmed up for a while, then lined up to do a practice run. Cole walked over and leaned on the fence next to me to watch. It was an ugly run. Willow stumbled twice and Tawnie almost lost her stirrup on the last barrel. She loped home and circled at a trot. She stopped in front of us. "See what I mean? What do you think I'm doing wrong?"

Cole stood up straight and said, "Time to retire her." He walked away.

Tawnie's eyebrows angled. "What's Cole talking about?"

"Your horse is favouring her front left leg."

"Like a sprain?"

"No. She's probably done."

"But she's only seven years old." Tawnie's face tightened as if she was on the verge of crying. I looked around to see if anyone else was watching. Seeing girls cry was one of my least favourite things in the world. Being the reason why they were crying was pretty much the only thing worse. Not that I hadn't made my fair share of girls cry. I just felt horrible doing it.

"I could be wrong. You should check with the vet," I said to make her feel better.

"Even if it's just a sprain, I can't ride her this weekend. Damn it." She dismounted. "I already paid for the hotel and I'm going to lose my entry fee too."

"You could borrow a horse."

The tears she'd been holding back made their way through her eyelashes. She wiped the back of her hand across her cheeks. "Do you know someone who has one?"

I stared down at the dirt to avoid making eye contact. Her sniffling was hard to ignore though. "I could talk to Ron Miller."

"Would you?"

I nodded, although I wasn't exactly sure why I had offered in the first place.

"Thanks, Billy. Let me know if he has anything." She waved with a big smile on her face before she walked Willow back to the arena opening. Her hips swayed with purpose as if she knew I was watching.

Damn it. A pretty girl cries and next thing I know I'm checking on getting a horse for her. Idiot. I wandered outside and over to the back pens. Ron was talking to a couple of guys, but he excused himself when he saw me. He walked over to shake my hand. "The face is looking good, Billy. How are you feeling?" He bent over and adjusted a gate hinge.

"A bit of a vision problem in one eye, but can't complain. Thanks." I tipped my hat back and scanned the pens. "Do you have any quarter horses that can run the barrels?"

He stood upright and adjusted his hat, always interested in talking business. "I've got a couple back home and one mare here. My daughter trained her, but she's never competed."

"Tawnie Lang needs a horse for the weekend. Her horse came up lame."

"Ten thousand dollars."

I laughed. "I don't want to buy her. I was hoping Tawnie could just borrow her, show her off for you."

"Nope. I don't want her getting injured."

"I doubt Tawnie can afford to buy her. She was upset about losing her entry fee."

"Then I guess I can't help you."

I shouldn't have cared. All I had to do was go back and tell Tawnie he didn't have anything for her to borrow. Losing her entry fee wasn't that big of a deal. On the other hand, if Ron gave me a good deal, I could buy the horse, let Tawnie show her off, and sell her for a profit. "How old is she?"

Ron smiled and tilted his hat up, glad that I was interested enough to not let it go. "Four."

If the horse was fast, I'd be able to flip her before the weekend was over. If she was slow, I'd be paying for board until I found a sucker to buy her. Tawnie wasn't as good of a rider as Shae-Lynn and there was a possibility she wouldn't show off the horse's full potential. I decided to negotiate a backup plan, so I wouldn't get stuck with a horse I couldn't sell. "Seven thousand, but I want to see her run in competition first. If Tawnie wins on her, I'll buy her."

"If Tawnie doesn't win?"

"Consider it a loaner."

He took his hat off and scratched his head. He took his time thinking, which was obviously his negotiation style. "She must be some girl. You can have your trial run, but I want eight thousand if she wins."

"Deal." I shook his hand. "And it's not about a girl. It's business."

"Sure. Sure." He smiled knowingly. "You want to see the horse?"

Damn. Maybe it was about the girl. If it had really been about reselling the horse for a profit, I would have thought to check her out first. Shaking my head because I couldn't believe I'd just done something so Cole-like, I said, "Yeah, that would probably be a good idea."

We walked over to a paddock and he put a bay quarter horse

on a lead. He walked her around so I could watch her gait and then he brought her close. I ran my hand over her spine and down her legs. She was a nice horse.

"What's her name?"

"Stella."

I checked her teeth and looked at her face. "Hey, Stella. Are you fast?"

She bobbed her head up and down as if she understood me. Ron laughed. "I taught her to do that." He gave her a pat and handed me the lead. "You better hope your brother wins so you can pay for her."

"Yeah, don't worry about it," I said, although I was worried about it. I led Stella over to the parking lot and wandered around until I found Tawnie's truck and trailer. She was bent over wrapping Willow's leg. "Hey, I got you something."

She spun around and her expression transitioned between shock and joy. "Oh, she's gorgeous."

"Her name's Stella. Ron said you can use her for the weekend."

Tawnie bounded over and launched herself at me. She wrapped her arms around my neck and knocked my hat off in the process. "Thanks, Billy." Before I had a chance to register the fact that she was hugging me, she stopped, and lunged over to pick my hat up off the ground. "Sorry." She brushed it lightly and handed it back to me.

I held it in my hands and watched as she inspected Stella. The smile on her face made her even more beautiful. Knowing that I put that smile on her face felt pretty good.

"I'm going to go see if the barrels are still set up," she said excitedly. "If I can get some arena time, do you want to come over and watch?"

"Sure."

"What's your phone number? I'll text you if I can get a run."

I told her my number and watched her type it into her phone. "Thank you so much."

I put my hat back on and tipped the brim at her. "Don't mention it."

She led Stella across the field towards the arena. I watched her hair sway across her back for a while, then headed over to our trailer to wait for her text. Shae-Lynn's family motorhome was parked next to us and she was standing near her horse trailer, brushing Harley.

"Hey," I said.

She stood up, but kept brushing. "Hi. I thought you were quitting the rodeo in order to pursue non-redneck careers."

"Retired, not quit. Cole convinced me to come along for this weekend only. It's his first ride back since his shoulder injury."

"I'm sure it didn't take too much convincing to get you to tag along. You were literally born at a rodeo."

"Only because my dad and all his buddies, including your dad, were too drunk to drive my mom to the hospital."

She smiled at the memory of our dads retelling that story every chance they got, then her expression turned more serious. "It won't be easy to get it out of your blood."

"I don't even miss it." I leaned in and gently tugged her braid. "You changed your hair."

"Yeah." She seemed unsure whether I was teasing her.

"It looks good."

Her cheeks blushed as she tucked a few flyaways behind her ear. "Thanks."

I studied her face for a while. "Is something else different too?"

She shrugged one shoulder. "No. I'm the same as I've always been." Her big green eyes shifted to meet my stare.

There was something different about her, but I couldn't put my finger on it. "Is your mom inside?"

"No. She's touring with my dad. It's just Lee-Anne and me."

"Your dad agreed to let his daughters' tour around on this circuit without chaperones?"

"He doesn't know. He thinks we're back in Calgary."

I chuckled and shook my head, wondering how that was going to go when he found out and the shit hit the fan. "That's probably not a good idea with all these cowboys around."

"What difference does it make if we're home by ourselves with a bunch of ranch hands, or on the circuit by ourselves with a bunch of rodeo cowboys?"

"He can fire his ranch hands for messing with either of you."

She seemed surprised that I even had an opinion on the subject. "We're not kids anymore. We can take care of ourselves."

I watched her for a while, still trying to figure out what was different about her. "That was a good practice run you had earlier."

She smiled, maybe from the compliment I gave her, or maybe from the memory of the last conversation we had when I gave her barrel racing advice. "Someone told me Harley was dropping his shoulder on the first barrel. My times have been improving since I corrected it."

"Hmm. Do you always take other people's advice?"

"Only if they're right."

"You're welcome," I said, kind of cocky.

Her eyes darted over to connect with mine and she seemed like she was going to say something sassy about my arrogance, but instead she said, "You look different."

"Yeah, they had to reconstruct my cheek and jaw bone."

She nodded her approval. "You look good."

I laughed. "What does that mean? Are you saying that the bull kicked the ugly out of me?"

"No." She snuck one more glance, then went back to grooming. "You look more like your dad."

She was the only person who wasn't afraid to talk about my dad around me. It seemed strange to hear her do it so casually, but for some reason I didn't mind it coming from her. I pushed my hat back and watched her pick Harley's front left hoof. "Hey, I don't know if Cole ever thanked you, but I want to thank you for what you did."

She stood and leaned against Harley's neck to give him a hug. "You don't need to thank me. I'm just glad you're both okay now." She slid her hand over Harley's coat and ran her fingers through his mane. "How much school did you miss?"

"Two terms."

"Are you planning on going back?"

I nodded, although I hadn't handed in the forms to reapply after my medical leave of absence. "What have you been doing since I saw you last?" I asked.

"I took some music theory and sports psychology courses at the University of Calgary."

"Great. You'll be able to diagnose me when you finish your degree."

She laughed. "I think I can already do that."

"Really? You think you've got me all figured out?"

"Yeah, I do." She threw the hoof pick in the grooming tray. "I think I have your brother figured out too."

"I doubt that. There's a whole team of professionals who haven't been able to figure him out." I turned out of habit as if I was going to spit.

Her eyebrows angled together, and she tilted her head when I didn't actually spit. "You're not chewing tobacco."

"I quit."

"Really?" She sounded legitimately surprised.

"Yeah, some girl told me it was repulsive."

She laughed, and seemed a bit smug that I took her advice. "Have you quit saying *ain't* too?"

"Only hicks say *ain't*."

She rested her cheek against Harley's cheek as she massaged his neck. "Do you always take other people's advice?"

Usually, no. I gave Harley a pat, wondering why I had taken her comments about me being hick to heart. I didn't have an explanation, but she was waiting for me to respond, so I stole her comment from before. "Only if they're right."

I meant for it to be funny, but it didn't make her laugh. It seemed to make her get lost in thought. Her sister Lee-Anne bounced up and shoved me in the shoulder to interrupt. "Billy Ray Ryan, did you really buy a barrel horse for Tawnie Lang?"

Shae-Lynn frowned and ducked under the rope to brush Harley's other side. I glanced at Lee-Anne. "Who told you that?"

"Who didn't tell me that? Everybody's gossiping."

"There's nothing to gossip about. Tawnie's just trying her out for the weekend. If she doesn't win, Stella goes back to Ron."

"So, if she wins, you're going to buy the horse?"

I pulled the brim of my hat down and kicked at the dirt. "Well, I have to."

Shae-Lynn threw the brush in the grooming tray and walked behind the horse trailer where I couldn't see her. Lee-Anne shook her head in a consolatory way as if she thought I was the stupidest person on the planet. My phone buzzed with a text. It was from Tawnie.

"I have to go." I stepped around Harley to see where Shae-Lynn went. She wasn't around. "Tell your sister I said bye."

"Yeah. See ya," Lee-Anne said, more amused than she should have been. It was just business.

On my way to the arena, Cole, Tyson, and Tyson's cousin Blake caught up to me. Cole twisted my ear painfully and forced me to lean towards him. "Did you just drop eight thousand dollars on a horse for a chick who you are not only not sleeping with, but you have never even gone on a date with?"

"Ow. Let go."

He released my ear and punched me in the shoulder, hard. "Where are you going to get eight thousand dollars from? I'm not paying for it."

"Don't worry about it. She has to win for the sale to go through." I turned to look at Blake, who I hadn't seen since I used to compete in the bigger rodeos. "What are you doing on this circuit?"

"I broke my collarbone. I decided to hang out with you sorry ass excuses for cowboys for a while and give my big cousin some pointers." He mussed up Tyson's hair.

"Watch it or I'll break your other collarbone," Tyson warned.

Tawnie and Stella were setting up in the alley as we walked over to the ring. They took off from the gate and she ripped around the first barrel. All four of us stepped forward and leaned on the fence to watch. She turned the second barrel with no air between and actually gained momentum. She skimmed the last barrel and then let the reins out and kicked home. We all looked up at the clock.

The contents of my stomach turned.

Cole and the Wiese boys laughed.

"Looks like you bought your girl a fast pony," Cole said as he slapped my shoulder. "Better go find eight grand somewhere."

"Shit."

Chapter 3

Cole was thrown on his first two outs, so he didn't qualify for the finals. We had to stay until Sunday, though, to find out whether I was going to owe Ron Miller eight thousand dollars that I didn't have for a horse I didn't want. I'd already asked around to see if anyone was in the market to buy a barrel racing horse, but nobody was. Shae-Lynn was leading Tawnie going into the championship round, so I wasn't too concerned. Stella was fast though. She was almost too fast for Tawnie's riding ability. If Shae-Lynn rode her, they'd definitely be able to tear it up on the bigger circuits.

Cole and the Wiese boys weaved through the crowd, making their way up to where I was sitting in the grandstand. "You look like you're going to throw up." Cole laughed and sat down next to me. "I thought I was the one who was supposed to do stupid impulsive things."

"It must run in the family." I tugged on my shirt collar to try to relieve the strangling feeling in my throat. The more I thought about it, the more I realized what a bonehead decision it had been. If Tawnie won and I didn't find a buyer before the weekend was over, I'd have to come up with the eight thousand for Ron and extra to transport, board, and feed the horse.

"What's the plan if she wins?" Cole asked. "Are we going to make a run for it?"

"I'll find a buyer, eventually, but she's not going to win. Shae-Lynn was looking good in practice."

He smiled as if he wasn't so sure about that and watched Lee-Anne entertain the crowd with her trick riding.

Tyson tilted his head as she rode hanging upside down off the side of her saddle. "How does she bend like that?"

"I bet she's bendy in all sorts of ways," Blake said. "That is a definite asset."

"Forget it," Cole told him. "She has a boyfriend back home."

"I bet she does." He smiled in a sleazy way. "Look at that flexibility."

When she finished, they all stood up hooting and hollering. The rest of the crowd wasn't really paying that much attention. They were mostly only there to see the bulls that were coming up later. When the ground crew entered the arena to set up the barrels, I shifted around on the bench, looked up, and prayed, "Come on, Shae-Lynn."

Unfortunately, Tawnie and Shae-Lynn were the last two of eight riders, so I had to sit there trying not to puke through the other ones. When the silhouette of Tawnie mounted on Stella entered the alley, I had to close my eyes. I didn't want to wish her any bad, but I really hoped she would make a mistake. I opened one eye and peeked. Stella took off as if she'd been struck in the butt by lightening. Tawnie had to fight to get her to slow down enough to get around the first barrel. They flew around the next two barrels. When she ran home, I literally felt a blast of air as they raced by us.

"Yee haw!" the announcer shouted over the loud speaker. "If you blinked you missed Tawnie Lang on her new mount, Stella. Look at that time. She just blew the competition right out of the water. Ladies and gentlemen, this is as good as barrel racing gets. Give that pretty lady another round of applause. She has posted the fastest time of the weekend." I glanced over at Cole, nervous as hell. He smiled at me in a goofy way as the announcer blabbed on, "With only one competitor left to ride, this is shaping up to be quite the race. We've got Shae Roberts on Harley. She was last year's top earner in prize money and she was in first place coming into this round. She is going to need a fast time to stay there though."

"I can't watch." I buried my face in my hands, only for a second, then looked up when the hooves pounded against the dirt. Harley ran fast, but Shae-Lynn didn't approach the pocket properly and Harley dropped his shoulder way too early on the first turn. She picked it up around the other two barrels and then raced through the finish line. It wasn't going to be a fast enough time though. Shae-Lynn immediately jumped off Harley and walked him out of the arena without even waiting for the time to be posted.

"What was that?" Cole mumbled, partly perplexed, but mostly amused.

"It almost looked like she threw that on purpose," Tyson said after the scoreboard confirmed that she dropped to second place.

I was too stunned to say anything. I just sat there staring at the barrels.

"We're going to watch Ty from behind the chutes. You coming?" Cole asked.

When I didn't respond, he shrugged and then rushed to catch up to the other guys. I sat there all through the bulls and I was still sitting there after the grandstand had emptied. Eventually, Ron found me and climbed up. "Looks like you bought yourself a horse."

I tilted my hat back and rested my elbows on my knees, still speechless that Shae-Lynn messed up.

"If I knew Stella was going to be that fast in competition I would have charged you more."

"I don't actually have the money right now, but I'm good for it."

"You better be. I'm going to run five percent interest on it until you pay it off, so don't take too long."

"You can keep her until I get the money. I don't even have a trailer or anything."

"I don't want her. You're going to have to figure something out."

31

I rubbed my face and sighed. "Yeah. All right."

He chuckled at my misery as he climbed back down the bleachers.

I got up and went outside to find Tawnie. Shae-Lynn was walking back from the concession stand with a sandwich and a bottle of water. I ran to catch up with her. "Hey, what happened?"

She shook her head. "I just wasn't feeling it today. Harley might have an upset stomach or something."

"Harley was fine."

Her eyes darted to meet mine for a second, then she stared down at the grass as she continued walking. "I can't win them all. Stella's a good horse."

"The guys think you did it intentionally."

"They do, do they?"

"Did you?"

"Why would I lose on purpose?"

"You tell me."

"I just wasn't feeling it today." She walked faster.

"Shae-Lynn, what's wrong?"

"For the millionth time, call me Shae." She started jogging at that point and I wasn't going to chase after her, so I went to find Tawnie. She was brushing Stella.

"Hey Billy. Did you watch the race? She is such a good horse. I absolutely love her. Too bad she has to go back to Ron."

"Actually, I bought her from him."

The comment took her off guard and she processed it for a few seconds. "You don't even have a trailer. What are going to do with a horse?"

I took my hat off and ran my fingers through my hair, hoping she was willing to do me a favour since I did her one. "Would you be willing to take her?"

"I would love to, but I can't afford to lease a horse."

I paced, trying to come with a solution that wouldn't end up with me having to buy a trailer and find a barn to board at. "If you cover the cost of boarding her, we can call it even."

She eyed me suspiciously. "You're going to just let me use your horse for nothing?"

"Well, you could give me one percent of your earnings on her if that makes you feel any better."

"One percent? That's it? Are you serious? I'll give you ten percent."

That was easy. "Fine."

She squealed and launched herself at me for another hug. I was ready for it, so I squeezed my arms around her to make it last a little longer. "Thank you, Billy. I'll take good care of her, and you can have her back whenever you want." She rested her hands on my shoulders, which gave me a good angle to check out her cleavage. She bit the corner of her lip for a second. "We should go out and celebrate."

My body reacted a little to the warmth of her hands and the scent of her perfume. I smiled. "Yeah. That's a good idea."

"All right. I'm going to ask someone to watch the horses. Then I need to go back to the hotel to get cleaned up. Rochelle said everyone is going to bar called Stetsons. I'll meet you there later."

I nodded, tipped my hat, and watched her ass as she spun and walked away.

Back at the camper, I showered and dressed in clean clothes. Cole came in as I was ironing my shirt. "Where you going?"

"To the bar."

"With who?"

"Nobody," I said because I didn't want him giving me the gears.

"Yeah, right." He unbuttoned his shirt and unbuckled his belt. "Wait for me. I'm coming with you." He hopped into the shower and took forever.

"Hurry up," I yelled through the door as I buttoned my shirt.

"Settle down. You don't want to get there too early and be waiting."

"I'd like to get there before it closes."

Fifteen minutes later, he stepped out of the bathroom wearing a towel around his waist, smelling like a piña colada from his shower gel. "What are you worried about? You know girls take forever to get ready. I can guarantee she won't be there before you — especially if she likes you."

"What does that have to do with anything?"

"Everyone knows that a girl who doesn't put any effort into looking good on a first date isn't into you. Who is it, by the way? Tawnie?"

I didn't say anything.

"That girl better thank you for buying her a damn horse. Here, take these." He threw a handful of condoms at me.

"I didn't buy her a horse. I bought a horse that she is just going to ride."

He shook his head, not buying it, then looked in the mirror to apply a moisturizer.

I sat back and stretched my legs along the dinette bench. "I can see why you know so much about women. You pretty much are one."

He threw the cap from the moisturizer bottle at me, then winked at himself in the mirror as he put some sort of product in his hair.

"Oh my God. Who cares what your hair looks like? You're going to be wearing a hat."

"The hat comes off at the end of the night, and I fully intend for some pretty girl to be seeing how my hair looks underneath it." He sprayed cologne in the air. "Speaking of which, if I bring a girl back here, you need to find somewhere else to sleep."

"No way. Get a room."

"I bought this camper. You have two options: leave or listen."

I rolled my eyes in exasperation. "Just hurry up."

Chapter 4

We got to the bar at eleven o'clock because Cole was hungry. I knew he hadn't eaten all day, so we went for dinner first. The band was pretty decent and a lot of people were dancing. I scanned the room for Tawnie, but didn't see her. What I did see was Tyson and Blake sitting at a table near the back with Lee-Anne, her best friend Rochelle, and Shae-Lynn. Blake had his arm draped across Shae-Lynn's shoulder. She looked up at me for a second, but when she noticed that I was already looking, and not impressed that Blake was hanging off her, she turned her head to take a sip of beer and watch the dancers.

"Isn't he a bit old for her?" I asked Cole as we stood at the bar to get drinks.

"Who?"

"Blake."

Cole checked over his shoulder and shrugged, unconcerned. "He's twenty, same as you. Isn't she almost nineteen?"

I frowned and glanced at the table again. Shae-Lynn didn't seem comfortable. Blake seemed smug. The bartender slid two beers over.

"What are you doing?" I asked Cole. "You know you can't drink."

He rolled his eyes like an irritable teenager before he handed me both beers. He leaned over and yelled at the bartender, "Can I get a Coke too? My keeper says I can't have a beer." As he waited, he looked at me. "I forgot my wallet."

I shook my head, not surprised, and pulled out cash to pay the bartender. Cole grabbed his drink and headed towards the table where everyone else was sitting. I downed half a beer before following him. A guy asked Rochelle to dance, so Lee-Anne moved over into her seat and invited me to sit in her chair. I handed her the second beer.

"Thanks." She tipped it back to take a swig. "You bought a fast horse for Tawnie."

"I didn't buy it for her. She's just riding it."

"Mmm hmm." She tilted the bottle up for another sip.

Blake leaned over and whispered something in Shae-Lynn's ear that made her smile. He placed his empty bottle down on the table and stood with his hand extended towards her. She slid her hand over his and followed him out onto the dance floor. As they two-stepped, I finished my beer and signalled the waitress to bring me another one.

Rochelle was back, and Lee-Anne was telling her a story that had something to do with her boyfriend, TJ. I wasn't really listening. Blake and Shae-Lynn danced for three fast songs, and based on how much she was smiling, she must have been having a pretty good time. When a slow song came on, she said something to Blake before walking off the dance floor. He followed her to the bar, ordered a beer for himself and a bottled water for her. They stood at the bar for a while, talking. When he turned as if he was going to head back towards the table, she glanced at me. When he noticed that she was hesitating, he reached over and held her hand to lead her back to the table. I downed the rest of my drink and signalled the waitress to bring me another one.

Once they were sitting, Blake draped his arm over Shae-Lynn's shoulder. She stared at the table. He stared at me. "So, Billy, when are you going to start riding with the big boys again?" he asked.

I was definitely going to get into it with him. I shook my head.

"I'm retired."

"Why? Did you get sick of me always taking home the buckle?" He laughed at his own joke. Nobody else did.

"Check the record books, Blake. You never won shit when I was competing against you."

He leaned over to shout at Cole. "Hey, who won more when we went up against each other? Billy or me?"

Cole smiled, happy to get into the middle of a disagreement. "You already know the answer to that question. Billy's the best God damned bull rider in the country. He's got a case full of buckles at home to prove it."

"Was," Blake mumbled.

"When do you expect your collarbone to be healed enough get back to trying to catch my records?" I asked, partly because I wanted to rub it in his face that I was still ranked higher than he was. Also, because I didn't think he was good enough for Shae-Lynn, and the sooner he shoved off the better.

He shrugged. "I don't want to rush it. Besides, I kind of like hanging out here with Shae." He squeezed his arm to pull her into his chest. "Maybe I'll take the whole summer off. What do you care anyway? You quit."

"I retired." An urge to punch the smug look off his face flashed through me and I had to cross my arms to resist the impulse. Cole obviously knew I was on the verge of jumping the table because he grinned and moved his drink so it wouldn't get spilled when I did.

Shae-Lynn pushed off Blake's ribs and sat up straight as if she sensed their closeness was what I was pissed about. Interestingly, she was wearing the same old jeans and tank top that she had on when I saw her coming from the concession stand. Her hair was pulled back into a ponytail and she didn't have any make-up on, except maybe that cherry lipgloss. Her lips did look shiny. Lee-Anne had on dark jeans with rhinestones over the seams, new looking boots, and a sparkly low cut top. Her hair was sprayed to the point that it didn't move when she did.

37

Blake abruptly got up to say hello to someone he knew. It was a pussy move because he knew I could take him, and would have, if he hadn't broken the tension. I leaned in and asked Lee-Anne, "How long did it take you to get ready?"

"Shut up."

"What? I'm not trying to insult you. It's a serious question."

She eyeballed me scornfully, but when she realized I wasn't joking, she answered, "Forty-five minutes. Why?"

I turned my head back to look at Shae-Lynn, who obviously spent no time getting ready. "I was just wondering."

"Relax, Billy Ray," Lee-Anne said. She shoved my shoulder, trying to loosen me up. "You've been so serious since —" She checked my expression. "Since, you know." She took another sip of beer. "Sorry. I shouldn't have brought that up. I just miss good time Billy."

"Yeah, well, good time Billy has responsibilities now." Blake returned to the table and sat on the other side of Shae-Lynn, away from me. I turned so I could have a private conversation with Lee-Anne. "Are you okay with her dating someone older?"

"Blake? Yeah. Why not? He's a total sweetheart."

"He's an asshole."

"To you maybe. He's sweet to her. He always has been. He's been following her around like a puppy dog for years."

"How long have they been dating?"

"Since tonight. He's asked her out a million times and for some reason she finally said yes."

Arms wrapped around me from behind and a girl's voice whispered in my ear, "Guess what?"

I twisted to see that it was Tawnie.

She kissed my cheek and her chest squished against my back. Her breath smelled like beer. "I got a sponsor. Jordan Outfitters has offered to pay for all my travel expenses for the rest of the season. I also get all the boots I want."

"That's great."

"It's all because of Stella." She squeezed my neck and kissed my ear.

"Congratulations," Lee-Anne and Rochelle said at the same time.

"That's great news." Shae-Lynn stood and yanked Blake by the hand. "You can have my seat. We're leaving."

Blake tipped his hat at all of us, then eagerly hurried to keep up with her. I watched them leave out the front door. Tawnie sat down in Shae-Lynn's chair and told us all about how the Jordan rep had approached her at the hotel and had her sign some papers. She was really excited.

After a while, Tyson asked Lee-Anne to dance, Rochelle wandered over to the bar with a guy, and Cole never came back from a trip to the restroom because he was chatting up a cute curly haired girl. Tawnie and I were alone at the table. Her tight black jeans and unbuttoned white top showed off all her curves. Her hair was hanging perfectly straight and it was so shiny.

"You look nice," I said, because the alcohol had kicked in.

Her smile was sexy. "Thanks. Do you dance?"

"I wouldn't be able to call myself a cowboy if I didn't know how to two-step, now would I?" I stood and led her by the waist to the dance floor. When I spun her to face me, the small of her back arched under the pressure of my palm. She smiled and slid her hand over my biceps to rest it on my shoulder. As we moved across the floor, wafts of wild lavender breezed over me. I spun her around and her hair fanned out catching the light. The cowboys loitering around the edge of the dance floor all angled to watch her move.

We spent the rest of the night two-stepping until the DJ announced last call and played a slow song. Tawnie stepped in close and our belt buckles clinked together. She slid her palms up over my abs and let them linger on my chest as she leaned in and pressed her lips to my neck pulse. My heart raced, and she must have felt it because she tilted her head back and smiled. I spun her around, then pulled her body close again. She giggled and it seemed like she was waiting on me to kiss her when Cole came over with the curly haired girl under his arm. He handed me the keys to the truck. "Molly's going to drive me back to the camper." He winked, then left.

Tawnie and I finished the dance, and the house lights came on, but she didn't step away. "Did you drive here from the hotel?" I asked her.

"I took a cab. I can catch a ride back with Rochelle."

"Rochelle left when Cole did. I can give you a lift if you like."

She studied me. "How much have you had to drink?"

"I'm fine," I said, although I was feeling pretty buzzed.

Her left eyebrow lifted slightly and a smile stretched across her face. She tucked her hair behind her ear and tugged my hand to invite me to follow her. We walked outside and I opened the truck door for her. She didn't talk as we drove. When I pulled up in front of the hotel and parked, she didn't make a move to get out.

"Which rodeo are you entering next?" I finally asked to break the silence.

"Falkland. How about you?"

"I'm retired."

"Cole said you were going to be his manager."

"He's delusional."

She looked as if she wanted to ask more, but she just nodded. She turned her head and stared at me for a while. "Aren't you going to kiss me?"

I smiled at her forwardness. "Well, if we're going to do that, we should do it properly." I took my hat off and placed it on the dashboard, then got out of the truck and walked around the front to the passenger side. I opened the door and held her hand to help her out. She ran her palms up my chest and hung her arms casually over my shoulders. I stepped close and leaned in to kiss her. Her full lips were soft and her mouth tasted like peppermint mixed with beer.

After we kissed for a while, she slid her hands down and

unbuttoned my shirt. Then she tugged at my belt buckle. She backed into the truck and reclined on the bench seat, smiling. "Get in here," she said.

"Uh." My eyes scanned her body. I scratched my head. It only took two seconds for my hormones to decide that it wouldn't hurt to postpone the official retirement until after one last rodeo one-night stand. "Wouldn't you rather go to your room?"

She shook her head and took her shirt off over her head. "We can't. I'm rooming with Rochelle."

Although doing it in a truck was something I did a lot when I was younger, years of rodeoing, and at least ten serious injuries made me less flexible and less enthusiastic about doing it in cramped spaces. She looked unbelievably hot though, so I knelt in with one knee and angled my other foot on the floor to close the door behind me. She clutched the fabric of my shirt and pulled me down onto her. My back kinked and my hamstring locked up, which made me wince before I was able to readjust and lean in to kiss her. She kicked her boots off and slid her jeans down. There was a blue flying sparrow tattooed above her hip bone. I looked up to see if anyone was around. Fortunately, the windows were steamy. "Do you have a boyfriend or anything that I should know about?"

"No. Do you have a girlfriend?"

I leaned in and kissed her. "No, not at the present moment."

Her hand reached down and she tugged at my jeans to release the fly, one button at a time.

"Are you sure you want to do this in a truck?"

She laughed. "Stop talking and get to work."

I smiled and reached down to pull her thigh up. "All right. You asked for it."

She giggled, grabbed the back of my hair, and kissed me hard. Her back arched and she stretched her arms above her head. I kissed down her neck towards her cleavage, then ran my hand over her ribs. After kissing my way across her collarbone, I stopped to catch my breath. She opened her eyes. The expression on my face, whatever it was, made her smile before she removed her bra and moved my hand down between her legs. I ran my fingers over the silky fabric and slid her underwear down. "Sit up," she whispered and moved to straddle my lap.

The condoms Cole gave me were in my jeans on the floor, but she didn't ask me to wear one, so I moved my hands and rocked her hips forward. She leaned her head over my shoulder. Her breath tickled my skin, becoming heavier and faster as she moved up and down. My left hand slid over her curves and she dug her fingers into my neck. She was going too fast, so I held her hips and slowed her down to let her feel the difference between the back and forth rise of riding a horse versus the rock and roll grind of riding a bull.

When she got the hang of it, the expression on her face changed and her breaths turned into soft moans. She pressed her palms against my shoulders and leaned her head back. The visual of her hair cascading down her back and her chest rising made every cell in my body react. Her moans got progressively louder as I explored her body with my mouth. She bounced for a while then curled forward, tensed up, and held her breath. Her body shuddered before she let out a little whimper. After two more shudders, she exhaled and slowly rocked her hips.

We sat there for a while just breathing heavily and I already regretted it. Eventually, I pushed her hair back to see if she felt the same way. It didn't seem like it. She opened her eyes and slid her hands up along my jaw to pull me in close. I felt her exhale before she leaned in and whispered in my ear, "Thank you."

Feeling guilty, I kissed her and took one more look at her body before I moved out from under her.

Once she was dressed, she held up her hands. "God, I'm trembling. I can still feel that everywhere." She looked at me. "That was good — really good."

Without responding, I put my jeans back on and buttoned

42

my shirt.

"I've never, um, you know; I've never enjoyed it quite like that before. If you know what I mean," she said.

"Really?" Shit. That was only going to make it worse when she clued in that it wasn't meant to be anything more than one time in a truck.

"Do all the girls you've been with enjoy it like that — to that intensity?"

"As far as I know, unless they were faking."

"Jesus, you can't fake something like that." She combed her fingers through her hair and checked her makeup in the mirror.

I smiled, feeling a little cocky, and put my hat back on.

"Call me." She gave me a peck on the cheek.

I nodded, although I had no intention of ever seeing her again, and turned the engine on so I could roll down the window to get the windshield to clear up. She hopped out of the truck and ran across the parking lot to a room on the first floor. She fumbled through her purse for the key card, then opened the door. She waved before she went inside. I pressed the defogger button. As I waited for the windows to clear, a girl came out of a second floor room and ran along the veranda to the stairs. When she reached the sidewalk, I noticed that she had strawberry coloured hair.

"Shae-Lynn?" I shouted out the window.

Her head spun to see who had called her name. She was crying. I left the truck engine running and got out.

"What's wrong?"

"Nothing." She wiped her palms across her face. "I'm fine."

"You don't look fine. What happened?"

"Nothing. What are you doing here?"

"Dropping someone off."

"Who? Tawnie?"

I frowned and looked up at the door on the second floor that she came out of. "Is this where Blake is staying?"

"I have to go. Lee-Anne's going to be worried about me."

"I'll drive you."

"No thanks." She rushed across the parking lot headed towards the highway.

"Shae-Lynn, get in the truck. I'm not going to let you walk along a pitch black highway."

She waved her arm over her head in a don't-worry-about-me way and kept walking. I hopped in the truck and pulled out onto the highway. I drove slowly on the shoulder behind her with my head hanging out the window.

"Leave me alone, Billy."

"I'm going to drive two kilometres an hour all the way back if you don't get in the truck."

She kept walking. A couple cars passed and honked.

"Uh, Shae-Lynn, I'm pretty sure it's not all that safe for me to be driving like this."

"Then go," she snapped.

"I'm not leaving you here, so unless you want to witness me getting killed when a semi-truck rams up my ass, I suggest you get in the truck."

She stopped and looked up at the sky. After an eighteen-wheeler honked at us, she shook her head in exasperation, then got in the passenger side.

"What happened?" I asked again as I shoulder checked and pulled out into the lane.

"None of your business."

"Did Blake hurt you?"

She stared out the side window for a while before she mumbled, "No."

"I'm going to beat the truth out of him if you don't tell me."

"It wasn't that big of a deal. He wanted more from me than I felt like giving, so I left."

"Didn't he offer to drive you back?"

She didn't answer.

"What an asshole. I'm going to beat his ass."

44

"I didn't give him a chance to offer to give me a ride. I just left."

"I didn't see him running after you."

She shook her head, unimpressed. "What kind of guy expects a girl will sleep with him after one date? A girl doesn't do that unless she is a complete slut. You know that, right?"

I glanced at her and gripped the steering wheel, wondering if she saw right through me and already knew what I'd done with Tawnie.

"Why would he even think I was like that?"

"He was just hoping you were. You did go back to his room with him."

"So? He said we were going to watch a movie." She glared at me and her lip curled. "You think it's my fault."

"No."

"Is 'let's watch a movie' code for 'let's have sex?'"

"No, not necessarily."

"Do you hope that girls will be slutty enough to sleep with you after just one date?"

I winced, positive that she had already figured it out. What the hell. If she already knew I was a dirt bag, I might as well be honest with her. "If a girl is going to offer sex on the first date, I'm not going to turn it down. But I don't expect it."

"Do you ever end up liking the girls who give it away on the first date?"

I knew what the answer was, but I didn't say anything. My non response obviously confirmed what she already suspected. She sat back and stared out the passenger side window. We drove for a while in silence before I said, "I'll take care of him."

"No." She pointed at me in a threatening way. "I don't want you talking to him about it."

"I'm not going to *talk* to him about it."

"I don't want you fighting with him about it either."

I turned into the arena grounds and drove over the grass field. Most of the participants had left, so there were only a few campers

45

and trailers speckled around.

"I'm serious," she said. "If you do anything, I will never speak to you again."

"That's too bad, but I guess that's the way it's going to have to be."

She groaned and fought to hold back a scream. "Don't be an asshole, Billy."

"Making sure Blake knows that it's not okay to treat you like that doesn't make me an asshole."

She stared at me, letting what I said sink in. Her expression fluctuated and I had trouble reading it before she said, "He didn't do anything wrong. He was just too eager. I want to forget about it. Promise you won't do anything."

"What do you care what I do to him? You weren't even into him in the first place."

The crease deepened between her eyebrows. "What makes you say that?"

"I could tell."

"How?"

"I just could. Turns out Cole might actually know as much about women as he claims to."

She rolled her eyes to disagree. "You guys don't know anything."

"So, you did like Blake?"

"No, and I don't want everyone knowing that I was stupid enough to go to the hotel room with him. It's embarrassing and it makes me look bad. Please don't make it into a big deal." She started crying. "Promise?"

I didn't like seeing her cry, so I nodded.

"Say it."

Although Blake needed to be set straight, the hurt tone of her voice was killing me and I wanted to make her feel better, so I gave in. "I promise."

Satisfied that I'd given her my word, she got out of the truck, swung the door shut, and ran over to the motorhome. There was a little red truck parked in front of our camper, which meant I

46

had no place to sleep. I stretched out on the bench seat and spent the rest of the night thinking about Tawnie, Blake, and Shae-Lynn.

By the morning, the only thing I had figured out was how I was going to handle things with Blake, while still keeping my promise to Shae-Lynn. The door to the camper opened at about six and Cole kissed the curly haired girl goodbye. As she got into her little red truck, I walked over to the camper.

"Hey," he said, still sounding half asleep. "Did you sleep in the truck?"

"I wouldn't call it sleeping." I stepped inside and undressed to take a shower. "You have to drive back to Saskatoon. I'm too tired."

"I don't want to go all the way home," he whined. "Can't we just go straight to Vancouver Island?"

"I'm not going with you. This was a one time deal."

He frowned and sat at the dinette. "What happened with Tawnie?"

I leaned on the bathroom doorframe, not intending to answer. "How well do you know Blake?"

He shrugged. "Same as you do. Why?"

"He tried to take advantage of Shae-Lynn and left her to walk home by herself along the highway. I had to pick her up."

"Is she all right?"

"I don't know. She wouldn't really talk about it."

Cole shook his head and his fingers tightened into fists. I smiled because I knew my plan would work just fine. He glanced out the window in the direction of the Roberts' motorhome, already plotting to defend her honour. There were a bunch of empty beer bottles on the table in front of him.

"You know you shouldn't drink when you're on that medication."

"I didn't," he said as he cleared them off the table. "That chick was a lush."

"She drank six beers all by herself?"

He smiled the kind of smile that made it hard to stay mad at him. I shook my head, tired of being his babysitter, then closed the bathroom door.

"Hey, you didn't answer the question about Tawnie," he shouted through the door.

I turned the water on so I couldn't hear him.

Chapter 5

Cole drove for the first four hours back to Saskatoon, then we stopped for lunch. He went to the restroom in the restaurant and while I was sitting at the table waiting for the waitress, my phone rang.

"Hey, Mom."

"You didn't call yesterday. I was worried."

"Sorry. We're fine. Cole didn't win any prize money."

"I heard you bought a horse."

Shit. I had seriously forgotten about that. It hadn't occurred to me that it was going to be hard to never see Tawnie again if she was taking care of my damn horse. I rubbed the stress in my neck, cursing the rodeo gossip grape vine that worked at the speed of light. "How'd you hear that?"

"Doreen Roberts called yesterday. She'd been talking to Lee-Anne, so I got the whole story. What are you going to do with a horse?"

"I don't know. She's fast though. I can probably resell her for a profit if she does well in the next couple competitions."

"Why don't you get Shae to ride her? She's better than that other girl."

It was a good idea, but she'd never go for it. "Shae-Lynn's got Harley."

"How are those little Roberts girls doing?"

"Well, they're not so little anymore."

"I hope you're keeping an eye on them around all those rowdy cowboys now that their mom's not with them. Their dad doesn't even know they're touring."

"They're fine."

"How's your brother?"

I looked up and saw him coming back from the restroom. "He's right here. You can talk to him yourself. Love you." I handed the phone to Cole as he sat down across from me at the table.

"Hey, Ma." He took his hat off and scratched his head as he listened to her. "Tell them to reschedule it…Why can't they do it earlier? … I don't care if that's the only time the psychiatrist is available. I'm already registered for Luxton… I've been fine in case you hadn't noticed…Whatever." He sat back and slouched down. "No… It's a waste of time…" He rolled his eyes and sat back up to lean his elbows on the table. "Listen, Mom, I know you're just trying to help, but I'm twenty-two years old. I don't need my mom confirming doctor's appointments for me — especially when I'm not sick." He shook his head while he listened. She talked for a long time then he said, "Yeah. Bye." He hung up and handed the phone back to me. "Why'd you do that? You know I hate talking to her about that kind of stuff. Now I'm upset." He stood, put his hat on, and left the restaurant.

I ate by myself to give him time to cool off. Then I ordered him a clubhouse sandwich and took it back to the truck. He was sitting in the passenger seat with earphones in, so I climbed into the driver's seat and headed towards the Saskatchewan border.

I worked my ass off once we were back in Saskatoon — on the ranch six days a week and bartending most evenings. On the Tuesday before Cole was supposed to leave for the Luxton rodeo, he showed up at the ranch as I was coming off shift. The owner's fifteen-year-old son wanted to get on the circuit, so Cole and a couple other local riders were allowed to ride the rough stock whenever they wanted in exchange for giving the kid a few pointers.

"You want me to go with you to that hospital meeting tomorrow?" I asked.

He reached over the side of the truck bed to grab his bull rope. "Nope. I'm not going."

"Why not? Just tell them you're doing fine and be done with it."

"Mind your business, Billy."

"Mind your business, asshole." I turned to walk to my truck.

"We're practicing on Wide Load today." His tone changed the way it always did when he wanted something from me. "You want to stay and coach?"

"No."

"Come on, you're the only one who has ever ridden him."

"I'm retired."

"If you get on a bull I'll go to the meeting tomorrow."

I shook my head, not interested in his manipulation, and kept walking. "I have to get to the bar."

The Palomino was already busy when I got to work. The owner was helping the servers, so I picked up the slack. At about ten o'clock, a girl leaned her elbows onto the bar and squeezed her arms to accentuate her cleavage. It caught my attention. When I looked up at her face, I realized I knew her. Although she and Lee-Anne were best friends because they spent so much time on the road with each other, I'd technically known Rochelle for longer. We'd been in the same class every year since kindergarten. She never liked me all that much. "Hey, Rochelle. That is a very nice top you're wearing."

"Shut up."

I smiled and slid her a vodka cooler on the house. "You're always so mean to me. Remind me why that is."

"Grade nine. We had to do a presentation on our hobbies. You did yours on bull riding. Dean Kline asked if you were ever scared. You said no, because whenever you got nervous about falling off you would imagine landing on two giant soft pillows like Rochelle's."

I chuckled as I remembered. "That was funny. Get over it."

"It wasn't funny, you jackass. It was humiliating."

"Why? It was a compliment."

"I was fourteen. Having boys only pay attention to me because of the size of my chest was embarrassing. It made me self-conscious."

"For your information, the teacher gave me a zero on that presentation and," I pointed at her impressive cleavage overflowing her low cut top, "You're obviously not self-conscious anymore."

"Shut up. I'm not here to discuss my emotional scars. I'm here because someone wanted me to deliver a message to you."

I poured a mixed drink for the guy who was standing beside her. I took his money then turned to look at her. "Who's that someone?"

She slid an envelope across the bar. It had my name written across it in curly writing. I handed two beers to a guy and took his money, then flipped the envelope over and opened it. Rochelle scrutinized my face as I read the note.

Billy, Here is your cut from my first win on Stella. She's doing great. Thanks again for letting me ride her. I guess you've been too busy to call, but I just wanted to let you know that I can't stop thinking about you, or our night in Coleman. I'd really love to see you again, Tawnie.

Rochelle was still watching me to see how I was going to react, so I tried to not show any expression. I put the note in my back pocket and served a few more customers. Her second drink was done before I was able to get back to her.

"Do you have a message you'd like me to pass on to her?" she asked.

"No. Thanks."

Her eyebrows angled. "Why haven't you called her? Were you just using her?"

52

"No offence, Rochelle, but it's not really any of your business."

"Well, it kind of is when she calls me crying every night upset because you haven't called her."

A guy was shouting an order at me, but I ignored him. "What's she crying about?"

"She likes you, obviously. Girls don't do what she did with you in a truck unless they really like a guy. You know that, right?"

I rolled my eyes, not surprised that even the women weren't clear with what meant what, and I shook my head because obviously there was no such thing as privacy on the circuit. "I can't believe she told you that."

Rochelle made her eyebrows dance up and down. "Apparently you're quite something."

"Shit." I turned around and pulled two cases of beer from the cupboard to restock the bar. When I turned back around, an older guy who was already pretty gunned was leaning with his arm over Rochelle's shoulder and talking too close to her face.

I couldn't hear what he was mumbling, but she said, "No thanks," and pushed his arm away.

He went in for another sloppy hug and was trying to cop a feel, so I reached over the bar and shoved him. "Why don't you go sit down, buddy?"

He stumbled back a little and frowned at me. "What's your problem?"

"She said no. You need to go sit down."

He stared me down for a few seconds, but must have realized he couldn't take me. He flipped me the bird and staggered away.

Rochelle took a sip of her vodka cooler. "Thanks."

"Don't mention it."

She checked the time on her phone. "I need to get going." She closed her purse. "Just so you know, Tawnie is really sweet and she's coming off a bad break-up. I realize you're not really the boyfriend type, but it would be good if you could at least be nice to her. I don't want her to end up feeling like a worthless piece of shit."

"I'll call her."

"Good man. I'll see you around." She stood and started to walk away.

"Hey, Rochelle."

She paused and looked over her shoulder.

"I'm trying to be a better person, so I would like to apologize for hurting your feelings when we were in junior high."

She turned to face me, tilted her head to the side, and closed one eye as if she was contemplating something. After a while, she said, "All right. I forgive you."

"Thank you." I winked. "But you do have to admit you have the nicest rack in town."

She shook her head in disappointment. "Geez Billy. Why did you have to go and ruin a perfectly good truce?"

I shrugged in mock innocence. "It would feel weird if you didn't treat me like I was an asshole."

"Yeah, that would feel weird." She chuckled, then left.

The bar closed at two and I didn't get out of there until closer to two-thirty. I drove back to my mom's house and sat in my truck looking at my phone. I had an uneasy feeling in my stomach. Finally, I took a deep breath and scrolled through my contacts to find Tawnie's number. Before I had a chance to call her, my phone rang. The call display showed, Shae-Lynn's name, so I answered. She was crying.

"What's wrong?"

She had to inhale a couple times before she was able to speak through her crying, "My mom and dad were in an accident."

"Are they all right?"

"My mom's in the hospital with a concussion and a broken arm. My dad just has cuts and bruises. They're fine, but the trailer rolled and they had to put two of the horses down." She started sobbing heavier.

I didn't know what to say, so I just sat there listening to her cry. Eventually, she calmed down a little and sniffled. "I'm sorry to call you so late, but I really needed someone to talk to. You're the only person I thought might still be awake. I'm sorry if you were sleeping."

"I was awake. Where's Lee-Anne?"

"She got on a plane to meet them down in Texas. I had to stay here to take care of the animals. It's really quiet in the house when nobody else is here."

"You mean scary?" I chuckled. "Do you want me to come over to keep you company?"

"Yeah, would you?" She sounded as if a smile had crossed her lips. "It's only a seven-and-a-half hour drive."

"Okay."

She paused as if she was worried I would really do it. "I was joking."

"I know. How about I just talk to you on the phone until you either feel better or fall asleep?"

"Really? You don't mind?"

"Sleep is overrated."

She hesitated again as if she was reluctant to impose. "Do you have an unlimited long distance plan?"

"Yeah, we can talk all night if we need to."

"Are you working, or on a date or something? I don't want to keep you from anything."

"I just got home from a shift at the bar."

"Are you sure you don't want to go to sleep?"

"I can't fall asleep right after I get home anyway. You're doing me a favour to keep me company."

"Okay. Um." She inhaled and thought for a few seconds to come up with a conversation starter. "Are you going with Cole to Luxton?"

"No, he's on his own. Are you still going?"

"I don't know." She sighed, reminded of why she called in the first place. "I guess I'll have to wait and see what happens with my mom. She might not feel well enough to come with us."

"A concussion won't stop her."

"Oh? You're a concussion expert?"

I chuckled. "Actually, yes."

"Oh yeah, I forgot all the —" She stopped abruptly and made a squeaking sound. "Oh, my God."

"What?"

"I heard a noise," she whispered with panic in her voice.

"I knew you'd called because you were scared, not sad."

"I'm both, Billy. I freely admit that. If you were here and heard what I just heard, you'd be terrified."

"It was probably nothing. You should turn the TV on so the house won't seem so quiet."

"I'd have to get out of bed and walk to the living room to do that. What if there is already someone hiding in one of the closets?"

I laughed because she sounded dead serious. "Why would someone be hiding in your closets? Either they'd be busy burglarizing the house or attacking you, not hiding."

"Thanks. That helps a lot. Remind me not to call you the next time I'm holed up in my room, scared to death."

"How are you ever going to move out of your parents' house and live on your own if you're too scared to stay by yourself?"

She gasped as if she couldn't believe I had the nerve to mock her. "Look who's talking. You live at your mom's house, tough guy."

She had me there, but I didn't live at home because I wanted to. "I had my own place before my dad died. I only moved back to take care of my mom."

"Yeah." She dragged the word out, unimpressed. "I heard about 'Billy Ray's Hideaway'. I wouldn't exactly say you were living there all by yourself. Rumour has it you took a different girl home every night."

Jesus, rodeo gossip was worse than ever. "I don't know who you've been getting your information from. I occasionally entertained a lady friend I met at work. It wasn't every night."

"Just admit that you don't like being home all alone either."

There was some truth to that, but not because I was scared to be alone. "Having another person around has its benefits, but we're probably not talking about the same benefits."

"Okay. That's enough. Spare me the details of your sordid love life."

"You want to explain how a girl who can get on a horse and chase a raging bull around an arena is scared to stay in a house by herself?"

There was a pause as she thought about it. "I do better if I don't have any time to think about the danger."

I smiled, knowing that well. "Cole's like that too."

"How's he doing?"

"He's all right."

She was quiet for a while before she asked, "Do you think you'll ever go back to riding?"

"Nope," I said without hesitation.

"But you were so good at it."

"Yeah, that was then." A tense sigh released along with the words.

"Before your dad's accident?" She paused, waiting for me to respond. I didn't, so she asked, "Have you talked to anybody about it yet?"

I rubbed my palm over my face trying to erase the memory. "What's there to talk about?"

"You can talk about how it made you feel to watch it happen; or you can talk about how you feel now that you have to take care of your mom and your brother; or you can talk about how it scared you so bad that you can't ride anymore."

The air in my lungs leaked out in a long and slow exhale. The same way I always breathed right before I got in the chute. "I'm not scared and I don't want to talk about the rest of it."

She fortunately surrendered the quest to fix Billy and changed the subject. "How's Stella?"

"Good, I guess. I haven't talked to Tawnie."

"Oh." She seemed surprised and paused before she changed the

57

subject again by asking me a question about the ferry to Luxton. I plugged the recharger for my phone in and turned the truck engine on long enough to top the battery up.

We talked for the next two and a half hours about pretty much everything. When the sky started to lighten, she yawned.

"You ready to go to sleep now that it's morning?"

She laughed. "Yes, but now I have to get out of bed and go feed the animals."

"Yeah, I should go inside and get ready for my day job."

"Sorry to keep you up all night."

"It's all right." I watched the sun peek up over the horizon, surprised that I didn't feel tired at all.

"Thanks, Billy."

"Don't mention it." I hung up then went inside. There were six beer bottles on the kitchen table, and since my mom wasn't a drinker, I knew it was Cole. I checked his room, but it looked as if his bed hadn't been slept in. He wasn't on the couch either. I knocked on the bathroom door. "Cole?" There was no answer, so I tried the doorknob. It was locked. "Cole. Open up," I shouted through the door.

Mom opened her bedroom door and tied the belt to her house-coat. "What's going on?"

"Didn't the doctor say you should start using your chair in the house?"

She raised her eyebrow in her notorious scolding expression. "I can still get around in my own home, thank you. I'm not an invalid. What's going on?"

"Did Cole stay here last night?"

"He was here when I went to bed." Her irritation at me transitioned into concern.

I rattled the bathroom doorknob and knocked again. Mom disappeared into her room and returned with a hairpin. She wiggled it in the hole of the doorknob. Eventually the lock clicked and she pushed the door open. It only opened about four inches then stopped as if it hit something. She poked her head in.

"Oh, Jesus. He's passed out on the floor." She stepped back and let me push the door with my shoulder. I was able to open it wide enough for her to slip through. She crouched down and moved his legs so I could open the door all the way. "Oh, Billy, he doesn't look right. You better call the ambulance."

Chapter 6

At the hospital, I wheeled my mom's chair up to a table, then sat down across from a psychiatrist, two doctors, and a social worker. The social worker folded her hands on the table and smiled at us in a pleasant way that made me uncomfortable. The bald doctor helped himself to a cookie from the plate on the table. The other doctor watched Cole come into the room with a nurse and sit beside me. Cole looked like shit. His hair was messy, his face was pale, and the smell of beer was still noticeable on his breath. The psychiatrist was reviewing the file and tapping her pen on a pad of paper as she read. Eventually, she looked up and smiled at us. "So, Cole. How are you feeling?"

"Fine."

"You gave your mom and brother quite a scare."

He looked down at the table and licked his lips.

"According to them, you were doing well until this incident occurred."

"This wasn't an incident. I just had a couple drinks."

"Yes, but you know that the medication you're on can not be taken with alcohol."

"So, give me a different medication." He sat back and crossed his arms in defiance. "All my friends and my brother drink, and I can't. It's affecting my quality of life."

"I'll quit," I mumbled so only he could hear me.

"Why?" He turned towards me. "So we both can't have any fun?" He looked back at the professionals across the table. "Just give me a different medication."

"But this one has been working so well," Mom said.

"Not really. I still feel like shit half the time. Billy has to drag me out of bed most days because I can't sleep at night. My stomach is always upset, and I get headaches that I never used to."

"Have you had any suicidal ideation? Intrusive thoughts? Unusual worries or obsessions?"

"Yeah."

They all looked up, intrigued more than concerned. "Which ones?"

"All of them," he said to mess with them.

"Can you be a little more specific, please?" the psychiatrist asked.

"Well." He stretched his legs out under the table and crossed his ankles as if he was getting comfortable, but his arms were still crossed. "I worry that I left the stove on even if I haven't used it, or sometimes I think I left the bath running even though I had a shower." He sat forward abruptly and rested his elbows on the table. "Is wanting to stab someone in the eyeball an intrusive thought? I get that sometimes. Oh, and I have to dress in exactly the same order every time or I think that something bad is going to happen to my mom."

"Did you dress in a particular order before your dad was killed?"

He smiled, amused by how gullible they were. "No. I put my left sock on first instead of the right. Damn. Do you think that's why he died? I never thought about that until you mentioned it. Way to go. Now I'm going to obsess about that until I get around to acting on the suicidal ideation."

I shook my head, tired of his antics, and Mom wrung her hands together.

The psychiatrist smiled at Cole in an unimpressed way once she figured out he was bullshitting. "If you aren't going to take this seriously, we won't be able to help you effectively. Do you want our help or not?"

"Not."

She wrote something on her pad of paper.

"Stop dicking around," I mumbled.

"Oh," he continued, enjoying it too much to stop. "I do have one real obsessive thought."

They all looked at him again. So gullible.

"I have sexual fantasies about my psychiatrist." He winked at her. "The images are very graphic. She's not wearing anything except little diamond nipple rings and black stilettos. She dances around for me and puts little blue pills on my tongue before straddling my lap. The images pop in and out, and in and out, of my mind. I actually don't mind though."

Fed up, Mom rolled her wheelchair back from the table and headed towards the exit. The nurse who had escorted Cole in opened the door.

Cole watched it close behind her. Then he glared at the psychiatrist and his joking tone changed. "Listen, I'll take medication to balance out my moods, but don't try to label me with more issues that I don't have. I'm not OCD, I'm not suicidal, and I'm not homicidal. I want to be able to drink, I don't want to get man boobs, I don't want my ability to perform sexually to be affected, and I don't want to have to take more pills to deal with side effects. If you don't have a medication that can do all that, I won't be taking anything."

"We need to ask you these questions to make sure we are using the best medication for your symptoms. If you don't have a particular symptom, simply say that you do not have that symptom. You don't need to play games with us."

"Okay, let me summarize for you. I get depressed and do nothing for a while. Then I get manic and do a bunch of crazy shit for a while. When I take your medication, I don't get depressed or manic, but I can't sleep or eat or drink alcohol. I'm really not convinced that your way is better."

The psychiatrist took a deep breath as if she needed to compose herself so she wouldn't lose it on him. "If you attended your weekly sessions, we would be able to monitor your symptoms better and adjust your dosages."

"Yeah, well, I'm busy."

I glanced over at him. "Cut it out," I said under my breath.

He sat back in the chair and folded his arms across his chest again. "I suppose you're going to give me something for belligerence."

She put the pen down and smiled, but seemed exhausted. "I wish it were that simple. There is an easy way to avoid these types of meetings if you dislike them so much."

"How's that?"

"Follow your treatment protocol and stop abusing your body."

He tilted his head and grinned at her, prepared to push her to her breaking point. "I like the abuse. What does that say about me?"

"It says that you're a twenty-two year old male who hasn't matured enough yet to know what's really important." Her tone made it clear she was losing her patience.

"So, because you spent something like twelve years in university, you think you know what's really important to me?"

She paused as if she was contemplating walking out, but then asked, "What's really important to you, Cole?"

"Riding bulls and getting laid. If I can't do those two things I'd rather be dead. And yes, that is a suicide threat."

She lifted her eyebrows and did the unimpressed smile again. She rested her chin on her palm and tapped her finger on her lip as she stared at him, out of ideas.

"Cole, you almost died," the bald doctor said. "If you keep doing things like that, your liver is going to give out. You can't ride bulls if your liver gets damaged."

Cole actually seemed to hear that, but then he stood. "May I leave now? I've got a rodeo I need to get to."

63

They all glanced at each other to confer. The social worker finally answered, "Well, Cole, it's your life, but when you don't take care of yourself or take your mental health seriously, you burden your family."

"I don't hear them complaining."

The psychiatrist's eyes pleaded with me to speak up and tell him how much of a burden it was to deal with his shit all the time. I didn't say anything, so she said, "Your mother is struggling with multiple sclerosis, her husband was recently killed, and she had to sell the family ranch to pay off the debt. Even if she doesn't complain, I'm certain that having her eldest son purposefully do things that could seriously harm or even kill him, is something that causes her distress."

Cole left.

The other professionals all shifted their focus to me.

I put my hat back on.

The doctor said, "He needs to understand that mental illness is not something he can ignore. If he doesn't take his treatment seriously it will impact his ability to work, socialize, and eventually compromise his physical health."

I nodded. I'd heard it all before. It wasn't me who needed convincing.

"Your mother's MS is possibly exasperated by this stress."

"Yes, Sir. I know."

"Has he talked about your father's death with you?" the psychiatrist asked.

"No, Ma'am."

"Has he visited the gravesite yet, or done something else to say goodbye?"

"No, Ma'am. Not that I'm aware of."

"Closure is important and the fact that he refused to attend the funeral will make it difficult for him to process through his grief."

"Cole does things in his own way."

"I'm sure you can encourage him in the right direction."

I chuckled since that was highly unlikely. "Do you know why bulls buck?"

"Because you tie some sort of rope around its testicles."

"No. The flank strap sits on the abdomen. They buck because they want to. If they don't want to, they don't. You can't make them do shit if they don't want to."

She nodded, wrote something on her prescription pad, and ripped the page off. "Cole's not a bull. He can start taking this. It doesn't have the contraindications with alcohol, but I still don't recommend that he use any sort of substance. He has to wean off the other one slowly. He can't just abruptly stop taking it. Please monitor him and make sure he follows the directions." She slid the paper across the table.

"Can he ride this weekend?" I folded the prescription and put it in my pocket.

She shrugged. "If he feels like it."

"Is he free to go?"

"Yes."

I tipped my hat then left.

Cole was standing in the hall with his back against the wall waiting for me. His cockiness was gone.

"What the hell's wrong with you?"

"I'm crazy, remember?"

"No you're not. You're just an idiot." I punched his shoulder. "Get dressed. We have to go find Mom. You probably made her cry."

He frowned because he hated the idea of women crying as much as I did. "Do you feel like I'm a burden?" he asked, serious.

"I feel like you're a pain in the ass, but since you're my brother I guess I'll have to live with it."

Relieved, he wrapped his arm around my neck and gave me a strangle hug. "Thanks, man."

"Don't mention it. Let's go somewhere where it pays to be crazy."

"Yeah, baby."

Chapter 7

We landed at the airport in Victoria on Thursday evening and took a cab to the hotel. The hotel was close to the Luxton fairgrounds and was full of rodeo participants. We checked in and then walked past the pool. Lee-Anne and Rochelle were lounging on deck chairs in their bikinis, so Cole and I stopped to take a look. I felt a pinch on my waist.

"Hey, Billy. I thought you weren't coming," Shae-Lynn said as she bounced by us. Her sparkly pink bikini showed off her athletic body.

"I…" I pointed my thumb at Cole. "He, uh, I changed my mind."

"Are you coming for a swim?" she asked with a grin that I couldn't quite interpret.

"I didn't bring a bathing suit."

"That's too bad, unless you want to dive in wearing jeans and a pearl snap." She walked backwards for a few steps.

I was trying to figure out when she had gotten all grown up and it took me a second to focus back on the conversation, "Hey, uh, what's, how's your mom doing? You know, with her concussion."

"She's feeling better. Both my parents came with us."

"Do you girls want to join us for dinner?" Cole asked.

"We already ate, but maybe we'll see you later." She smiled, then waved.

I watched her ass as she walked away, which felt a bit weird since it was Shae-Lynn.

"Good Lord, will you look at that," Cole said. "Someone's all grown up." He shoved my shoulder. "I said look at it, not stare at it. What's wrong with you?" He pointed to where I was clutching at my chest.

I shook my head, not sure. "Do heart problems run in the family? I think I've got a murmur or something."

"Yeah. All the men on Mom's side keeled over from heart attacks."

"Great." I winced from the discomfort before I followed him to the room.

He flopped down on the bed and read through the welcome package. "Let's go to the midway," he said.

"You know I hate carnival rides."

"Who cares about the rides? They'll have mini donuts and girls."

"Underage girls. You need to be careful unless you're planning on getting arrested. Again."

"Hey, I've only been arrested for fighting, not perving."

"It's a slippery slope." I laughed as I sat on the chair and turned the TV on.

"Yeah, you would know, Mr. Grand Theft Auto."

"Hey, I borrowed that chick's truck for you. You're welcome."

He smiled appreciatively, then disappeared into the bathroom. He took forever to shower and get ready. We didn't arrive at the fair until ten and I was starving. After walking around for a while, I bought a slice of pizza from a stand. Cole left me there as he went to search for the mini donuts. While I was standing eating my pizza, I spotted a girl with long strawberry coloured hair at the shooting gallery. Her back was to me and she stood with a wide, slightly angled, stance as she shot a rifle at moving targets. She was wearing short cut-off jean shorts and a tank top. I walked up and watched from over her shoulder. She knocked every one down.

"Nice shooting."

She jumped a little and spun around to face me. "Hey." She tucked her hair behind her ears. "Thanks."

Before I had a chance to say anything else, Lee-Anne bounced around from behind me, stole my hat, and put it on Shae-Lynn's head. "Hey, Billy Ray. Where's your brother at?"

"The mini donut stand."

She smiled as if she was scheming something. "Mmm. That sounds good, doesn't it, Rochelle?"

"What?" Rochelle asked as she joined us. She was texting on her phone and not really paying attention.

"Mini donuts with Cole. We'll see you two later." Lee-Anne tugged Rochelle's elbow and they disappeared into the crowd.

Shae-Lynn put my hat back on my head. She glanced at me, then looked over at the people lined up for the Ferris wheel.

"Where'd you learn how to shoot like that?"

"My dad taught me. I think he secretly wished I was born a boy." The game attendant handed her a stuffed rabbit for winning.

"Remind me not to piss you off."

She smiled and hooked her thumbs through her belt loops. "Is Stella here?"

"No. Tawnie said she was racing somewhere else this weekend."

She nodded, but acted awkward as if she didn't know how to respond. Eventually, she changed the subject, "I was thinking about getting a drink. Do you want to get something?"

"Sure."

We made our way through the row of carnival games and out onto the grass where the bigger rides were. She pulled my elbow and stepped sideways to line-up in front of a freshly squeezed lemonade stand.

"I thought you meant a real drink." I chuckled and gave a ten-dollar bill to the girl who passed Shae-Lynn the cups of lemonade.

"I've got my own money." She handed me my drink and dug into her front pocket to pull out a five-dollar bill. She flapped it around trying to make me take it.

"It's fine. I got it."

She smiled and folded the money back in her pocket. "Thank you. I'll buy your ticket for the rollercoaster or something."

"No thanks. I don't like rides."

She laughed to tease me. "How can a bull rider not like midway rides?"

"I just don't. They make me want to throw up."

She tugged my hand and led me to a ride that was a bunch of chain swings suspended from a circular carousel thing. "You can do this one," she encouraged. "Look, there are children getting on it."

I frowned and studied the stability of the apparatus as she paid the attendant. The swings were only about three feet off the ground, so I sat down in the one next to hers and tested the chains for sturdiness.

She sipped her lemonade, then arranged her stuffed bunny so it was propped up next to her. "You ready?"

"What's it do?"

"Just spins around. Clip the lap belt."

A buzzer rang and music piped in as the entire carousel spun. After a couple rotations, the force from the speed pulled our swings outward until we were flying sideways. "Uh, how fast does this thing go?" I placed the lemonade between my thighs so I could hang on properly with two hands.

She laughed and raised her arms in the air, completely carefree. "Not much faster than this."

That's when the centre support of the carousel began rising. My fingers gripped the chain as I peeked over the edge at the receding ground. "Shit." My eyes clenched shut and every muscle in my body seized up.

Shae-Lynn laughed.

I opened one eye to check, and all I saw was sky whizzing by. "How high does it go? I'm feeling queasy."

Shae-Lynn's arm reached out towards me. She leaned her upper body over the edge of the swing in order to bridge the gap between

69

us.

"Careful. Don't. You're going to fall out."

"It's fine," she said with genuine calmness. "Grab my hand." Her hair swirled around in the wind the same way it did when she was riding Harley. The lights on the ride reflected in her eyes and made the gloss of her lips sparkle. She smiled and encouraged me to reach over.

I pried the fingers of my left hand off the chain and reached my arm out. It took two attempts before our hands connected. She pulled our swings close together and laughed as she used all her strength to keep us together. My eyes met hers and I kept staring.

"What?" She tilted her head to study my expression, wondering why I was acting weird.

Although I knew it was because I couldn't believe I had never noticed how beautiful she was before. I shrugged and said, "I don't know."

She lifted her eyebrows in a mischievous way as if she might have known what I was thinking, then she released her grip on my swing. She waved as my swing catapulted outwards and strained the chains to the point of creaking.

I clenched my eyes shut for the rest of the nauseating ride. Once the swings were lowered close enough to the ground for me to feel comfortable again, I said, "You're going to regret that, Shae-Lynn."

She giggled, collected her drink and bunny, and took off running. Once I got myself unfastened from the lap belt, I chased her and lunged to grab her by the waist with my left arm while attempting not to dump my drink with my right. She squealed and buckled over trying to loosen my grip.

"I told you I don't like rides because they make me sick. I think your punishment should be me chucking you in that dunk tank over there."

"No, no, no. I'm sorry. I'll never do it again." She laughed and squirmed until she was facing me. "I'm sorry." Her bottom lip jutted out in a pout that probably let her get away with murder when she used it on her dad. "I really am sorry. Do you forgive me?"

When I realized how close we were and what kind of message that might have been sending to the people watching us, I released her.

She winked, proud that she got away with the prank. "You're such a wuss." She took a sip of lemonade and was smiling until she saw something over my shoulder that made her expression change.

Blake slapped me on the back, stood next to Shae-Lynn, and squeezed his arm across her shoulder. "Hey, Shae. How you been?"

Instead of answering him, she glared at me and warned, "Don't."

When Blake noticed how intensely she was looking at me, he turned his head. "Am I interrupting something?"

Neither one of us answered.

He looked her up and down. "Do you want go on some rides, Shae?"

"No, thank you."

"I could win you a teddy bear or something."

She held up the bunny that she'd won for herself. "I've already got one, thanks."

He focused back on me and I could tell by the smirk on his face that he was going to try to provoke me. "I heard your brother got a weekend pass from the loony bin to come here."

I didn't respond because I had promised Shae-Lynn I wouldn't do anything to him.

He reached over and took a sip of Shae-Lynn's lemonade. She curled her lip and handed the whole cup to him.

"Don't you want any more?"

"No. I'm done."

I handed mine to her and she smiled before taking a sip. Lee-Anne walked around from behind me and leaned her elbow on Shae-Lynn's shoulder. She popped a mini donut in her mouth and talked around it. "Hey, Blake." She grinned at me as if she was waiting for me to clock him.

Cole and Rochelle joined us. Without saying anything, Cole

71

handed me his bag of mini donuts. He said "Hi" to Blake, then punched him across the cheekbone. The force made Blake fall backwards onto the grass and the lemonade soaked his shirt.

Shae-Lynn screamed. Lee-Anne clapped. Rochelle looked confused.

Blake held his face and tried to sit up. "What the hell, Cole?"

"That was for taking advantage of Shae and then making her walk home by herself from the hotel." He held his hand out so I would give his donuts back.

Shae-Lynn's mouth dropped open as she glared at me. "Billy."

"What? I didn't do anything."

"Really?" She propped her hand on her hip, pissed. "Who told Cole what happened?"

"I —"

Her anger melted into embarrassment and her voice cracked. "You promised me." She spun around and bumped into her dad's chest. The lemonade slipped out of her hand, fell to the grass, and splashed everywhere. She ducked around her dad and chucked the bunny on the ground before running away.

Mr. Roberts frowned as he assessed what was going on. "You took advantage of my daughter?" he asked Blake.

Blake scrambled to his feet and brushed the dust off his jeans. "No, Sir."

"Why do these boys think you did?"

"I don't know. I took her out on a date when we were in Coleman, but nothing happened. I swear."

Lee-Anne and I both winced when he said Coleman.

"I see." Mr. Roberts shot Lee-Anne a look that could have made a wolf high-tail it out of there. "Get," he said, and she and Rochelle took off. "You," he pointed at Blake, "I better not see you around either one of them again. Got it?"

"Yes, Sir." Blake walked away and left Cole and me standing with Mr. Roberts.

"Shae-Lynn's a good girl," I said.

"Yeah, and I'd like to keep it that way."

"She didn't do anything wrong. Blake's an idiot, but she handled it. I hope she's not going to get in trouble or anything."

"They were in Coleman when I was told they were in Calgary. I don't appreciate being lied to." He turned and walked away.

I considered telling him that their mom knew they were in Coleman and technically lied to him too, but I figured throwing her under the bus would only make everything worse. "Shit," I mumbled.

Cole offered me a mini donut, but I pushed his hand away.

"Hey," Tyson said as he walked up with a hotdog in one hand and beer in the other. "I just saw Blake. He called you both pricks. What did I miss?"

Cole shook his head to indicate it was no big deal. "Nothing. I just had to teach him a lesson on being a gentleman."

"Why? What did he do?"

"He messed with the wrong girl."

"Who? Tawnie?" He looked at me and took a bite of his hotdog.

"Shae," Cole said.

He nodded as if he'd already heard what happened in Coleman and wasn't surprised. He took another bite and spoke with his mouth full. "Some guys are getting together for a poker game. Do you want in?"

"Yeah." Cole shoved me in the arm. "You in?"

I wasn't sure what else I could do to convince Mr. Roberts to give Shae-Lynn a break without causing more problems, so I nodded. I picked up the stuffed bunny from the grass and followed them through the midway back towards the participants' lot. The poker game was being held in Mutt the bullfighter's camper. He was parked four down from the Roberts' motorhome and as we got closer, I noticed that the engine was running. "I'll meet you guys there in a minute," I said before I jogged over and found Shae-Lynn loading Harley into the trailer. "Hey, I'm sorry I told Cole. I didn't know he would do that."

"Yes, you did," she snapped.

"Okay, maybe, but I didn't know he would do it in front of your dad."

"Yeah, well, he did and now my dad's making me withdraw from the competition and go home." She closed the trailer door and slid the lock.

"You're almost nineteen years old. You can stay if you want to."

"And ride what horse? He owns Harley and his trailer."

I really wanted to offer to let her ride Stella, but I didn't even know where she was.

"Let's go, Shae," her dad shouted out the driver's window of the motorhome.

"Sorry," I said again and handed her the stuffed bunny.

She held it by the neck like it was dead. "Yeah, me too."

I reached for her elbow and made her turn to face me. "No. I'm really sorry you're going to miss the competition. If I knew that was going to happen, I wouldn't have told Cole."

"You shouldn't have told Cole anyway. You promised you wouldn't tell."

"I didn't promise that. I promised I wouldn't do anything to Blake."

"I told you I didn't want anybody to know. I thought I could trust you." Her voice wavered, on the verge of tears.

"He deserved it."

"No he didn't. Blake ran after me that night. He was going to walk me back to the motorhome, but I got into your truck before he had a chance to catch up. He apologized the next day and I forgave him."

"Why didn't you tell me that when we talked on the phone?"

"It shouldn't matter whether he apologized or not. You promised me." She jerked her arm to make me let go of her elbow and walked towards the door.

"Shae-Lynn, come on. You know I didn't mean for it to happen that way. I was just trying to do right by you."

"Doing right by me would have been respecting my wishes and keeping your promises. Leave me alone, Billy. I don't want to be friends with someone I can't depend on." She climbed the steps and slammed the door behind her.

They rolled out and I watched until they turned onto the main road and disappeared. I exhaled, not sure why it rattled me as much as it did. Eventually I wandered over to Mutt's camper. He offered us beers. Cole declined, so I did too. Mutt stared at us confused for a second, but then he must have remembered why Cole couldn't drink. "All right. Let's play some poker."

I sat down at the dinette table and threw my money on the table. "Everything okay?" Cole asked as he sat next to me.

"Yeah."

He always knew when I was lying, but he didn't push it, so either he didn't want to get into it in front of the guys, or he didn't care what was bugging me. He picked up his cards and bet. I didn't even look at my cards — I called. I lost.

Lots of girls thought I was an asshole and it had never bothered me all that much before. There was something about the disappointed expression on Shae-Lynn's face that I couldn't get out of my head.

After we'd been playing cards for about an hour there was a knock at the camper door. Tyson got up and opened it. I couldn't see her, but I could tell who asked, "Is Billy Ryan here?"

He turned and made his eyebrows dance up and down. "Someone's here to see you, Billy."

Cole had to slide along the bench to let me out. I didn't really have the option of avoiding her, so I stood and put my hat on. "Deal me out." I stepped out onto the grass and closed the door behind me.

Tawnie didn't say anything. It seemed as if she was waiting for me to explain why I never called. She was wearing her sky blue hat and a jean jacket that matched. I tried to come up with something to say, but I had no idea what the right thing was.

Eventually, I said, "I wasn't expecting to see you. I thought you were going to Falkland."

"I got mixed up."

"How's Stella?"

"She's good. You can come by and see her tomorrow." She shifted her weight to her right foot and hooked her thumbs in her back pocket. "Did you get my note and the cheque?"

"Yeah. Thanks."

It was a little too dark to tell for sure, but her eyes seemed a little glassy as if she was going to cry. "You must have been really busy."

"Yeah. I was working two jobs and my brother was hospitalized, so it was kind of chaotic."

"Hospitalized for what?"

"Uh, he had something like an allergic reaction."

She shifted her weight to her left foot and sighed. After staring down at the ground for a few seconds, she glanced up at my face. "It felt like maybe we shared something special, and you're acting as if you wish it never happened. Did I do something wrong?"

I pushed my hat back and looked over my shoulder at the camper. Five guys were crowded in the window watching us, so I reached over and grabbed her hand. "Let's go for a walk." I led her around the back of the bull pens and sat on the edge of a picnic table. The music and buzzers from the rides of the midway seemed loud. She stood facing me hugging herself as if she was cold. "I'm sorry I didn't call you. I just don't date girls from the circuit."

"But you have no problem sleeping with them?"

"Dating long distance is too complicated. It doesn't work."

"Are you saying you'd be interested in dating me if we lived in the same town?"

The answer was no, but I figured that wouldn't go over that well. I turned my head out of habit to spit tobacco. It must have looked strange since I had nothing to spit. Her eyes were definitely watery at that point. "I didn't know you were interested in dating. I figured you only did what you did because you felt like

76

you owed me for Stella."

"You think I slept with you because you let me ride your horse?"

I shrugged because it was a logical assumption.

"If that were the case, I would technically need to sleep with Ron Miller."

I chuckled at the thought of her sleeping with a guy almost thirty years older than her. "That's sick."

She smiled a little and wiped the tears from her cheek.

"I didn't mean to hurt you. I just didn't think you wanted it to be more than what it was."

"So, in your mind I'm the type of girl who goes around thanking guys by sleeping with them?"

I shrugged. "I really didn't have any other information to go on. What was I supposed to think?"

"I don't know. Oh my God. You're right." She got choked up again and pressed her palms over her eyes. "I'm so stupid." She dropped her hands and stared at the empty rodeo arena. "It never occurred to me that you would think I was a trashy buckle bunny. I know you're not going to believe me now, but I'm not a slut. I've only been with one other guy, and he was a long-term boyfriend." She held her stomach. "Oh God, I feel sick. I'm sorry I screwed things up between us. I'm so embarrassed." She spun around and walked fast.

"Tawnie." I chased after her and reached forward to grab her elbow. She flinched as if she thought I was going to hit her or something. I let go of her arm and she relaxed. Her face was turned to the side, so I gently held her chin and rotated it to make her look at me. "If it wasn't to thank me for Stella and you don't normally do that sort of thing, why did you sleep with me?"

"I wanted to," she answered without even needing to think about it.

"You hardly know me."

"I know." She covered her eyes with her hands again. "God, what's wrong with me? You must think I'm such an idiot."

77

I wasn't sure how I felt.

She dropped her hand. "I had a huge crush on you when we were on the junior circuit. When I saw you again, I realized I still had a crush on you. Then when we were dancing at the bar, I could feel your heart racing. I hoped you felt the same way about me. Maybe it was because I didn't know when I was going to see you next, or maybe it really was because of Stella. Obviously, I made a mistake by rushing things and if I could take it back I would." She tipped the brim of her hat down and kicked at the dirt. "I feel like I'm going to die of embarrassment, so if we could just forget that it ever happened, that would be great."

I stared at her for a while, then I said, "I had a crush on you back on the junior circuit too."

She looked up, surprised. "Really?"

"Yeah. You disappeared and I always wondered what happened to you. I was about to go over and talk to you when I saw you again last season."

"Why didn't you?"

"A bull stomped my face in. That probably sounds like a made-up excuse, but it really happened."

She laughed.

We were standing on the empty spot on the grass where the Roberts' motorhome had been parked. The script of Shae-Lynn giving me shit ran through my mind as I took my hat off and ran my hand through my hair. The old Billy would have made up an excuse for why he couldn't see Tawnie again, but I really wanted to hit the reset button and prove that I could be a stand up guy. "What do you say we have a redo on Saturday night at the dance?"

She nodded enthusiastically. "Okay. Can we pretend like Coleman never happened?"

I laughed and admitted, "There are a few things about Coleman I wouldn't mind remembering if that's all right with you."

She shoved my shoulder and then rested against my chest for a hug. Her hair smelled like lavender scented shampoo and my mind created an image of what she must have looked like stepping out of the shower all tanned and slick. My palm slid up her arm and over the slope of her shoulder to just below her ear. She closed her eyes and tilted her head to lean into the support of my hand. My thumb caressed her cheek.

"I've been dreaming about your touch since the last time I saw you," she whispered.

I gently pressed my lips to the silky softness of her neck.

"I should get going," she whispered and pulled away as if she was worried the night would end up the same way as it did in Coleman if she didn't leave.

"Do you want me to walk you back to the hotel?"

She shook her head as if she thought it was a bad idea, but smiled as if she wouldn't mind if I did. "I'm fine thanks. You should go back to your poker game."

"All right. I'll see you tomorrow."

"Tomorrow," she repeated before she turned and walked away.

My phone buzzed in my pocket. I watched her walk until she turned the corner, then read the text from Tyson. "Shit," I mumbled and rushed back to Mutt's camper.

Chapter 8

On Saturday afternoon, Cole eased into the chute to set up for his go. I pressed my foot against the bull's shoulder, but didn't pull the rope. Cole looked up at me to see what I was waiting on.

"No pressure, but I owe eight thousand dollars plus interest on a horse I don't even want, and you lost your twenty thousand dollar camper in a stupid bet. You need to hang on to this bull."

"Yeah, I got it. Pull the damn rope," he grumbled around his mouthguard.

I pulled it, then slapped him three times on the back, a little harder than was necessary.

He tucked his chin and nodded.

The bull initially shot out of the gate and went into a series of tight spins, but one of the bullfighters smacked his head and forced him to rear up and start bucking good. He pulled out every move to try to throw Cole, but nothing worked. Cole was in the zone and he had the best ride of his life. The buzzer rang and he hopped off clean.

We all looked up at the scoreboard. He got a ninety-two, which was his personal best and only two points shy of my personal best. He turned and pointed at me before he climbed the fence and waved his hat at the crowd. After he'd showboated for a while, he jumped down and shoved me in the chest. "How was that, baby?"

"It was pretty good, but you're going to need to do it again tomorrow in the finals — and every time after that for the rest of the season if we're going to pay our bills."

"Yeah, yeah. Don't worry." He took my hat off and hit me with it. "Stop being a buzz kill. That was a personal best."

I slapped his back. "You did good. Dad would have been proud."

He smiled and watched the last two riders. They did all right, but Cole kept his lead. "Let's go celebrate."

"I can't. I've got a date."

He raised his eyebrow, ready to give me the gears. "With Tawnie?"

"Maybe."

"Well, well, well. Look who's acting like a proper gentleman. Find out if she has a friend who wants to help me celebrate."

"You don't need me to find your dates for you."

"Good point." He jumped up onto the outer railing of the grandstand and climbed over into the first row. A girl put her arm over his shoulder and kissed his cheek. He leaned over and shouted, "Don't wait up."

"Just make sure you can ride in the finals."

He smiled in a way that made it seem like he wasn't making any guarantees. Then he turned to talk to the girls who had crowded around him.

Tawnie was expecting me at eight, so I went back at the hotel, got cleaned up, and was ready to go by seven forty-five. My mouth was watering for some chew, so I popped three pieces of gum in my mouth instead. At five to, I walked down the hall and took the elevator to the third floor where Tawnie was staying. Before knocking, it occurred to me that I should show up with flowers or something. I turned around and went down to the lobby. The gift shop didn't have flowers, but I bought a box of chocolates and went back up to the third floor.

I knocked and heard her moving around inside before she opened the door. She looked mind blowing in tight white jeans and a white blouse that was tailored to show off her flat stomach. Her hair was curled in big bouncy waves. I was at a loss for words, so instead of speaking, I handed her the chocolates.

She smiled at my lack of coolness and disappeared to put them in the room. "Where are we going?" she asked as she stepped out into the hall and closed the door behind her.

I blinked about five times before I was able to speak. "Um, I researched online and found a steak house that's supposed to be pretty good. You're not a vegetarian, are you?"

"No, I like steak." She smiled again and seemed a little worried about why we were still standing in front of her door. "So, should we go then?"

"You look really nice," I finally said.

She closed her eyes and shook her head, embarrassed. "Thank you." She hooked her arm around my elbow and made me walk down the hall.

The cab was already waiting outside the front entrance of the lobby, so I opened the door for her and watched her ass as she slid in. After telling the cab driver the address of the restaurant, I glanced over at Tawnie and searched for something to talk about to break the awkwardness. "You and Stella posted a good time today."

"Yeah, I don't hardly have to do anything. She's just fast."

"You might have even beat Shae-Lynn if she were here."

"What happened to her? I heard she had to withdraw."

I shrugged, not wanting to gossip about it because it would bother Shae-Lynn if even more people knew.

Since I didn't answer, she asked another question, "Have you guys been friends for a long time?"

"I've known her since she was a baby. Her dad and my dad were friends. They grew up together in Saskatoon."

"I thought she was from Calgary?"

"They moved there about ten years ago."

She nodded and seemed unsure where to take the conversation from there. She tucked her hair behind her ears.

"Where are you from?" I asked to help her out.

"Originally, Winnipeg, but I moved to live with my grandparents in Edmonton after my parents were killed in a fire."

"Oh, sorry to hear that."

She looked into my eyes for a brief second, then stared down at her purse on her lap. "I heard you lost your dad."

"Yeah." I shifted in the seat and hoped she would move on to the next topic.

"He died in a wreck?"

My neck muscles tightened and my heart rate sped up. I figured it was probably better to make it clear right from the start that we weren't going to be talking about my dad, so without sugar-coating it I said, "I don't talk about it."

"Sorry." She bit at her nail until she came up with a less touchy question to ask. "What do you take at university?"

"I was taking business courses mostly, but I haven't been able to go back yet since I have other priorities right now."

"Like your brother?"

I inhaled and tipped my hat back. Avoiding touchy questions wasn't going to be possible if she wanted to know about my family, so I decided to get it over with. "What have you already heard about him?"

"That he's crazy and if you don't take care of him he gets himself into trouble." She looked over at me again, with caution. "That's just what I heard. I don't know what the real story is."

"That's pretty much accurate."

"What's wrong with him?"

"He has bipolar disorder."

"Don't they have medication for that?"

"Yeah, but it doesn't always work. And even when it does work, he doesn't always take it."

The cab pulled up in front of the restaurant, thankfully. I paid the driver and we got out. There was a bit of a wait, but I had made a reservation, so the hostess took us in right away. Blake and Tyson were already there with two girls. They were sitting at a table for four across from where we got seated.

"What's wrong?" Tawnie asked me.

"Nothing."

She looked over her shoulder. "Would you rather go somewhere else?"

"No, this is fine." I took my hat off and hung it on the back of my chair.

"Are you embarrassed for them to see us together?"

"No. Why would I be embarrassed to be seen with you?"

She shrugged insecurely. "I don't know. You're acting uncomfortable."

"It has nothing to do with you. I just don't like Blake all that much, and I'd rather not get into it with him here."

"He's nice. Why don't you like him?"

"He messed with the wrong girl."

Tawnie's expression changed, and she looked as if I slapped her or something. Her cheeks turned red.

"What's wrong?"

She shook her head and stared up at the ceiling blinking back tears. "Well, he didn't try to mess with me, so obviously there is some other girl you care enough about to get all worked up over."

I frowned and ran my hand through my hair. I hadn't meant for it to sound the way it did. "It's not like that."

"What's it like?"

The waiter came over to take our order, took our menus, and left. Tawnie tapped her fingers on the table as if she was still waiting on me to answer the question. I tore off some bread and offered the basket to her. She shook her head and then took a sip from her water glass. She eventually sat back in her chair and crossed her arms. "Do you have a girlfriend? Don't lie to me."

"No."

"Who's this girl you care about?"

"It doesn't matter. I told you; it wasn't like that."

84

"Do you want it to be like that with her?"

"I'm on a date here with you. If I wanted it to be like that with her, I'd be on a date here with her, now wouldn't I?"

"I don't know. Maybe she just wasn't available." She leaned her elbows on the table and rubbed her palms over her forehead. "Or, maybe she's just not easy. Shit." She looked up at me. "I want to go."

"We just got here."

"Yeah, I suddenly feel sick to my stomach." She stood and rushed towards the door.

I got up and cancelled our order, then asked the hostess to call us a cab. I stepped out into the parking lot, but couldn't see Tawnie. I wandered around the side of the restaurant and out to the sidewalk. Eventually, I spotted her leaning against a street light. I walked over and touched her arm, which made her flinch. "What was that all about in the restaurant?"

"I don't want to be some girl you just hook up with."

"I know."

"But you like someone else."

"I never said that."

"You didn't deny it either. You can't treat me like trash."

"I'm not treating you like trash. I asked you out to get to know you better. I don't date girls unless I like them. If I just wanted to sleep with you, I wouldn't take you out for steaks first."

She frowned, unconvinced, and chewed at her fingernail.

I stared at her trying to figure out what her problem was. "Did someone mess with you or something?"

After a long hesitation, she nodded.

"What happened?"

She mumbled, "I don't want to talk about it."

I stepped in to wrap my arms around her. She relaxed into my hug. We stood that way until the cab pulled up.

"Do you want to go back inside?" I asked.

"The cab's already here. Let's just go to a drive-thru or something."

That was fine with me, so I smiled and opened the door for her. My phone buzzed as she was sliding in. I read the text and mumbled, "Shit. Not again."

"What's wrong?"

I got in and told the driver to take us back to the hotel.

"Did you forget something?" Tawnie asked.

"Yeah, my brother."

When the cab pulled up in front of the hotel, there were already two cop cars there. Rochelle met me on the curb. "I told the hotel management that I already got a hold of you, but they still called the police."

"Thanks for letting me know. Where is he?"

She pointed up to the first floor roof. Cole was buck naked and dancing in a raunchy way with the flag pole.

"Jesus." I glanced at Tawnie to gauge her reaction. She stared up at him with an expression that was a mixture of amusement and disgust. When she looked over at me, it switched to pity. I walked over to where the cops were shouting up at him. "He's my brother. I'll take care of it."

"What's he high on?"

"He isn't high. He has a mental illness." I climbed up on a trashcan, so I was closer to the roof. "Hey, Cole." He stopped grinding on the pole. "Let's go to the dance. Tawnie and one of her friends are going to come with us."

"Is she as good looking as Tawnie?"

"Yeah."

He looked around the crowd of people who had gathered in the parking lot. Then he spotted the cop cars. "Why are the police here?"

"There was a burglary or something. You should go on inside and get dressed so we can go."

"Where?"

"To the dance with Tawnie and her friend. How did you get up there anyway?"

He looked around and frowned, disoriented. "I don't know. What are you all staring at?" he shouted.

"Hey, Rochelle," I said over my shoulder. "Can you get everybody to move inside, please?"

She nodded and herded people into the lobby. Tawnie must have paid the cab driver because he drove away and she followed Rochelle under the awning where Cole couldn't see them.

"Tell those cops to leave," Cole shouted.

"They can't leave until you come on down." I hopped off the trashcan and walked underneath where he was.

"Are they going to arrest me?"

"For what? Just come down so you can get dressed and go to the dance with us."

After about a minute of staring up at the sky, he turned around and mooned us as he bent over to grab the downspout. He dropped his legs over the edge of the roof and hung for a second before jumping barefoot onto the pavement. One of the cops tensed up and hovered his hand over his holster, which made Cole back away. "Why's he going for his gun?"

"He's not. You just look a little crazy right now since you're not wearing any clothes."

He glanced down at his nudeness and chuckled as if he was surprised. "Are they going to take me to the hospital?"

"Not unless you want to go."

"I can't. I have to ride in the finals tomorrow. We need the money."

"No. We'll be okay. You don't need to ride tomorrow if you don't feel like it."

He crouched in a fighting stance and spread his arms out like he was acting out a scene from a ninja movie. He made weird yelping sounds.

"Settle down, Cole."

"Tell the cops to leave or I'll take them out with my mad black belt skills. Whaaaa."

"You don't have a black belt. If you don't settle down, I'm going to call Mom."

"No. Don't call her." He stood up straight and relaxed his arms at his side.

The cop beside me suddenly rushed Cole and tackled him to the ground.

"What the hell?" I shouted.

Cole fought really hard and punched the cop in the face a couple times before launching him against the cruiser. The other cop had no choice but to try to restrain him. Even with two cops beating on him, Cole was not surrendering. Eventually, he broke free, scrambled to his feet, and backed away. The cops both stood. The twitchy one pulled out his taser.

"Don't tase him. Just back off," I said and stepped between them and Cole. "Hey, look at me." Cole's eyes were wide and he wasn't focused on me. Blood from his nose was smeared all over his chest. "Cole. Look at me." He blinked, then frowned when he saw me standing in front of him. The tendons in his neck stretched tight and his chest heaved. "Cole, you need to calm down."

"They attacked me. I'll kill them if they come near me."

"No, you won't. You can't say that to a cop."

"I can say whatever I want." His voice got louder and he pointed at them with jabbing motions. "This is a free country. These fascist pigs can't tell me what to do. Who gave them the authority to take away my freedom? Last time I checked, I didn't live in a police state. I don't have to acknowledge a repressive totalitarian authority. As far as I'm concerned, they're just a bunch of Nazis who can go fuck themselves."

I looked over my shoulder at the twitchy cop. "Can you put that taser away? You're agitating him."

"I'm going to kill you, fucking Nazis," Cole shouted and moved in their direction.

The cop raised the taser gun and fired. The electrodes flew by my cheek and the darts insert into Cole's shoulder. He collapsed and convulsed grotesquely. His back arched and his face grimaced with each bolt. "He's down, God damn it. Stop it. He's down."

The cop released the trigger and Cole contorted one more time before writhing around in pain. He groaned, then tried to get up.

"Stay down." I knelt beside him and dug my fingers into his arm. He tried to get up again, so I pulled his ear. "Stay down or I will beat you myself."

He rolled over and groaned again. "Fucking pigs."

"Shut up." I looked up at the cop who was more level-headed and said, "He needs to go to a psychiatric hospital, not jail."

He nodded and spoke into the radio that was hooked to his shoulder. He called an ambulance, then crouched beside me. "Hey, Cole. I need to put some restraints on your wrists. If you cooperate, I'll make sure they're nice and loose. You're not going to jail. We're just going to take you to the hospital and make sure you're all right. Your brother can stay with you the whole time."

"Fuck you, pig." Cole spit in the cop's direction.

I leaned my elbow on Cole's cheek, ground his head into the cement, and spoke right up against his face, "Shut your God damn mouth and be cooperative or I'm leaving you here by yourself. You understand?"

His face contorted as if I'd stabbed him, and he stopped fighting.

"Put your hands behind your back," I said. He did it, so I took the pressure off his face.

By the time the ambulance arrived he had calmed down a little and he said, "Sorry, Billy. I don't feel good. Something's wrong with me. Don't tell Mom. Sorry."

I exhaled stress, and helped him sit up. "Don't worry. I'll take care of everything. It's going to be okay."

Chapter 9

Three days after the incident in Victoria, I was driving home from my shift at the bar when my phone rang. I checked the message once I was parked in the driveway at my mom's house. "Hey, Billy. It's Shae. Um, I guess you're still at work, or maybe you're sleeping. I heard about what happened with Cole in Victoria. Um, yeah, so I'm just calling to see how you're doing. I know we kind of left things weird, but I want you to know that you can always call me if you need someone to talk to. Always. Okay, so call if you want to. Or not. Yeah. Okay, bye."

I went inside and showered. After making myself a sandwich, I lay on my bed and called her back.

"Hey," she said.

"Hey, I got your message. Did I wake you?"

"No, I just turned my light off."

"Do you want me to call you back in the morning?"

"No, it's okay." Something about her voice was as soothing as someone singing a lullaby. It instantly relaxed me. "Were you working?"

"Yeah. I just got home. I was surprised to hear from you. I thought you weren't going to talk to me ever again after the whole Blake thing."

She hesitated before she responded, "That was the plan, but

then I figured you were probably upset over what happened with Cole. I owe you an all night phone call."

"I'm not upset."

"You should be. It sounded terrible." Her tone was both apologetic and appalled.

"It wasn't that bad."

"How's he doing?"

"A little better. My mom flew out to Victoria to be with him so I could come home and work."

"So, you're all alone in the house?"

"Yeah, it's pretty quiet."

"You mean scary," she teased.

I laughed. "Nah, I don't get scared." I fluffed up my pillow and propped my head against the headboard before taking a bite of sandwich.

"Liar. You were scared on that midway ride."

"I was sick, not scared."

"Oh, really? So, nothing scares you?" she challenged.

"Not that I know of."

"That's not normal."

"What scares you?" I asked.

"Rattlesnakes, tsunamis, algebra, cancer, the entire concept of childbirth, getting struck by lightning, staying home alone — as you know — and fog. Just to name a few."

I laughed, both at the items on the list and how quickly she was able to rifle them off. "Tsunamis? You live in the Prairies."

"Some of my fears might be slightly irrational."

"Slightly," I teased.

She chuckled, then after a comfortable silence she changed the subject. "Stella won, eh?"

"Did she? I haven't talked to Tawnie since Saturday night." I took another bite of the sandwich.

"How did your date go with her?"

Rodeo gossip was unbelievable. When was I going to remember

that everything I did was public knowledge? "Uh, it was probably the worst date she's ever been on. Is there anything you girls don't gossip about?"

"No, not really. Is the gossip why you don't normally date girls on the circuit?"

"It has more to do with not living in the same towns. I don't do the long distance thing that well."

"So, you plan on meeting the girl of your dreams in Saskatoon?"

I laughed because that was kind of unlikely. "I don't know. I don't really see myself getting married anyway."

"Why?"

"Because I don't want to be like my dad." I popped the last bit of sandwich in my mouth and got out of bed to take the plate back to the kitchen.

"I liked your dad. Why don't you want to be like him?"

"He was a shitty husband. He cheated on my mom pretty much every time he went out of town."

"Really?" she sounded genuinely shocked. Obviously she was too young to remember that rodeo gossip, or maybe only Cole and I knew about it.

"Don't tell your mom. My mom doesn't know." I washed the plate, then poured myself a glass of milk.

After she spent some time processing that my dad wasn't who she thought he was, she said, "Technically that's something you're scared of — becoming like him."

"It's not a fear. He just wasn't someone I admired."

"Does my dad cheat on my mom?" she gasped as if it just occurred to her that it might be possible.

I'd never heard any rumours about Trent, but maybe he was just better at hiding it. Or, maybe he was a stand-up guy. "Not that I know of, but maybe that's why your mom travels with him so much." I finished the milk and walked down the hall. "Can you hold on one second?" I placed the phone on the bathroom counter and quickly brushed my teeth. "Sorry about that," I said after I picked the phone back up and crossed the hall to my room.

"I wonder how a person knows for sure if they're with the right person." Her voice lowered a little. "Have you ever been in love?"

"No." I climbed back into bed and propped the pillows behind my back. "Have you?"

"Um, yeah."

"What's it feel like?"

She took a deep breath and was quiet for a while. "Well, when you can't be together, it feels like getting kicked by a horse in the chest."

I laughed because I knew firsthand how bad that hurt. "Then why would anyone want to fall in love?"

It sounded as if she rolled over under her sheets. "They can't help it. It just happens."

"When you are together, does being in love feel better than having sex? Because if it doesn't, I'll just stick to what I've been doing."

"Um, actually, I wouldn't know."

I smiled at her innocence. "I told your dad you were a good girl. He'll be happy to know it's true."

"He told me you said that."

"It obviously didn't help. He still made you withdraw from the competition."

"That was because we lied to him."

"Your mom knew you were there. She should have just told him she gave you permission."

"The deal was that she would let us go by ourselves, but if Dad found out, we weren't allowed to tell him she knew. It would have been a win-win if he hadn't somehow found out. Ahem."

I chuckled at her not so subtle accusation. "You shouldn't lie. It always comes back to bite you in the butt."

"I guess you would know."

"I'm not a liar."

"No? I heard you tell your mom you weren't chewing tobacco

93

when you were."

"White lies don't count."

"Yes, they do. Hold on a second." It sounded as if she was stretching to do something before she said, "You know, retiring from bull riding is no guarantee that you won't be anything like your dad. If you really want to be a better man it's going to take more than that."

"Yeah? You've got me all figured out?" I reached over and turned off the lamp next to my bed. "Did you also figure out how my brother got himself onto the roof of the hotel and why he was pole dancing in his birthday suit?"

"No. That's a mystery. It must have been so embarrassing."

"Cole doesn't care about stuff like that when he's doing it."

"I meant embarrassing for you."

"Oh, is that why you really called, because you feel sorry for me?"

"Pretty much. I mean, not that I think you should be embarrassed or anything. It's not like it was your fault, but if it were Lee-Anne up there doing some naked pole dancing and I had to tackle her to the ground, I would die."

The visual of that made me grin. "If it were you and Lee-Anne wrestling around, it wouldn't have been embarrassing. It would have been hot. The police would have just let you go at it."

"Jesus. Don't let my dad hear you talking like that."

I laughed. "I'm just saying; people would have paid money to see it."

"I'm pretty sure people would have also paid money to see you wrestling around with Cole's bare ass hanging out."

"Yeah, it must have been quite the sight. I wonder if it's on YouTube."

"I thought people knowing about what happened with Blake and me was embarrassing, but what happened to you is way worse." Her tone wasn't joking anymore. She was genuinely sympathetic. "No offence."

"I don't care about the embarrassment. I just worry about him."

I pulled the blanket up over my shoulder and closed my eyes, surprised that I was about to talk seriously about it with her. "If I hadn't been there they definitely would have arrested him, and they might have even shot him. He was really out of control."

"You can't always be there. Even if you are there, something could still happen to him. He's not your responsibility and it won't be your fault."

I exhaled slowly and felt my real feelings surface. "I'll feel like it's my fault and if I don't do it, no one else will."

She seemed to sense that I had opened up in a way that rarely happened, and her voice became even more gentle and sensitive. "Were you scared of him?"

"No, just concerned he'd hurt someone else and I wouldn't be able to stop it."

"Well, there's nothing more you could do for him that you don't already do. It's up to Cole to take care of Cole."

I reached up and rubbed my forehead because all the honesty was giving me a headache. That was as much opening up as I was capable of. "Can we talk about something else?"

"Sure," she said without hesitation. "Who's your favourite singer?"

Relieved that she understood me well enough not to push things, I smiled and answered, "Bruce Springsteen."

"Shut up. Are you seventy years old?"

"His music is timeless."

"Old," she teased.

"Timeless."

"What's your favourite meal including dessert?" she asked as if she was reading it off a card.

"Shepherd's pie and apple crisp. What are your favourites?"

"Carrie Underwood, lasagne, and Key Lime pie."

I laughed.

"What? Those are all good."

"I'm not laughing at that, although Carrie Underwood is a joke.

I'm laughing because I just heard a noise outside that would have made you pee your nightie, or whatever you sleep in."

"Ooh. It's probably a murderer who's going to break in and chop you up with an axe. By the way, I can't believe you just sass mouthed Carrie. And, I sleep in a tank top and boxer shorts, not a nightie. Who sleeps in a nightie, Bruce Springsteen lovers?"

"One of those loose tank tops that guys wear, or a tight, stretchy one that girls wear?" I asked, distracted by the image of both.

"What difference does it make?"

"I was just wondering." I decided on the tight, stretchy one.

"What are you wearing?"

"Nothing."

"Liar," she said, but her tone made it seem like she was considering the possibility that I told the truth.

"I swear."

"Well, your axe murderer is going to be in for quite a surprise."

"I'm pretty sure it's just some raccoons getting into the garbage."

"Maybe you should go outside and scare those coons off."

"I can't. I'm busy talking to a pretty girl about her sexy night-wear and questionable taste in music."

She was completely silent on the other end of the line. I couldn't even hear her breathing.

"Are you still there?"

"Mmm hmm."

"What's wrong? Are you falling asleep?"

"No." It sounded as if she sat up in bed. "Um, I should probably let you go, so you can get some sleep."

"No way. You owe me an all night call."

"Oh." She seemed surprised that I wasn't going to let her off the hook. "Are you admitting that you're upset?"

I smiled when I realized I was willing to admit it to her if it meant she would stay on the phone with me. "Maybe a little bit."

"All right hold on." It sounded as if she threw the phone on the bed. Then the sheets rustled and her feet pattered across the

96

floor. A door squeaked and a few seconds passed before she came back on the line. "Pink or blue?"

"Pink or blue what?"

"Nail polish. If we're going to be up all night, I might as well do my nails."

"Pink. I like it when girls have pink nails with white tips."

"That's a French manicure."

"Do that one."

"All right."

We talked until the sun came up and I never got tired. I just felt relaxed. She sounded relaxed too. I stretched and looked out the window. "Do you have a job you need to go to?"

She yawned. "Yeah, I have to be there at eight-thirty."

"What do you do?"

"I work at a daycare."

"Do you like it?"

"Yeah. It's fun and they schedule my shifts around my rodeo events."

"Where are you competing next?"

She checked the schedule. "Leduc."

"All right. I'll see you in a week."

"You're going? You think Cole is going to be well enough by then?"

"No. He can't ride, but I still need to go so I can pay Ron Miller for Stella and deliver Cole's camper to Mutt. He lost it in a poker hand."

"Mutt shouldn't take it. It's a bit unethical to take a bet like that from someone who has a mental illness."

"That bet had nothing to do with his mental illness. It had to do with his stupidity." I sat up on the edge of my bed and rested my elbows on my knees. "Thanks for talking to me all night."

She stole my line and said, "Don't mention it."

It sounded cute. "Have a good day, Shae-Lynn."

"Yeah, you too, Billy Ray. Bye."

Chapter 10

It was just over a six-hour drive to Leduc from Saskatoon. I left earlier than I needed to because I wanted to be gone before my mom came home with Cole. I was worried he would get all upset that I was taking the camper to Mutt. I only had half the money I needed for Stella, so I borrowed the rest from my dad's insurance settlement and transferred it into my bank account to cover the cheque I wrote for Ron Miller.

I arrived on Thursday just before five o'clock and parked in the competitors' area next to Mutt's truck. By the time I got out of the cab, he was already giving the camper the once over. "Hey, Billy. She's a beaut."

"Yeah, she was good while she lasted." I unhitched it and handed over the keys. "Take care of her." I looked at the camper one last time. It wasn't a good feeling to hand over something worth twenty thousand dollars. It made me want to puke actually. I tipped my hat, then walked out to the back pens looking for Ron. He was sitting on the top rail of a fence, reading through some documents. "Hey."

"Hey, how's your brother?"

"They discharged him from the hospital today. He's probably home by now."

"Do you think he'll ride again this season?"

"I doubt it." I pulled the cheque out of my shirt pocket. "Here's your money."

He took it and folded it into his wallet. "She's doing good, eh?"

"Yeah."

"You should let Shae ride her. Tawnie's not good enough to really show buyers what Stella's capable of."

"Yeah, I'll think about it. So, we're square?"

"I'll have my lawyer send over some papers for you to sign, but we're square."

"All right, see you around." I started to walk away.

"Billy."

I turned to face him.

He took his hat off and scratched his head. "Um, I'm not sure if it's really my place to mention this, but Cole owes some people quite a bit of money."

"I know. I just gave Mutt the camper. We're square."

"He also owes Tyson's Uncle Lyle."

"For what?"

"Lyle runs some illegal betting on the side. The rumour is that Cole's been getting in deeper over the past couple weeks."

"How deep?"

"Twenty, maybe thirty thousand and the juice is running."

"Jesus Christ." I took my hat off and paced back and forth. The nauseous feeling returned. "What happens if they can't collect?"

He shrugged. "I don't know, and I don't want to know, but it's probably not good."

"I can't believe Tyson didn't tell me."

"I don't think he knows. Blake does though. He's the one who got Cole into it."

I shook my head and patted my pockets hoping that a pack of gum or better yet, chew, would materialize.

"We're sponsoring a special event at the stock show this year. All the rankest bulls. One hundred thousand dollars goes to the last man standing in each category. If Cole can't ride, you could."

"I'm retired." I turned and kept walking. "Thanks for the heads up on Lyle."

"Think about riding. You don't want to owe the wrong people," he hollered.

Tyson didn't return my text, so I wandered around looking for either him or Blake. I was just exiting the arena when Tawnie saw me. She walked over with her hands shoved in her back pockets. "So, are we going to repeat this every time?"

"Sorry I haven't called. I've got some serious issues that I'm trying to deal with. My mom needs me to help her, and with work, and taking care of my brother's shit, I don't have time to make a long distance relationship work."

"Why didn't you just call me and say that? I would have understood."

"Sorry." I hung my head and looked down at my boots because I really didn't want to talk to her.

She stepped closer and I felt her arms slide around my neck. "Maybe I could help, or if you just want to talk, I'm a good listener."

I stood there for a long time just feeling the rise of her body as she breathed. Eventually, I said, "I'm sorry, Tawnie. You seem like a really nice girl, but I can't do this." Then I walked away.

"Billy."

I kept walking.

Tyson and Blake weren't anywhere on the grounds, so I got in my truck and drove to the hotel that most of the competitors were staying in. The girl behind the lobby desk looked at my belt buckle and smiled. "Welcome. How may I help you?"

"Could you please tell me which room Tyson and Blake Wiese are staying in?"

"I can't tell you the room number, but if they're staying here I can call the room for you." She moved the mouse on the computer and typed something on the keyboard. She scrolled through a list then shook her head. "They must not be staying here."

"All right. Thanks."

"Do you need a room?"

"Yeah, I guess I do." I pulled out my wallet. "Just one night." While she was typing on the computer, I texted Tyson again to ask where they were staying.

She slid the key card across the counter. "I get off at eight if you've got no plans."

I glanced at her. She was good looking even in the unflattering beige uniform she was wearing. "Uh, I've got some business I need to take care of. Thanks anyway."

She smiled and wrote her name and number on the back of one of the hotel business cards. "If you change your mind, we're all going to a bar called The River."

I tucked it into my shirt pocket and took the stairs to my room.

I waited around in my room until ten o'clock, then caught a cab to The River. If Tyson and Blake were in town, they'd be at the bar. It was really busy and the first person I recognized was the girl from the hotel. She was dancing with a group of girls on the dance floor. I didn't want her to see me, so I stood at the far side of the bar and ordered a drink.

There was no sign of Tyson or Blake, but a champion bronc rider named Nate Nashlund stepped up to the bar to order a round of six drinks. "Hey Billy, I didn't see you hiding there. How the hell are you?"

I shrugged. "Been better."

"Sorry to hear that. Are you riding this weekend?"

"No. How about you?"

"Yup. First one back in a while. It'll be my last though."

"Why? Are you retiring?"

"Yeah, I'm opening up my own veterinary clinic in Calgary. I won't have time for rodeo."

"Congratulations. Seems like not that long ago when you found out you got accepted to vet school."

"Yeah, life's crazy fast. I graduated, bought a house, and signed

102

the lease on the clinic all in the same month. Now I just need to find myself a nice girl and I'll be set. Speaking of which, I've got my eye on one right now, so I should get back to the table. Do you want to join us?"

"No thanks. I'm trying to track down the Wiese boys. You haven't seen either of them, have you?"

"No, not tonight. Nice seeing you, Billy. Take care." His hands were big enough to wrap around three glasses each. He squeezed them together and picked up all six drinks. It was impressive.

"Yeah, you take care too. Good luck with everything."

As he disappeared into the crowd, Tawnie stepped up beside me. She looked at me with one eye open and the other one drooping. "Hey," she said. She had to steady herself by leaning her elbow on the bar. "Who was that? He's dreamy."

"Nate Nashlund."

"Oh, my God, really? I heard he's the perfect man — smart, brawny, funny, romantic, rich."

"Yeah, he's perfect. How much have you had to drink?"

"Just a little bit," she slurred and held her fingers up to indicate a tiny amount.

"You need to ride tomorrow. Maybe you should shut it down for tonight."

"Maybe you should mind your own business. I'm celebrating."

"Yeah? What are you celebrating?"

"I'm single. The guy I wanted to date doesn't like me, so I'm going to find myself a different cowboy. Do you want to celebrate my singleness with me? Maybe Nate Nashlund would like some company." She waved the bartender over. "I'll have a shot of tequila." She turned to me. "What do you want to drink?"

"Nothing."

She pouted. "Don't be a party pooper."

I scanned the bar searching for Rochelle, hoping she would come over and take care of Tawnie. I couldn't see her. The bartender slid Tawnie's shot across the bar. He didn't make her pay for it.

She glared at me, then threw her head back to drink it. The girl from the hotel stepped up behind Tawnie and leaned her elbows on the bar to shout at the bartender. As he mixed her order, she glanced over and saw me. "Hey," she said in a sexy way.

I nodded, and Tawnie turned to see who I was saying hello to. "Who's that?"

"She works at the hotel."

"Are you here with her?"

"No."

"She's giving you the fuck-me look. Maybe you should offer to give her a ride back to the hotel in your truck." She reached over and took a sip from my beer before she whispered in my ear, "So you can fuck in your truck like a duck who got hit in the head with a puck because he has no luck and forgot to duck then he fell in the muck like a schmuck." She laughed at herself. "You suck, Billy."

"Maybe you should stop drinking before you embarrass yourself."

"I already embarrassed myself by sleeping with you." She pointed at my chest and lost her balance a little bit. She turned and said to the hotel girl, "He's not that good in bed, honey. Don't waste your time."

The girl gave Tawnie a *you're pathetic* lip curl, grabbed her drinks, and left.

Tawnie turned back towards me and leaned on my shoulder. "I just said that to get rid of her. You're really good in bed. Really, really good." She stood on her tiptoes and tried to kiss me.

I pulled away. "You're getting sloppy, Tawnie. You need to find Rochelle and go back to the hotel."

"Don't tell me what to do. You're not my boyfriend. Even if you were my boyfriend, you couldn't tell me what to do. I can do whatever I want, whenever I want. Don't forget it."

My phone rang. It was Tyson. "Excuse me. I have to take this." I walked away from Tawnie and she stumbled once I wasn't there to lean on. "Hey, Ty. Hold on a second. I need to go somewhere quieter." I walked down the hall where the bathrooms were and leaned against a vending machine. "Hi. Sorry. Are you in Leduc?"

"No. I had to skip it because of work. What are you doing there? Are you competing or is Cole?"

"Neither. I came to deliver the camper to Mutt." Two girls exited the ladies' washroom and gave me the eye before walking down the hall. "What do you know about the betting your uncle does on the side?"

"I try to know nothing about it, why?"

"Blake got Cole involved, and apparently he owes a lot of money."

"How much?"

"Maybe thirty thousand dollars."

"Shit. I didn't know. I would have told you if I knew."

Tawnie staggered down the hall towards me. She smiled and leaned her body against mine. I wedged my left hand against her hip and pushed her back so our bodies weren't touching. "I need your uncle's phone number so I can get it straightened out." Tawnie leaned in and sucked on my earlobe. I jerked my head away.

"I only have Blake's number on me right now. Do you want that, or do you want to wait until I can get his dad's number?"

Tawnie's hand slid down below my belt buckle and over my fly, then she fondled me. I grabbed her wrist and moved her hand, but she used her other hand to pop the buckle. "Cut it out."

"What?" Tyson asked.

"Not you. Sorry. I've got a drunk chick molesting me."

He laughed.

"It's not funny."

"Who is it?"

"Nobody." She kissed my neck and used her left hand to unbutton my fly. "Shit," I mumbled.

He laughed again. "You want to call me back when you're not so distracted?"

"No. Give me Blake's number."

"Hold on. I have to look it up in my contacts."

Tawnie's hand slipped down into my jeans and she massaged me. "Please, stop," I said and lifted her hand out.

"Me?" Tyson asked.

"No, not you."

Tawnie dropped down to her knees and pulled the waistband of my boxer briefs down to expose my increasing erection.

"Shit. What are you doing?" I protested.

"Okay, you ready?" Tyson asked.

Tawnie leaned in and the warmth of her mouth slid along my skin. "Damn. Tyson. Just text it to me. I gotta go." I hung up and put my hand on the top of her head. My brain was telling me to make her stop, but my body was telling me to let her go at it. I closed my eyes and put pressure on her head to make her slow down. "Shit." I leaned back against the vending machine and clutched her hair as she moved back and forth repeatedly.

A girl's voice gasped, "Holy shit."

I opened my eyes and turned my head. Lee-Anne was standing in the hall gawking at us. Tawnie's head kept bobbing.

"Billy Ray Ryan and Tawnie Lang, you have just officially earned the title of trashiest couple on the rodeo circuit." She reached to her side and covered the eyes of the girl who had just stepped up from behind her. "You shouldn't see this, Shae."

I pushed Tawnie's forehead away and she fell back against the wall, slumped into the corner. Shae-Lynn stood next to her sister and watched with wide eyes and a gaping mouth as I tried to stuff my hard dick back into my jeans. She made a weird wheezing sound as her gaze darted between Tawnie and me. Her hand clamped over her mouth and her eyelids squeezed shut before she turned and rushed back down the hall towards the bar.

Lee-Anne kept staring at me with the biggest grin on her face. "That was so totally awesome. And gross."

Tawnie moaned.

Lee-Anne shook her head in complete disapproval before she

106

spun around on her heel and trotted down the hall shouting, "Rochelle! Hey, where's Rochelle at? She's going to want to hear this." She disappeared around the corner.

I wanted to sneak out the back door and drive back to Saskatoon to leave all the bullshit behind forever, but I couldn't leave Tawnie lying there, passed out. I picked her up and draped her over my shoulder like a sack of feed. She moaned again as I kicked the back door open and walked out to the street and hailed a cab. The driver didn't look overly thrilled to be helping me take a passed out girl back to the hotel, but he didn't say anything.

I didn't know what room she was staying in, so I took her to my room and dropped her on the bed. She leaned over the edge and puked on the floor. I cleaned it up with a towel and threw it in the bathtub to wash it out. When I stepped back into the room, she was sleeping. The sad thing was that she still looked ridiculously beautiful. I sat on the chair and turned the TV on. Tyson had texted me Blake's number, but it was too late to call him, so I watched infomercials until I fell asleep.

At seven in the morning, I woke up with a kink in my back and my left leg had pins and needles. I called Blake and woke him up.

"What?" he grumbled.

"Did you get my brother messed up in side betting?"

"Who is this?"

"Who do you think it is?"

"Cole got himself messed up in side betting."

"Exactly how much does he owe?"

"Last I heard it was about forty-seven thousand."

I stood and paced. "What the hell? You know he's not stable at the moment. Why'd you let him get in that deep?"

"I didn't let him do nothing. He made his own bets. He's a big boy."

"You should have told me."

"I'm not his guardian, and I'm fairly certain you aren't either."

Enraged, I tugged at the roots of my hair to prevent myself from going off on him. "How long until it needs to be paid off?"

"I can talk to my dad about Cole being crazy. He'll probably give him an extension, but the juice will be running, so I wouldn't take too long."

"What happens if he can't pay it?"

"You don't want to know," he said, then hung up.

"God damn it."

Tawnie sat up startled as if she didn't know where she was. She saw me pacing and frowned. "What's wrong? Why are you swearing?"

"I got problems that have nothing to do with you."

"What am I doing here?"

"You got really drunk and passed out. I brought you back here because I didn't know which room you were staying in."

"Did anything happen?"

I winced a little and turned to stare out the window.

"What? What happened?"

"You don't want to know."

"What's that supposed to mean?" She stood up to look down at herself and seemed confused. "Did you put my clothes back on?"

"They were never off."

"Then whatever happened couldn't have been that bad."

My face winced again. "Oh, it was pretty bad."

"Jesus Christ. Just tell me what happened."

"You went down on me in the bar, and Lee-Anne and Shae-Lynn saw."

Her expression froze and it looked as if she stopped breathing. "In the bar?"

I nodded, wishing to hell it hadn't happened.

"Why didn't you stop me?"

I glanced at her, wondering the same thing. "I tried."

"Bullshit." She bolted into the bathroom and slammed the door. A few minutes later, she swung it open again and stood with her hands on her hips as if she was waiting for me to say something.

I stared at her for a long time, then I said, "I'm going to ask Shae-Lynn to ride Stella."

"What?"

"I need to. Sorry."

"You need to. What's that supposed to mean?"

"I just need to. It's complicated."

She shook her head. "She's the girl, isn't she?"

"Which girl?"

"The girl who Blake messed with and got you all worked up over."

"It's not like that. I need to sell Stella to help pay off my brother's debt. Shae-Lynn's a better barrel racer than you and I need her to ride Stella so I can attract a buyer who's willing to pay a lot of money for her. It's just business."

"Fine," she snapped. "I don't want to ride your horse anyway." She started crying, but quickly wiped her tears.

"Please don't cry. This isn't about you. I need the money."

"Fine. Talk to Shae and have her come by my trailer to pick Stella up."

"Thanks, Tawnie."

"Screw you, Billy." She picked up the lamp and threw it at me. The cord ripped out of the wall and the shade bounced off me. The ceramic shattered when it hit the ground. "Don't thank me. I'm not doing it to help you. I'm doing it because I don't want anything to do with you, which includes riding your stupid horse." She swung the door open and left.

I exhaled and took my phone out of my pocket to call Shae-Lynn. She didn't answer, so I texted, *Please call me. I need to talk to you.*

No.

It was an instant response that felt like a hoof to the shin. Although I knew full well she'd be disappointed in me and maybe even disgusted by what she saw at the bar, I had spent the night hoping she'd miraculously forget about it and let me off the hook. No such luck. I stared at her message for a while, then left the hotel room to go track her down.

Chapter 11

Shae-Lynn was tacking Harley by their motorhome. When she saw me approaching, she lunged towards the door as if she wanted to escape from me. I stepped sideways to block her and grabbed the handle. She turned back around and ducked under Harley's neck so he was between us. She didn't say anything. She lifted the saddle pad and put it on Harley's back.

Mrs. Roberts stepped out of their motorhome and smiled at me. "Hi Billy. How's your mom?"

I moved out of her way. "I haven't talked to her since she got home. She was in Victoria because Cole was in the hospital there."

She made a sympathetic expression and lowered her voice, "I heard about that. I'm so sorry."

"It's fine."

"Well, tell her I said hi. I'll call her when we're back in Calgary."

"Yes, Ma'am."

"I'm going to the coffee shop. Do you want anything?"

"No. I'm fine, thanks."

"Shae?"

"No thanks, Mom."

She seemed to sense that there was some sort of tension between Shae-Lynn and me, but instead of prying, she said, "I'll see you later," and walked away.

I rested my elbow on Harley and watched Shae-Lynn, still not sure how to make things right. "Aren't you going to look at me?"

She shook her head adamantly and lifted the saddle.

"Your nails look nice," I finally said to try to smooth things over.

She glanced at her pink nails with the white tips, but my compliment only seemed to make her more irritated before she slid her hand along the cinch to tighten it.

Getting her to respect me again wasn't going to happen anytime soon, so I cut straight to the reason I was there. "Will you ride Stella for me?"

"No." She turned and grabbed the bridle from where it was hanging on a fence post. She slid it over Harley's ears and buckled the straps.

"Please. I just found out that Cole owes almost fifty thousand dollars in gambling debts. I need to sell Stella. If you ride her in the next couple of competitions, I'll get the best price for her."

"No." She unhooked Harley from the fence and led him towards the back field behind the arena.

I walked with her. "Why? Because you're mad at me?"

"I'm not mad at you, Billy. I don't want to ride a horse in competition that I've never ridden before."

"You don't have to ride her today. Just take some practice runs on her and see what you think."

"No thanks. Are you done? I need to warm up." She stopped walking and stood with her back to me. She leaned against Harley's shoulder.

Even though I knew exactly why, I asked, "Why won't you look at me?"

"I can't."

I wanted her to say it, so I pressed, "Why?"

"Because."

"Because why?"

"Because I want to remember you as the guy I thought you were. I want to remember the guy who is sweet to his mom and would

112

give his left arm to his brother if he needed it; the guy who's a good enough friend to stay up all night talking to me so I won't be scared; and the guy who is stupid enough to buy a horse for a girl he has a crush on. If I look at you right now, all I'm going to see is a hick asshole who let a really drunk girl give him a blow job in the bathroom hall of a bar." She waved her hand in front of her eyes as if she was trying to wipe the disgusting image off her eyeballs. "I don't want to see you as that guy."

It felt better to hear her say it and she was right, but I didn't want it to be true anymore than she did. "Come on, Shae-Lynn. I'm still that other guy."

She shook her head, not buying it.

"It was just sex. It didn't mean anything," I said, more to convince myself than to prove it to her.

"Yeah, well, sex is supposed to mean something. It's supposed to be something intimate and private between two people who love each other. I don't know what that was." Although she still hadn't looked me in the face, I could see that her neck and cheeks were flushed.

"I'm sorry that it offended you, but I can't take it back."

"No, you can't." At least we agreed on one thing.

"I'm still the same person."

She shook her head at the realization that me being the same old Billy was exactly the problem. "When are you going to smarten up? You can't keep using women and throwing them away. One day you're going to wake up and realize you're all alone and miserable. Everybody except you will have moved on."

"I didn't use Tawnie."

"No? Really?" She focused on my belt buckle and the frustration in her voice went up a notch as she gave me shit. "So, does that mean it's serious? Are you guys dating? Have you made a commitment to be with her for longer than the maximum of two nights you normally date a girl for?"

I swallowed hard. "No."

"Then you used her. I thought maybe you had it in you to be a stand up guy, but obviously I was wrong."

That one stung, but I knew she was right and I didn't want our friendship to be ruined because I was an idiot. "So, you're never going to look at me again?"

She jammed her boot into the stirrup and grabbed the horn. She hopped up, then swung her leg over Harley's back. "I have to warm up. Good luck trying to find someone to ride Stella." She clicked her tongue and gave Harley a kick.

It felt as if they trampled me. Partly because she'd stood her ground and refused to let me get away with the same old bullshit I'd been pulling for years. But mostly because I respected her opinion, and the confirmation that she hated me as much as I hated myself hurt like hell. I had to bend over and rest my hands on my knees as I gasped for oxygen.

After a few minutes of wheezing and wincing, Lee-Anne rode up on her horse, Misty. "Are you all right, Billy Ray?"

"Nope." I stood up and clutched my chest.

"What's wrong? You're a bit young to be having a heart attack."

"I've got stress. I think it's killing me." I flinched from the pain as I looked up at her. "Sorry about what you saw last night."

"Yeah, you should be. I don't think I'll ever get that scandalous image unetched from my mind. Too bad Shae wouldn't let me tell anyone. It would have been good enough gossip to get people to stop talking about your brother's meltdown."

"You didn't tell anyone?"

"No. Shae wouldn't let me."

I glanced over and watched Shae-Lynn trotting on the other side of the field. "Why'd she do that?"

Lee-Anne smiled as if she pitied me. "I guess she likes Tawnie and didn't want anyone to think badly of her." She pulled her reins to the side and clicked her tongue to get Misty to walk on. "See you around, Billy Ray."

I watched as she galloped to catch up to Shae-Lynn. She said something to her and Shae-Lynn turned her head to look at me for a second. I was still holding my chest. It felt as if someone was squashing my heart with their bare hand. It hurt worse than when the bull caved my face in. I inhaled repeatedly and forced my legs to take steps.

Eventually, I made my way to where Tawnie was parked. Stella was tied up to the trailer, but not tacked. Tawnie was sitting in the passenger seat of her truck with the door open. She looked up at me, then went back to reading the magazine that was on her lap before she said, "What's wrong with you? You look like shit."

"Shae-Lynn said no." I leaned on the truck door. "You can ride her."

"I'm not riding her. Shae still has to come get her. I'm not taking her."

"She can't. They only have a two-horse trailer. Why don't you ride her?"

"I can't show my face around these people again. I'm sure Shae and Lee-Anne told everyone what they saw. I'm probably going to lose my sponsor."

"They didn't tell anyone."

She glanced at me and frowned. "How do you know?"

"Lee-Anne told me. Nobody else knows but them."

"I don't want to ride Stella. I'm too hungover to ride. I'm going home and I'm not taking your horse with me."

"Please keep her until I find a buyer. I'll pay you for boarding her."

"No." She flipped through the magazine pictures.

"Then lend me your trailer. I'll take her back to Saskatoon and board her there."

"You'll have to drive it all the way back to Edmonton to return it."

"Fine," I said, too exhausted to fight about it.

She glanced at me. "All right. Get your truck." She hopped out of her truck and unhitched the trailer.

As I was walking to my truck, Shae-Lynn rode up from behind me and slowed down. She didn't look at me, but she said, "You can take Stella to the ranch. My dad's there. I'll train on her this week and decide if I want to ride her in competition."

"Really? Thanks, Shae-Lynn."

"Shae," she corrected me and then galloped away. When she was halfway back to the warm-up field, Nate stepped out from the row of campers and waved her over. She turned Harley and stopped in front of Nate. They talked for a while. Nate's hand rested on her knee the entire time. When the conversation was over, Nate stepped back with a big grin on his face. She turned Harley back around, then glanced briefly in my direction before transitioning into a trot.

Chapter 12

It was only three hours from Leduc to the Roberts' ranch in Calgary, so I got there before lunch. Shae-Lynn must have called her dad to tell him I was coming because he was expecting me. He met me at the truck and shook my hand as I got out.

"Hey, Mr. Roberts."

"Call me Trent."

"Yes, Sir."

He slapped my shoulder and wandered around to the back of the trailer. "I hear you've got a fast mare you want Shae to ride."

"Yes, Sir."

He opened the trailer and backed Stella out. "Brody," he shouted over to a ranch hand who was unloading bales of hay from a flatbed truck. "Come take Stella. You can put her next to Skeeter."

Tawnie had written all the information about Stella's feed and schedule on a piece of paper that I handed to Brody. He led Stella into the barn. Trent walked over to yell at a bunch of guys sitting on the fence around a corral. "Are any of you donkeys planning on getting some work done today?"

They all looked at him, smiling. "It's lunch time, Sir," one of the guys shouted. "Jeremy's about to have his first go on a bronc. You might want to watch."

"Jeremy needs to mend fences this afternoon. If he gets hurt, you all are going to be doing his work for him." Trent climbed the rails and sat on the top one to watch.

I climbed up next to him.

"When was the last time you rode?" Trent asked me.

"Saddle broncs?"

"At all."

I shrugged. "Ten months ago."

"About when your daddy died?"

I shrugged again, then watched Jeremy ease down onto a horse in the chute. It bucked in the chute and Jeremy jumped off. He took a deep breath and eased himself back in. He took forever to nod and he didn't even look set when he finally did. The gate swung open and Jeremy flew off before the horse took one step out of the chute. He caught some good air, but the dirt was soft, so he landed fine and crawled to get out of the way. Everyone laughed and his face turned red.

"Load him up again," Trent shouted.

Jeremy raised his hands in surrender. "Once is enough for today, Sir."

"It isn't for you. It's for Billy."

"No thanks, Mr. Roberts," I said, firm on my decision.

"Get over there before I whup your ass."

My muscles tightened and my blood rushed, but I fought to sound calm. "I'm retired."

"Really? Why would one of the best young bull riders out there want to retire?"

"I've got responsibilities. I can't go around getting myself killed."

He chuckled, not buying it. "You could get killed in your truck. Are you going to retire from driving?"

"I don't need to ride bulls."

"You don't need to, or you don't want to?" His tone transitioned from good natured ribbing to a serious lecture.

"Both. I don't have it in me anymore."

"So, you quit."

"No. I retired."

He studied my face as if he was deciding the best approach to take with me. Fully aware that if my dad were around, I wouldn't have been allowed to stop riding because of a wreck, he challenged me, "You ride that horse and prove you're not scared, then I'll let you officially retire." He shoved my shoulder. "Get."

"I can't. My vision still isn't right from my last injury."

"That's no excuse. There are legally blind riders out there." He glanced sideways at me. "Your daddy used to always say that you came out of your mama with your right arm in the air."

"Yeah, he told everybody that story. It was a lie and it don't mean nothing." The whole 'make your daddy proud' angle, wasn't going to work.

"You were born to ride."

"There's more to life, Trent."

"Seems like a waste of talent."

I shrugged and turned my head wanting to spit chew juice. Instead, I just stared down at the dirt.

"Are you sure you don't want to prove to yourself that you can get back in the saddle?"

"I've got nothing to prove. I didn't lose my nerve."

He nodded, but knew I was full of shit. "If you say so."

I'd had enough, so I climbed down and walked towards my truck.

Trent shouted at the guys, "Never mind. Get back to work before I fire you all." His boots hit the ground and the gravel crunched as he followed me. "You want some lunch before you head out?"

"Are you going to try to have a heart to heart about my dad and how I need to get back in the saddle?"

"Hell no. I barely even have heart to hearts with the wife." He slapped my shoulder. "Come on. I make a pretty good grilled cheese." His phone rang before we got to the porch, so I waited for him. I didn't hear the first part of the conversation, but when his tone changed, I started to listen. "Where'd they take her? ... I'll be there as soon as I can." He hung up. His expression seemed as if he was angry, scared, and upset all at the same time. "I have to go to Edmonton." He patted his pockets as if he was looking for his keys. He rushed into the house and then a minute later ran back out towards his truck. "Brody!"

Brody stepped out of the barn and pushed his hat back. He took one look at Trent and asked, "What's wrong?"

"Shae was in a wreck."

"What?" I said. My hand reached for the porch railing. "Is she okay?"

"I don't know. I have to meet them at the hospital in Edmonton." He pointed at Brody. "You need to run things while I'm gone. Call me if you have any problems." Brody nodded. Trent's phone rang again. "Okay. Yeah … Okay." He hung up and looked at me.

"Get in. I'll drive," I said as I ran to my truck.

He hopped into the passenger side and made more phone calls as I gunned it down the dirt road. I couldn't see anything behind us because of the cloud of dust the empty trailer was creating.

"What happened?"

"I don't know all the details," he said as he dialled to make another call. "Harley slipped going around the second barrel. Shae was thrown and Harley came down hard on her. The paramedics were treating her as if she had a spinal cord injury."

"Jesus," I mumbled and pushed the accelerator to the floor. My hands started to shake and my lungs felt as if Harley landed on me too.

Chapter 13

Trent and I made it to Edmonton in just over two and a half hours because I was driving like a maniac. Lee-Anne and her mom were in the hospital waiting room when we arrived. Trent hugged Mrs. Roberts first and then kissed Lee-Anne on the forehead. Lee-Anne glanced at me and smiled. Her eyes were red and swollen from crying.

"What did the doctor say?" Trent asked.

"They're still doing tests," Doreen said and sat down wringing her hands together. "We can see her once they bring her back from having the MRI done."

Trent paced around. Lee-Anne sat down beside her mom. Then Nate came in the room holding three coffees in his giant hands. He gave one each to Lee-Anne and her mom and offered the third one to Trent. Trent declined, but shook Nate's free hand. They talked about what happened in the ring and how Nate had been the first to reach her. If he hadn't had medical training and told everyone what to do, someone might have mistakenly tried to move her and made the injury worse. Lee-Anne glanced at me and it felt as if she was checking my reaction to Nate being there. Or, maybe she was just wondering why I was having trouble breathing. I leaned my back up against the wall and blinked a couple times. When that didn't stop the room from spinning, I left and sat on a bench in the hall. I leaned my elbows on my knees and hung my head trying to force oxygen into my lungs. The door opened, footsteps crossed the hall, and Lee-Anne stopped in front of me.

"You okay?" she asked.

I shook my head without looking up at her.

She sat down beside me.

"Did you see it happen?" I asked and glanced at her.

She nodded and started crying. "I felt so helpless, seeing it happen and not being able to do anything about it." She looked over. "You know."

I nodded. "Yeah. Unfortunately, I do know." I sighed and leaned back to stare up at the ceiling. I swallowed down the lump that was swelling in my throat. My eyes burned and I felt tears trying to push forward.

She touched my arm sympathetically before she hugged her knees into her chest.

"Is she dating him?" I asked even though it was obvious.

"Mr. Wonderful? Not officially. They were hanging out together at the bar last night though."

"He's kind of old for her, don't you think?"

She shrugged. "Shae skipped being a teenager and fast-forwarded straight from little girl to young woman. She's already looking for a guy who is serious, stable, and works hard doing admirable things. Nate's that guy."

"Yeah. He's perfect for her," I said, although it didn't feel good to admit it.

She checked my expression and seemed to be reading into it, but since I didn't even know what I was feeling, she gave up. We sat without talking for what felt like hours before a doctor walked down the hall and went into the waiting room. We both stood and followed him. He shook hands with Trent and updated them on Shae-Lynn's condition. Flashbacks to when the doctor came in to tell Cole and me that our dad was dead kept distracting me from what was being said. All I heard at first was the word *paralysis*.

Doreen covered her mouth with her hands as she started sobbing. Then I heard the word *temporary* and Trent squeezed his arm around her. The doctor stood and said, "You can see her now."

The three of them, along with Nate, got up to follow the doctor. I didn't move. Lee-Anne turned to look over her shoulder. "Are you coming, Billy Ray?"

"No. You go ahead. I should probably get going."

She walked over and wrapped her fingers around my hand. Her expression was incredibly serious when she said, "Billy, she'll want to see you."

I stared at her for a while, considering it, before I looked down at my trembling hands. "I don't think I can handle seeing her all messed up."

She squeezed my hand tighter maybe trying to steady them. "The doctor said she's going to be okay once the swelling goes down. She's going to be all right."

"I can't. Sorry."

She frowned and it seemed as if she was debating something before she released the grip on my hand. "Okay. I'll tell her you were here. Thanks for driving Dad."

I nodded, then left.

Tawnie's house was twenty minutes outside of Edmonton. I headed straight there from the hospital to drop off the horse trailer. It was dusk, so it was hard to see the addresses on the mailboxes. I eventually found hers, pulled up the long dirt driveway, and parked in front of the farmhouse. She stepped out the screen door and onto the front porch as I got out of the truck. "Have you eaten?" she asked.

"No. I'll get something on the road." I unhitched the trailer.

"I made roasted chicken. It's almost done if you want to come in."

"No thanks. I need to get going," I said and opened the driver's door.

"You're not going to drive all the way to Saskatoon tonight,

123

are you?"

I pushed my hat back and leaned on the door. "I might stop somewhere along the way if I get tired."

"You can stay here if you want. My grandparents are away on a Caribbean cruise."

I shook my head. "I have to work tomorrow."

She leaned on the porch railing and smiled. "Sorry about throwing the lamp at you this morning. Stay for dinner. I won't hurt you. I promise." She turned and went back into the house.

I stood staring at her through the window as she moved around in the kitchen. Shae-Lynn's voice replayed in my ear about how I used girls and that if I didn't learn how to have a relationship that lasted longer than two nights I was going to end up alone and miserable. My stomach growled. Having dinner didn't mean anything, except that maybe I had it in me to be a stand-up guy. I closed the truck door and walked over to the porch. The screen door squeaked when I opened it. It was a heritage farmhouse and most of the furniture looked as if it was original to the house. I took my hat off and hung it on the back of the dining chair.

After we finished eating I helped her with the dishes. She handed me a plate to dry and asked, "Did Stella settle in okay in Calgary?"

"Yeah. They'll take good care of her."

"Is Shae going to train on her this week?"

I looked over at her. "Didn't you hear?"

"What?"

"Shae-Lynn was hurt real bad. Harley slipped and landed on her."

"Oh my God." She dropped the plate she was washing into the soapy water. "I didn't know. Rochelle called a couple times, but I thought she wanted to ask what happened between you and me, so I didn't call her back. Is Shae going to be okay?"

I shrugged.

She watched as I rubbed the spot on my chest that felt as if it was being repeatedly kicked. "Sorry I freaked out when you told me about asking Shae to ride Stella."

I exhaled and placed a glass in the cupboard. "It's understandable that you were upset. I should have given you some warning. It was a dick move."

"She's your horse. You can do whatever you want with her." She rinsed a pot and placed it upside down in the rack. "I overacted because I was embarrassed by what I did in the bar, and I was jealous about Shae. I shouldn't have thrown the lamp at you. It was a crazy bitch move."

I laughed at her honesty. "Well, if it makes you feel any better, you're not the craziest bitch I've ever met. A girl tried to stab me once."

"Why? What did you do to her?"

I smiled and stacked another plate in the cupboard. "I slept with her sister, but in my defence, they were twins. I never knew which one was which."

She chuckled, but her smile faded a second later and her tone became serious. "I don't want to be so reactive. I never used to be, but the guy I used to date was really abusive and it messed me up. I act insecure around guys now."

"Abusive how?"

"In every possible way."

"How long were you together?"

"We dated for almost five years and I lived with him for about six months. It was a disaster. He talked me into paying all the bills because he said he was saving his money to buy a house for us to live in when we got married. I was naïve enough to believe him. I was also stupid enough to let him convince me to drop out of my college classes so we could travel." She laughed. "We never went anywhere. The money disappeared and I couldn't get a good job because I didn't have my degree. He was controlling and it got to the point where he would slap me around if I hung out with my friends or bought an outfit he didn't approve of."

"Why did you stay with him?"

"He was a sweet talker, and obviously I'm a sucker."

"How did you eventually leave?"

"One night he got rough because I was like twenty minutes late getting home from work. He pushed me down the stairs and I broke my arm, so my grandpa dragged me out of there. Mitch stalked me after I left and I still have a restraining order against him."

My phone buzzed in my pocket, but I ignored it.

"The whole thing really affected my self-esteem. I'm sorry."

"You don't need to apologize."

"I don't want to be insecure and needy." She ran her hands through her hair and exhaled. "I just haven't got my confidence back yet."

My phone buzzed again and it occurred to me it might be Lee-Anne calling about Shae-Lynn. "Sorry," I mumbled and took it out of my pocket.

"Don't worry about it. Answer it."

It was a text from Cole. *Where are you? Did you take my camper? Call me.* I stuffed my phone back in my pocket and leaned against the counter as she emptied the sink. My phone buzzed again and she looked at me. I pulled it out to turn it off and noticed that it was a text from Blake. *Call me, shit head.*

"You have that look on your face again."

"Which look?"

"The one where you get that serious line between your eyebrows. You get it when you're worrying."

"I have a lot on my mind."

"Yeah, I can tell. You've been clutching at your chest as if you're about to have a heart attack, and your jaw muscles keep tensing as if you're chewing tobacco. Is there anything I can do to help?"

"No. Thanks."

She opened the freezer. "Ice cream makes everything seem better. Do you want some?"

I arranged the cutlery in the drawer next to the oven. "Sure."

She scooped two bowls of ice cream and then we went outside to eat it on the porch. She sat on a rocking chair and I sat in the porch swing. I finished mine and balanced the bowl on the railing so I could sit back and relax in the swing.

"It's nice here," I said as I stared out at the pasture beyond the barn. The grass appeared silvery in the dusky sky.

"Yeah, it's peaceful. I missed the quiet when I was living in the city."

"We used to have a place like this, but my mom had to sell it after my dad died. I used to go for walks at dusk just to listen to the world slowing down." I closed my eyes and inhaled the fresh air. "Shae-Lynn's not going to be able ride Stella, so you can if you want to."

She rocked for a while before she answered. "Let me think about it. I'll let you know." The sky got darker and the air cooled off. "Billy," she said so softly I almost didn't hear her.

"Yeah."

"This feels nice, doesn't it?"

I didn't answer, but it did remind me of a time when I didn't have so many problems.

"Don't you ever think about settling down with one girl?"

I shrugged, because although I hadn't ever really thought about it, I knew I probably should make a plan for my future, like Nate had done.

"If you did settle down, it could feel like this all the time."

"I can't leave Saskatoon right now with everything going on with my mom and brother."

"You don't have to. We could date long distance for a while and if it gets serious, I'll move there. It's not like I'm tied to Edmonton." She studied my expression, maybe hoping for something that wasn't there. "You can stay tonight if you want."

Shit. I shouldn't have stayed for dinner. I stood and said, "I have to work tomorrow."

"Call in sick. I'll worry if you're driving at night."

"I already miss way too many work days with all the events. I can't afford to get fired."

She sighed as she stood. "Your hat's in the dining room. Hold on a second. I'll get it." She disappeared inside.

Through the screen door, I heard what sounded like her gasping. Then she said, "You can't be here."

"Yeah? Who's going to stop me?" a man's voice replied.

Chapter 14

I opened the screen door, walked down the hall, and stood in the archway to the dining room to see who Tawnie was talking to. There was an athletic looking guy sitting at the head of the table.

"Who's your dinner guest, Tawnie?"

"None of your business, Mitch. You need to leave before I call the cops."

"Go ahead. I'll be done with what I'm about to do before the cops get here."

Tawnie stepped closer to me and it seemed as if she was checking which exit was nearest.

"She asked you to leave," I said.

"Shut up."

I stepped into the dining room and stood in front of Tawnie. "Go call the police." She turned and her feet pounded against the floorboards as she ran up the stairs. I stared at Mitch. The chair scraped across the floor behind him as he stood.

"You think you're a tough guy?" he asked.

"I'm not looking for a fight. You just need to leave. You're trespassing. And from what she's told me I'm going to assume you're also violating a restraining order."

"You picked the wrong girl."

"She doesn't want anything to do with you. You need to accept that and move on."

He laughed and walked along the side of the dining table towards me. He was as tall as me and a little broader. His breathing was shallow and getting faster. "This is between her and me. You need to mind your business, cowboy."

"Making sure she's safe is my business."

He rubbed his hand over his mouth. "I hope you enjoyed fucking her because it's the last thing you're ever going to do." He winced as if the thought of her being with someone else stabbed him.

I smiled to provoke him and widened my stance. "I did enjoy it. Thoroughly."

He launched himself through the air and tackled me to the ground. His fist made contact with my jaw, but I wrestled him onto his back and rammed my knee against his chest. I punched him with a left hook.

He was out.

I stood and kicked his motionless body. Tawnie appeared in the archway with the phone pressed to her ear and stared at Mitch. I put on my hat and sat on a dining room chair to wait for either the police to arrive, or for the asshole to come to. Tawnie rushed into the kitchen and returned with a bag of frozen peas. "Here," she whispered away from the phone. "Put this on your face. I'm so sorry."

"It's not your fault." I pressed the bag against my hand. It was already throbbing from punching him so hard.

"How long until an officer is going to be here?" she asked the person on the phone. "Mitchell LaPorte...Tawnie Lang...Yes, but there's a restraining order." She frowned as she paced back and forth listening to the person on the other end of the phone. "He entered my house without permission. He attacked my friend." Mitch groaned and moved a little, which made her hop back. Her breathing sounded as if she was being choked. "Can you please tell them to hurry?"

He groaned again and tried to move, so I stood over him. "Stay put, or I'll knock you out again."

He rubbed his jaw and shook his head. "Damn. What did you hit me with?"

"My bare fist, and there's plenty more where that came from if you ever go near her again. Got it?"

He shook his head again and rolled to lie on his back.

The police arrived ten minutes later and arrested him. One cop escorted him to the cruiser and the other one interviewed us. By the time everything was done, it was after midnight. Tawnie walked over and hugged me. "You can go. I don't want you to get fired on my account."

"Maybe you shouldn't be here all by yourself."

"It's fine. I already called one of my girlfriends to come by and sleep over. She'll be here any minute." She stood on her tiptoes and kissed me. "I'm glad you were here. Thanks."

"Don't mention it." I took my hat off to run my hand through my hair.

She reached up and ran her finger over the crease between my eyebrows. "Don't worry. I'll be fine." Headlights from a compact car turned up the driveway. "There she is now. Go."

I kissed her cheek before I went out to my truck. I plugged my phone in to recharge it. There were ten text messages from Cole asking where I was. Three from Tyson telling me that Blake was trying to get a hold of me. There was also one voice message from Shae-Lynn saying that she couldn't sleep in the hospital and she was wondering if I would call her. I listened to her message again because the sound of her voice made the stressful feeling in my chest disappear.

I drove back to the hospital.

Shae-Lynn was lying in bed, staring up at the ceiling, when I popped my head into her room. There was a metal brace holding her head in place and she looked uncomfortable.

"Hey," I whispered and closed the door behind me so none of the nurses would realize I snuck in.

Her head didn't move, but her eyes rolled to the side to look at me. She smiled. "Hey. I thought you already went back to Saskatoon."

"No. I had some stuff to do."

"I wouldn't have called if I thought you were actually going to come by. Lee-Anne said you were having a hard time being here because it was bringing up memories of your dad."

"I'm okay now that I can see you're going to be okay."

"This is your idea of okay?" she joked.

"Well, at least you're conscious. And I'm glad you're able to look at me again. Have you gotten over what you witnessed at the bar last night?"

"God, was that only last night? Feels like forever ago."

It did feel like forever ago, but I hadn't forgotten it. "Do you think you can start seeing me as that other guy again?"

She sighed and her eyes closed in a long blink. "Well, I had this teacher once who said life was like one of those desk calendars that has an inspirational quote on each page." She looked at me. "You know those ones you rip off at the end of every day?"

I nodded because my mom had one from the eighties near the phone for taking messages.

"He told us to start each day fresh and positive, like a new page on the calendar — learn from your experiences and mistakes, but leave any guilt, regret, worry, disappointment, hurt or anger in the past."

"Does that mean you forgive me?"

"It means I would like to leave my feelings about that particular incident in the past. Tomorrow's a new day. Hopefully you learned something from it."

"Don't let drunk girls go down on you in a public place where people whose opinion you care about might see?"

She smiled at my attempt at humour. "I guess that counts as learning from your mistakes. You care about my opinion?"

"Yeah. I do. What did you learn?"

"That you're an idiot."

I relaxed, glad we were back to the comfortable place we had been before I screwed up. "But you still called me when you couldn't sleep."

Her cheeks turned a little pink and she looked up at the ceiling. "You're the only person I know who would be awake this late."

"Where's your family?"

"The motorhome is out in the parking lot. I told them I wanted to get some sleep, but then after they left, I was wide awake. You don't have to stay."

"I don't mind. I can stay until you fall asleep if you want." I dragged over a vinyl-covered armchair and sat down. "Where's Nate?"

The corner of her mouth turned up into what may have been a grin. "He had to go back to Calgary. He's opening up his own veterinary clinic."

"Yeah, I heard. That's awesome." I tried to say it without sounding bitter, but it didn't quite work.

"He's a really nice person."

"I know. I didn't say he wasn't."

"Then, why are you making that expression like you want to beat him up or something?"

"I'm not. I'm happy for him. I'm happy for you."

She didn't seem convinced before she asked, "Were you just with Tawnie?"

I didn't want to admit it because she was going to think I was using Tawnie again. I avoided making eye contact for as long as I could before I met her gaze. She was going to find out anyway, so I said, "Yeah. I had to return her trailer."

"You only went to return the trailer?"

"Well, someone I know mentioned that maybe it was time for me to try having a relationship that lasted for more than two nights, so I hung out for a while. We had dinner."

"Hmm. Do you always take that someone's advice?"

133

"That someone knows me pretty well and I'm pretty sure she's right."

She inhaled and stared up at the ceiling for a while before exhaling. "You and Tawnie in a committed relationship. Good for you." Her eyes closed as if it was too much effort to keep them open.

"How are you feeling?"

"Paralyzed."

"That's not funny. It's not normal to joke when you're laid up in the hospital not able to feel your arms and legs."

She opened her eyes again. "The pain medicine makes me seem calm. I'm actually freaking out inside my head, but by the time the terror reaches the surface, I feel numb."

"I wouldn't mind some of that medicine." It sort of sounded like I was joking, but I wasn't really.

"You'll have to start riding again so you can get injured."

"Never mind then." I chuckled.

Her tone shifted into something more serious, and she sounded scared when she asked, "Have you ever had an injury like this?"

"No, I try not to let the animal land on me." I kept it light to prevent her from thinking too much about it and worrying.

"Ha ha. I'll keep that in mind next time."

I pointed to the tube leading from the bed to a machine. "I do have some experience with a catheter, though — as a result of a horn to the groin."

"Fortunately, I can't feel it."

"Can you move your fingers?" I slid my hand under hers.

She squeezed very subtly. Even though her fingers barely moved, the warmth of her touch inched all the way up my arm. The sensation grew in intensity as she squeezed tighter. When the heat spread to my chest, my heart jumped as if I'd backed up onto an electric fence. When I flinched, her eyes met mine for a second before she moved her hand away.

"Did you feel that?" I asked.

Her voice was soft and her lips barely moved. "Yes."

I didn't know if she was referring to the physical touch or the shock, but the corner of her mouth turned up in a smile, which made me smile too. "How did you call me if you can't move?"

She pointed at her phone sitting on the bed next to her right hip. "My phone has a voice activated feature. I had never used it before, but it's pretty awesome."

"I tried to use mine when I first got my phone, but it just came up with a bunch of gibberish."

"That's because it doesn't understand hick accent."

I laughed. "Yeah, that must be it."

Her eyes rolled to the side to look at me. "Why do you look like you were in a fight?"

"It's a long story."

"You might as well tell me. I've got nothing better to do."

"I'd rather talk about good things."

She was quiet for a while as if she was searching for something pleasant. "I can't think of any good things right now. Can you?"

I moved the chair towards the end of the bed so she wouldn't have to strain her eyes so much to look at me. I sighed. "I can't think of anything good right now either. We can play a game."

"I can't move."

"You don't have to. When I was a kid, my mom used to play this game with Cole and me on long car rides. She would sing a couple lines from a song and we would have to guess the song and artist. I can't sing, but I'll say the line."

"Bruce Springsteen."

I laughed. "You can't guess before I even say the line."

"Okay. Go."

I recited the lines and smiled as she tried to think of the song. "Sing it."

"I really can't sing."

"Everybody can sing; it's just not always in tune."

"There's more wrong with my singing than just being out of tune."

135

"Luckily for you, I know that it's Lee Brice. *Hard to Love.*"

"Good. Your turn."

She sang three lines with a voice that was mesmerizing.

I watched her face for a while before I recovered from the way the sound of her voice made my skin tingle. "I can't remember the name of the song, but it's by Dallas Smith."

"You only get a half point for that one."

"All right." I took my hat off and hung it on my knee before I said the line of lyrics.

She squished up her face. "Um, I know this one. My dad likes it. I would definitely know it if you gave me the tune. Can you whistle?"

"Not in tune."

"Give me a second. It's an old one. Is it Kenny Chesney?"

"No."

"Tim McGraw?"

"No."

"Brad Paisley?"

"No."

"Alan Jackson?"

"No."

"Toby Keith?"

"No."

"Ooh, I remember. It's Garth Brooks. *Friends In Low Places.*"

"You get minus ten points for that one."

She laughed, then licked her lips. "Is there still a cup of water on the counter behind me?"

"Yeah." I stood and held it so she could take a sip from the straw. "Do you need anything else?"

"Neural sensation."

"Hilarious." I sat back down and sighed because no matter how much we joked, it didn't change the fact that she was seriously injured.

She must have known what I was thinking because she said,

"Don't make that stressed face of yours."

I smiled to erase the tension. "You're the second person to say that to me today. Apparently I can't help it."

She exhaled and closed her eyes in a long blink. "I'm scared, Billy."

Hearing her say it crushed me, but I couldn't let it show. I leaned in and said, "Well, lucky for you, I don't get scared. I'll be brave for you."

She opened her hand so the palm was facing up. "Do you mind holding my hand again?"

I rested my elbows on the edge of the bed and wrapped my hand around hers. The warm sensation traveled up my arm to my chest again. I smiled when it gave me another little jolt.

"You do get scared." Her voice was quiet and sleepy sounding.

"Prove it."

"You throw up before every round."

I chuckled. "That's just food poisoning. I need to learn to stay away from arena hotdogs."

"Admit it."

"All right. I get scared sometimes. I admit it. We'll have to be brave together."

She smiled, proud that she'd got me to say it. "Thanks for being here, Billy."

"Don't mention it."

We sat quietly for a long time, then she said, "I'm sleepy now." She closed her eyes and her breathing slowed as she drifted off to sleep. I watched her sleep for a while before I pulled my phone out and texted Hank Pollert to tell him I wasn't going to be at work on time and would make up for it by staying late. He was going to be pissed, but I didn't feel like leaving. I put my head down on the bed and fell asleep still holding Shae-Lynn's hand.

Chapter 15

At five in the morning, a nurse came in and woke me up. I stood and kissed Shae-Lynn on the forehead. She opened her eyes and smiled. "Hey."

"Hey. They're kicking me out, and I've got to get home for work," I whispered.

"Okay. Thanks for staying."

"I'll call you."

She squeezed my hand one more time before I left. It took over six hours to get back to Saskatoon. I couldn't tell if Hank was more mad that I didn't get to work until lunchtime, or that I was so tired I was moving at half my normal speed. It took me until eight o'clock at night before I got all the work done. My phone buzzed the entire day with messages from Cole, but I ignored them because I didn't have the energy to deal with him.

When I finally pulled into the driveway at Mom's house, he came bursting out the front door. "Where the hell have you been? Mom's been worried sick."

"Edmonton."

He shoved me. "Where's my camper?"

"I gave it to Mutt."

He punched me in the same spot Mitch had already hit me.

"God damn it." I leaned over to spit blood. "Do not start with

138

me. I'm already pissed at you. If you provoke me, I might kill you."

"Not if I kill you first."

"What is your problem? You lost that camper to Mutt fair and square. And while we're on the subject, I also found out that you lost almost fifty thousand dollars in side betting. How do you plan on paying that off?"

He looked over his shoulder at the house as if he was worried that Mom might be listening. "I was planning on selling the camper, dumbass."

"That would have only covered half of it and you'd still owe Mutt."

"I don't mind owing Mutt. It's not like he's going to break my legs if I don't pay him in thirty days."

"I didn't know you owed those other guys."

"That's because it's my business. Not yours."

"Yeah, well, it becomes my business when you're locked up in a psych ward and they try to collect from me or Mom."

"If you didn't stick your nose in it, I could have paid them back and worked off my debt to Mutt. Just stay out of my business. I'll take care of it."

"Oh, really? Like you take care of everything else? You don't even have a real job." I shook my head, tired of his shit, and tried to push past him.

He shoved me back. "Stop acting like you're the only one who can fix things."

"I'll be happy to do that as soon as you stop acting like a God damn useless piece of shit who fucks up everything he goes near."

His eyebrows twitched slightly and his face tightened. "I said I would take care of it."

"I don't see how you can."

"I'll figure it out."

"Forgive me if I don't believe you," I yelled.

He pointed at me in a threat. "I'm getting really sick of your superior attitude. Just because Dad liked you better doesn't make you better than me."

"Yeah, well prove it once and a while."

He swung at me again, but I ducked and rammed my shoulder into his ribs to force him to the ground. I pounded on him and he fought back real hard. We rolled around on the grass — I was trying to get my arm around his throat so I could strangle him, and it felt as if he was trying to pull my arm behind my back so he could break it. The screen door slammed, and Mom shouted, "Cut it out!"

I rammed my elbow into his nose and he kneed me in the nuts. I groaned and rolled off him. We were both bleeding.

"What the hell has gotten into you two?" She stormed down onto the front lawn and grabbed Cole by his ear to make him stand.

"Ow. Nothing. We we're just horsing around," he muttered.

She let go of his ear and pushed his chest. "Don't lie to me." She stepped over and pulled the collar of my shirt to make me stand up. "What are you fighting about?" she asked me.

"Ask Cole. He's going to take care of it all, so he might as well start by telling you what he's done." I rubbed my sleeve under my nose to wipe away the blood that was dripping.

"He just got out of the hospital, Billy. Why are you beating on him?"

"Oh, poor Cole. I forgot. He's crazy, so he's got a convenient excuse for never taking accountability for anything."

"Billy," she gasped.

"What? I'm sick of it. He does whatever bullshit he wants, I suffer all the consequences, he apologizes, and then I keep going back for more abuse like a God damn idiot." I pointed at Cole. "Tell her what you did and figure out a way to get yourself out of it. I need to be at the bar in less than two hours. I'm going to take a nap. Don't bother me." I climbed the porch steps and slammed the screen door behind me.

There were envelopes from the bank and credit card companies on the counter next to a letter addressed to me from the University

140

of Saskatchewan. One of the bills had 'PAST DUE' and two of them had 'FINAL NOTICE' stamped in red on the outside. I didn't even bother washing up or changing. I dropped face down on my bed and didn't move.

When my alarm went off an hour and a half later, I rolled over. Every part of my body was in pain, and the brief nap made me even grumpier. I took a shower, then sat on the edge of my bed to call Shae-Lynn. There was no answer, so I left a message. "Hey. I'm working tonight at the bar. If you can't sleep, give me a call after two-thirty. Hope you're feeling all right. Take care."

I hung up and dialled Tawnie's number.

She sounded happy to hear from me.

"How are you doing?" I asked.

"Good, my girlfriend is going to stay with me until my grandparents get back."

"When do you think the cops will let him out of jail?"

"He's already out," she said as if she wasn't impressed, but wasn't surprised either.

"Really? How do they know he won't go by your house?"

"They don't."

Jesus. What's the point of having him arrested? "Maybe you should stay at your girlfriend's place instead."

"I can't. I have to take care of the horses."

I sighed and ran my hand through my hair. "Lock the doors and sleep with the phone next to your pillow."

"Yeah, yeah. Stop worrying; you're going to make that wrinkle between your eyebrows permanent."

I checked the clock and stood up. "Sorry to cut this short, but I have to go to work."

"It's fine. Thanks for calling."

"Don't mention it." I hung up and left the house.

As soon as I walked in the bar, I saw the one person who could make my weekend worse. He was sitting at a table by himself drinking a beer. He didn't notice me walk in, so I scooted behind the bar and started working, hoping to avoid talking to him. When he finished his beer, he walked over and sat on a barstool in front of me. I slid a bottle towards him and didn't bother asking for his money. Two girls who wanted body shots leaned over the end of the bar and shouted at me, so I left him sitting there. When I eventually looked back at him, he was staring at me. I sighed and walked over to talk to him.

"What do you want, Blake?"

"To make a deal with you."

"I'm not interested."

"You don't even know what it is."

"I don't care. I don't want anything to do with you or your dad. Cole's problems are his, not mine. Don't try to make them mine and don't go anywhere near my mom."

"I have an idea that could get Cole out of trouble without him actually having to come up with all the money."

"Not interested." I slid two beers to the guy next to Blake and took the money.

"Just hear me out." He leaned forward and rested his elbows on the bar so he wouldn't be shouting. "If you enter the winner takes all stock event —"

"I'm retired," I interrupted.

"All you have to do is ride one bull and Cole's debt will be erased."

"Not if I don't win."

"I'm not talking about the prize money. You just have to ride and Cole's debt will be forgiven."

"Why?"

He smirked, obviously assuming I was stupid enough to agree to a deal I didn't know anything about. "It just will be."

"How? Is your dad going to bet against me?"

"Just register and ride. You don't need to know all the details," he said, losing his patience.

"Is he expecting me to throw the competition somehow?"

He looked over his shoulder to make sure nobody was listening to us. "I didn't say that. Do you want your brother's debt to be erased or not?"

"Tell me how they're planning on fixing the betting."

"I didn't say it was going to be fixed."

I served a couple more drinks, then focused on him again. "So, all I have to do is ride my best. If I win, I take the purse and Cole's debt is erased. If I lose, Cole's debt is erased, just because."

Since it sounded like I was considering it, he smiled. "Yeah. It's a no-brainer if you ask me."

"I'm not interested."

Shocked that I turned it down, he pushed his hat back. "Are you crazy? That's a win-win."

"I don't want to be involved in whatever you and your dad are up to. I'd rather just pay him off fair and square."

"You're an idiot," he scoffed.

"If you say so. I have to get back to work. Are we done here?"

"Yeah." He stood and threw cash onto the bar to pay for his beer. "You should probably think about the offer. People you love could get hurt when the debt collectors come calling. When you change your mind, let me know."

"Don't hold your breath, and don't try to rope Cole into any deals either."

"They don't want to do the deal with him."

Although I wanted him to leave, I was also curious what made him offer the deal in the first place. "Why?"

"Cole's not as good as you."

"He's better than me. I haven't ridden in almost a year."

"You're still ranked higher than me."

I was beyond pissed off with his attitude, so I fired back, "That's because you suck shit."

"Yeah? Sign up for the event and put your money where your mouth is."

143

"Bye, Blake."

He sneered, tipped his hat, and left.

"Who was that?" the owner of the bar, Stephanie, asked as she stepped next to me to mix a piña colada for an older lady who was sitting at the bar by herself.

"Nobody. He rides on the circuit."

"You don't like him, do you?"

"Nope."

"I do." She pulled a bunch of bills out of her bra strap. "He tips well and he talked to Maurice, so I didn't have to." I looked over at Maurice, the town drunk who rambled on about the world coming to an end to pretty much anyone who would listen. Most people avoided him unless they could look past the crazy and see that he was just a lonely old guy who needed someone to talk to.

"What did he want?" Stephanie asked, referring to Blake.

I poured shots of whiskey. They were for three of the ranch hands I worked with at Hank's, so I didn't charge them. "He wants me to ride in a competition."

"You should. When you beat him it will knock that smug look off his face." She wiped the spills off the bar with a towel.

"I don't know if I can beat him anymore."

"Isn't riding a bull like riding a bike?"

"I don't know." And, honestly, I wasn't sure if I could do it anymore.

"You still got it in you," she said encouragingly and readjusted her top to show more cleavage. "You need to stop giving all those drinks away for free. You're going to put me out of business."

"This place is packed. I pull in more business for you than you know what to do with."

"Oh yeah, Billy Ray Ryan, hot bull riding champion working the bar at the Palomino." She laughed. "How long do you think that's going to be good for business?"

"Until I'm sixty or something."

"Yeah, I doubt that. Nobody cares about washed up rodeo

has-beens. Get back to riding, or start taking their money and pocket those tips while you still can." She whipped the towel at my ass, then walked down to the other end of the bar to flirt with a couple of her old-timer regulars.

My phone buzzed in my pocket. I never took calls when I was working, but it was Shae-Lynn, so I picked up.

"Oh, hey." She sounded surprised. "I didn't expect you to answer. I was just going to leave a message. I thought you were working."

"I am, but I can talk and work. Pouring drinks isn't exactly brain surgery."

"Aren't you going to get in trouble?"

I glanced over at Stephanie. She glared at me like a mother scolding her child. I shrugged innocently and smiled at her. "My boss likes me. She lets me get away with stuff." I slid two long necks across the bar to a guy who looked like an off-duty cop. I took his money and put it in the till.

"Is your boss pretty?"

"Uh, yeah. Her prime was before I was born, but she's still hot in a coyote ugly way."

"Have you slept with her?"

I laughed. "No. She's married and has three kids."

"Oh, I didn't realize that you have standards."

"You think I'm a man-whore?"

She thought about before answering, "More like a mustang."

"Mustangs can be gentled with the right handler."

She was quiet for a while before she said, "They have to want to leave their wild side in the past."

"Yeah, well living wild gets hard after a while. What were you going to say in your message?"

"Oh, just that they gave me some sleeping pills, so I probably won't be awake when you finish your shift. I didn't want you to think I didn't want to talk to you, because I did, or I do, or whatever."

I smiled at her honesty and leaned against the counter along

145

the back wall. "How are you feeling? Can you move any better?"

"I'm a bit stronger. I'm bored though."

Customers were lined up at the bar, but I didn't care. "Whenever I get laid up I read."

Shae-Lynn groaned, frustrated. "I read two books today cover to cover. It didn't help."

"You're not supposed to read so fast. The trick to being hospitalized is to slow down. Going to the restroom is your event for the morning. Taking a nap is your event for the afternoon. Getting a sponge bath is your event for the evening. Then you read one chapter and call it a day."

"I can't live like that. Besides, I'm pretty sure sponge baths from the nurse are a little different experience for me than they are for you."

I laughed. "Yeah, you're probably right." A girl shouted at me to get her a margarita, so I tucked the phone between my ear and shoulder as I mixed it. "When are they going to let you out?"

"Probably by the end of the week if I keep progressing."

The margarita girl paid me, but didn't tip. "Is your favourite colour pink?" I asked Shae-Lynn.

"Yeah, I guess. I like lilac too. Why?"

"It's a surprise. What's your lucky number?"

"Thirteen."

"That's not lucky."

"That's why I chose it. Nobody else chooses it, so it leaves more luck for me."

I turned my back to the line of people, so I wouldn't be distracted. "You're weird. Is there anything else that means a lot to you or brings you luck?"

"What are you asking for?"

"I told you; it's a surprise."

Stephanie shoved my arm. "Billy, either get off the phone or take it to the office."

"I can work and talk." I picked up a bottle of bourbon to prove it.

146

"Yeah, not with whoever that is."

"Hold on a second, Shae-Lynn." I covered the phone with my hand so she wouldn't hear me talking to Stephanie. "What are you talking about?"

"The ladies come in here to see Billy Ray Ryan working behind the bar. They buy drinks and leave big tips hoping that maybe he might want to take them home at the end of the night. If he's busy talking on the phone with his girlfriend acting all lovey-dovey, he kills the illusion."

"She's not my girlfriend and I'm not acting lovey-dovey. I don't know what you're talking about."

"I've seen you flirt with at least a thousand girls and I have never seen you smile like that. Trust me, you're killing the illusion. Take it into the office, cowboy." She shooed me.

"She's just a friend, but if you want me to take a break I will." I grinned at her and trotted around the end of the bar. Once I was in the hall that led to the office, I spoke back into the phone, "Hey, sorry about that."

"Did you get in trouble?"

"No, she just told me I could take a break if I wanted to talk to you for a while. She thinks you're my girlfriend."

"Oh. Doesn't she know you're not the boyfriend type?"

I sat at Stephanie's desk and put my feet up. "She must have noticed that I've changed."

"Right. I forgot you're trying the committed thing. I doubt you've changed enough in one day to make a noticeable difference."

I grabbed a pen and doodled on the pad of paper. "When I set my mind to achieving a goal, I learn fast."

"It's more important to do it well than to do it fast."

"I can do both."

She snorted as if she didn't believe I could do it, or she wasn't interested in the topic of conversation anymore. I couldn't tell. "How long are your breaks?"

"I don't know. I've never taken one before." I looked down at

147

the pad of paper and realized I was sketching a girl on a horse running the barrels.

When I didn't say anything for a while, she asked, "Have you put together an ad for selling Stella?"

"Not yet. I haven't had time. I'll get to it."

"I can do it if you want. How much do you want for her?"

"I was thinking about asking twenty, but you don't have to do it for me."

"It's okay. I have my laptop. It will give me something to do tomorrow. Maybe Tawnie should ride her again to show her off."

"Yeah, maybe," I said, then changed the subject. "If you won a hundred thousand dollars what would you do with it?"

"Are you thinking about entering the stock contractor event?"

"No, I'd rather work three jobs. I was just wondering what a person without money troubles would do with a hundred thousand dollars."

"Um, I would pay off your brother's gambling debt so you could stop worrying all the time. I would buy some art supplies for the daycare. I would buy my dad a new truck and my mom would probably like a kitchen reno. I would buy Lee-Anne a new saddle or something. If there were any left, I would donate it to the charities that I volunteer for. Oh, and I'd buy you a new pair of boots too."

"What's wrong with my boots?" I looked over at them, propped up on the desk.

"They're old and scuffed up."

"I like them that way."

"You can keep the old ones, but you should also have a nice pair for special occasions."

"Like for dates and things?"

"Yeah, like dates."

I smiled because I could tell by her tone that she was smiling. "You didn't mention that you would buy yourself anything with the hundred thousand."

"I don't need to. I would get the most pleasure from the money by seeing the people I care about happy."

"God, you're a nice girl. Maybe you'll rub off on me a little." I wrote her name under the sketch I had completed.

"Is that supposed to be some sort of sexual innuendo?"

I laughed. "No, if I meant for it to be sexual, I would have said something about me rubbing off on you."

Instead of responding to that, she said, "I should let you get back to work before you get fired." She took a deep breath and sounded so peaceful.

"I like how you do that."

"What?" she asked.

"You have a way about you that makes me feel at ease. I don't know how you do it, but I have a shit load of troubles and you make me forget all about them."

"That's nice of you to say."

"Well, it's true."

She was quiet, so I just listened to her breathing.

"Did I make you smile?" I asked.

"Yes."

"Good. Call me tomorrow so I can do it again."

She exhaled slowly before speaking. "Um, Billy, what are you doing?"

Although, I knew exactly what she was getting at, I asked, "What do you mean?"

"I mean, why?" She made a frustrated sound. "Ugh, I don't know. Never mind. Forget I said anything."

My heart sped up and Stephanie's office felt as if someone had cranked up a furnace. Admitting that I was without a doubt flirting with her, and acknowledging what was obviously going on between us excited and scared the shit out of me at the same time. "Shae-Lynn, I—" I rubbed my face trying to work up the nerve. "I, um. I don't know what to say. I just really like talking to you. If you don't want me to call, or if you think Nate wouldn't

149

like it or something, I won't."

There was complete silence on the other end of the line. Finally, she said, "I like talking to you too."

I smiled, happy that she said exactly what I wanted to hear her say. "All right then. I'll call you tomorrow. Good night."

"Night."

I waited for her to hang up before I did. Then I went back to work with a big goofy grin on my face.

Chapter 16

Two weeks later, I walked into the house after working at Hank's and my mom called me from her bedroom, "Billy, is that you?"

"Yeah."

"Do you mind coming in here for a second? I need some help."

I walked down the hall and opened her door. She was sitting up in bed, looking pale. "What's up?"

"I'm having an off day."

"Do you want me to take you to the doctor?"

"No." She dismissed my concern with a weak wave. "I'll be fine once I rest for a while."

"Why's it so hot in here? Did the AC break?"

"No. I just don't have it turned on. It's expensive to have it running all the time."

"Yeah, well, you're going to pass out in this heat." I turned the air conditioning knob on the wall. "Do you need anything else?"

"Maybe just make dinner for yourself and Cole. I also need my knitting bag off the top shelf in the closet."

The shoebox next to the bag of knitting supplies accidentally slid off when I moved it. I tried to catch it, but I ended up flipping it upside down. The contents, which were mostly photos and letters scattered on the floor. "Shit. Sorry."

She tried to stand, but she obviously didn't feel strong enough.

Her knees collapsed and she had to sit back down on the edge of the mattress. I gathered up the photos and letters into piles and stacked them back in the box. One caught my attention. It was a picture of my dad with a blonde woman sitting on his lap, kissing his cheek. He had a beer in one hand and his other hand was resting on the curve of her ass. I remembered her from when I was a kid. She used to sometimes make meals for Cole and me when we were touring with our dad. For a long time I just thought she was a friend of the family. It wasn't until I got older that I realized she was one of his mistresses.

"What is all this?" I asked.

"Nothing. Just some things that belonged to your dad."

I flipped through the other photos and read bits of the letters. They were basically love letters from a bunch of different women. "Why would you keep these?"

She shrugged. "They were obviously important to him, so I didn't want to throw them out. I would have buried them with him, but I didn't find them until after the funeral."

"Did you already know?"

"Of course. You know how people gossip on the circuit."

Yeah, I guess I'd always kidded myself into believing she didn't know what was going on all those years. "Why did you stay with him?"

She shrugged as if she felt she had no choice. "What was I supposed to do? I was nineteen years old with two babies, no job, and a tenth grade education."

I sat on the floor and leaned my back against the wall. Each photo had a different girl hanging off him. Cole and I were in a couple of the shots. It made me feel sick seeing how happy my dad looked with the other women, and he didn't care that he was acting that way in front of his kids. I tore up the photos one at a time. "You shouldn't have let him treat you like that." I ripped up the letters and threw the shreds into the box. "Why'd you let us tour with him by ourselves if you knew how he was carrying on?"

"He was a good dad. You know that."

I stood up and closed the lid. I placed her knitting on the bed. "A good dad wouldn't have taught his sons that it was okay to cheat on his wife or put them in the position of having to lie to their mom. I'm throwing this out."

Her eyes closed in a heavy, tired blink. "Can I get a hug?"

Feeling guilty for stressing her out when she was already having a bad day, I sat next to her on the bed. She wrapped her arms around my shoulders and squeezed. Her arms felt frail and it made me sad. "I love you, Mom."

"I love you, too." She brushed my hair back off my forehead. "I got a part-time job today."

"What? You don't need to work. I'm taking care of the bills."

"It's just an easy data entry job at the bank — a couple hours on Tuesday and Thursday mornings."

"Did the doctor say it was okay?"

She shrugged to avoid admitting that he hadn't. "I found out that your dad had some more debt I didn't know about. I had to use most of what was left from the insurance money to pay the collection agency."

"You still have what's left from selling the ranch, right?"

"No. I had to use that to pay for your medical expenses last summer. Not everything was covered by the insurance."

"Jesus, Mom. Why didn't you tell me? I would have taken care of it."

"I took care of it." She picked up her knitting needles. "There's nothing left now though."

"You don't have to work. I'll figure something out."

"I want to work. I feel better when I stay active." Her hands trembled to convey that the opposite was true.

"I've got over ten thousand in my tuition savings. That will keep us going for a while."

"No. You're going to school. It's going to be fine. I can apply for a loan at the bank or something."

I sighed and ran my hand through my hair, thinking about the fifty grand Cole also owed. The front door opened and footsteps crossed the wood floors of the living room.

"You go on and make Cole something to eat. I'm not feeling up to talking about finances right now, all right?" She slid up to rest her back against the pillows, then continued her knitting to end the conversation.

I watched her for a while before heading to the kitchen with the shoebox. Cole was standing in front of the fridge leaning on the open door as if he hoped a meal would leap out at him. "I don't suppose you found yourself a job today?" I snapped.

"Nope. Seems like nobody is that keen on hiring a mental case." He closed the fridge and sat at the kitchen table. "Why's it so damn hot in here?"

"Mom is trying to cut expenses by not running the AC. She just told me there's no money left."

"I'll sell my truck."

"That will only cover part of what you owe. Besides, you need your truck. I'm not chauffeuring you around."

"I'll drive Dad's truck."

I glanced over my shoulder in the direction of the door that led off the kitchen to the garage. The Chevy had been parked in the garage since we moved Mom into the house. I wanted to sell it, but Cole sat in it at least once a week smoking cigarettes and listening to the radio, so I hadn't yet. "Dad's truck guzzles gas," I said.

"Well, I'm not letting you sell his truck, so if we need the money, I'll sell my truck. What's for dinner?"

I looked in the freezer and took out some frozen ground beef. "Chilli. It's going to be a while though. Make some nachos as an appetizer." I put the meat in the microwave to defrost it, opened some cans of beans, and dumped them into the chilli pot.

Cole spilled tortilla chips out of the bag onto a pan. He diced tomatoes, then reached over to turn the garburator on. It made

154

the same horrific grinding sound that it had been making for two weeks. Then the water backed up into the sink.

"You promised you'd fix that." I mumbled, trying to restrain my frustration.

"I will. It needs a new part. I haven't had time."

"If you're assuming that if you procrastinate long enough I'll do it for you, don't. I'm not fixing it for you this time. Especially since you broke it by doing exactly what I told you not to do."

"A pepper is a vegetable. You said vegetables were all right."

"Not the damn stem and not with beer bottle caps. I told you a million times not to leave the caps in the sink."

"Whatever. I'll fix it. What's in that box?" He nodded to where I had left it on the counter.

"Nothing. Just some of Dad's old shit. I'm throwing it out."

"Don't."

"It's a box of love letters and photos of his mistresses. I already ripped them up. It's garbage."

"Oh." He grated the cheese for the nachos. "Don't throw out any of his rodeo stuff, or things from when he was a kid."

I glanced over at him, surprised that he was finally open to talk about Dad. "If you want to go through that stuff, it's in a wooden box in my closet."

"I don't want to go through it. Just don't throw it out."

"The psychiatrist said it might be good if you found a way to say goodbye and start to process your grief." I glanced at him to gauge his mood. "Since you didn't go to the funeral and you don't talk about it with anybody."

He opened the oven door and slid the pan of nachos onto the rack. "Are you listening to yourself?"

I shrugged because I knew it sounded preachy. "I'm only telling you what she said."

"I don't need to be told what to do. Just don't throw his shit out and don't sell his truck."

My phone rang. I didn't recognize the number, but I'd been

155

getting inquiries about Stella from the ad Shae-Lynn had posted, so I answered it. It was a woman who was interested, but it didn't sound like she was really ready to buy a horse. When I finished talking to her, Cole was eating scorched nachos and the chilli was exactly how I left it.

"Seriously? You couldn't at least brown the meat and put it in the pot?"

"I don't know how to make chilli. I burned the nachos for Christ's Sake."

I got a frying pan out of the cupboard and slammed the door shut. "Are you really useless or do you just pretend so nobody ever asks you to do anything?"

"It's a chicken and egg thing." He chuckled, taking it about as seriously as he took everything. "I can't remember which came first anymore."

"Well, you're not living with me forever, so you better learn how to at least feed your damn self."

"That's what drive-thrus and wives are for."

"Good luck getting a wife if that's what you think she's for."

"I wouldn't say it to her face." He smiled and shoved a crusty black stack of chips into his mouth.

I browned the meat in the frying pan, then mixed all the rest of the ingredients and spices in the pot. My phone rang again. I smiled because it was Shae-Lynn. We'd talked every day she was in the hospital, and we'd kept on calling each other even after she'd returned home to Calgary. "Hey," I said quietly. "Hold on one minute. I just need to go to my room."

Cole sensed the change in my mood and threw a potholder at me. "Who are you talking to?"

"None of your business." I threw it back at him and turned the element down. "Stir this every once and a while so it doesn't burn."

"Is it Tawnie?"

"No. Shut up." I walked out of the kitchen.

"Since when do you gab on the phone with girls?" he shouted

156

down the hall after me.

"Don't let the chilli burn. I'm going to be a while," I shouted back.

I knew Cole was going to let the chilli burn, but I didn't care. I stretched my legs out and leaned back on my pillows because I planned on talking to her for as long as she would let me.

Chapter 17

A serious buyer had contacted me and wanted to meet in Calgary to see Stella. Trent agreed to let me meet the guy at the ranch. He was going to be out of town, but he said he would let the girls know I was coming. I got a haircut and took the truck through the carwash before I hit the road.

When I drove up the gravel driveway and parked in front of the Roberts' ranch house, Lee-Anne was in the corral doing a shoulder stand at full speed on Misty. I walked over, leaned my elbows on the fence, and watched. She flipped right side up and did a few more tricks before she noticed me. "Whoa," she said. Misty stopped immediately. "Hey, Billy Ray. What are you doing here?" She rode over to where I was standing.

"I might have a buyer for Stella."

"That's good since your brother owes a small fortune to Blake's asshole dad."

I took my hat off and ran my fingers through my hair. I'd been trying not to stress about the debt, but it wasn't easy to ignore. "The buyer is meeting me here to take a look at her. Your dad said it would be okay."

She nodded as if she didn't know, but didn't mind either. "Yeah, it's fine. What time is he coming?"

"Around six o'clock."

"What time is it now?"

"Four-thirty. I came early to groom her."

"Shit. How did it get so late? Shae needs to get picked up at work."

"I thought the doctor said it was still too soon for her to go back to work?"

"He did, but she can't stand being cooped up. She went in for a couple hours today. She still can't drive, so I have to chauffeur her."

"I can put Misty away while you go pick her up if you want."

"Actually." Her face lit up like she had a bright idea. "I still have a couple other things I need to get done in the barn. If you don't mind picking Shae up that would help a lot. I'll groom Stella for you."

She was acting as though she needed to bribe me, but I was happy to get Shae-Lynn. I was looking forward to seeing her. "Okay, what's the address?"

"It's the big blue church on Clark right before you get to the strip mall. The daycare is around back." She smiled, then turned to walk Misty to the barn.

I opened the door to my truck and cleaned out all the empty drive-thru coffee cups. I threw them into the cooler in the back and wiped the dust off the dashboard with a rag. The cab still smelled like old coffee, but it looked a little neater. I stripped off the T-shirt I was wearing and put on the new button-up shirt that was hanging in the back window.

The church was a twenty-minute drive into town. I parked facing the fence that surrounded the playground area. Shae-Lynn was sitting on a bench talking to a little boy who looked as if he'd been crying. He nodded at something she said. She held his chin gently and said something else that made him smile. She tousled his hair before he got up and ran over to join some other kids who were lined up to go down the slide. After she watched him for a while, she turned her head and saw me sitting in my truck. Her expression was a mixture of surprise, confusion, and happiness.

159

I got out and walked over to lean my elbows on the fence. She reached for a pair of crutches resting against the bench behind her, hoisted herself up, and balanced with the crutches under her arms. She was wearing khaki shorts and a white polo shirt that had the logo for the daycare stitched on the chest. She made her way over to me and smiled in a way that made me glad Lee-Anne had sent me to pick her up.

"We discourage strange men from lurking around the outdoor play area," she said like a teacher.

"I'm here to pick someone up."

"Do you have some identification? We can't release the children to just anyone."

I pulled my wallet out of my back pocket and passed her my driver's licence.

She nodded as she read it. "William Raymond Ryan from Saskatoon, Saskatchewan. You're a far way from home, cowboy. What is the nature of your visit? Business or personal?

"Both."

"Do you have a criminal record?"

"Yes."

Shocked, she looked up at my eyes to check if I was being serious. "For what?"

"Not kidnapping."

Her expression shifted as if she just remembered something. "Did they arrest you for assaulting Tawnie's abusive ex-boyfriend?"

Although I already assumed she would hear about that, I shook my head and pushed my hat back to pretend like I was surprised. "Did Rochelle tell you that?"

"Maybe. Don't blame her. Tawnie's the one who blabs everything."

"I didn't get arrested for that. He did."

I could tell she was still curious about what I had been arrested for, but she let it go. "Who gave you permission to do today's pick up?"

"Lee-Anne Roberts."

"Why?"

"She was busy. You can call her if you don't believe me."

"I just might." She stared at me for a while and smiled as if she was impressed. "Did you just get a haircut?"

"Yeah."

"And is that a new shirt?"

"Yeah."

Her eyes scanned down to check the rest of me out. "Nice boots."

"Thanks. Some girl told me that my other ones were ratty."

"They were." She smiled, happy that I took her advice again. "Wait here a minute. I have to get my bag." She turned and pushed off the crutches to make her way over to the door of the daycare. One of the ladies she worked with said something to her and they both looked over in my direction. Shae-Lynn nodded at something that was said and the woman waved at me. I waved back to be friendly. It seemed to embarrass Shae-Lynn. She disappeared inside and came out a different door that led directly into the parking lot.

I rushed over to the passenger side of the truck and opened the door for her. She turned and handed me the crutches. The truck was too high off the ground for her to reach the seat, so I leaned the crutches against the side and lifted her by the waist to help her in. She had to use her arms to pull her legs into the cab one at a time. Once she was settled, I closed the door and laid the crutches in the back.

"Bye Shae!" a little girl shouted and waved from the back seat of her mom's car.

Shae-Lynn waved back as I hopped behind the wheel. The adoring way she was smiling made her look so beautiful. I was still staring at her when she turned her head to look at me. "What?"

"You seem good at your job."

She shrugged modestly. "It's just babysitting. It's not that hard."

"You make them feel special. I can tell by the way they look at you."

Her cheeks turned pink and she stared down at her hands folded in her lap. "Thank you." She snuck a glance at me. "What are you really doing here?"

"Kidnapping you. You should have followed through on that criminal record check." I backed the truck out of the parking spot and turned right onto Clark to head to the strip mall. "I just have to make a quick stop." I drove for a block and turned into the parking lot of the grocery store.

"Whose idea was this exactly?" she asked cautiously.

"I'm sort of flying by the seat of my pants." I hopped out of the truck. "I'll be right back. Don't run off."

"Ha ha."

I pulled out my phone as I walked across the parking lot and searched everything I needed to buy. I rushed up and down the aisles, then got in line. I could see Shae-Lynn through the window. She was talking on the phone. My phone rang as I was paying the cashier. It was Tawnie, so I let it go to voicemail and turned it off. When I returned to the truck, Shae-Lynn frowned as if she wasn't sure whether she should trust me. I put the two bags on the seat between us. She was still on the phone and said, "Okay, we'll see you in about twenty minutes, I think." She hung up and stared at me as I pulled back out onto Clark. "Lee-Anne said you're in town to show Stella to a buyer."

"Yeah. Your dad said it would be all right. I guess he forgot to tell you guys."

"I'm sure he wrote it somewhere in the fifteen pages of notes that he left for us. They'll be home again before I can even read through everything on it." She glanced down at the bags to snoop. "What are the groceries for?"

"Take a look."

She peeked in at the ingredients for lasagne and Key Lime pie. She smiled and seemed surprised that I remembered her favourite meal. "So, you think you're staying for dinner, do you?"

"I owe you a dinner for taking care of Stella."

"Actually, you owe me about four hundred dollars."

"Yeah, I know. I'll pay you back when I sell her."

"I'm just kidding. I wouldn't charge you. She's been a sweetie and Skeeter has decided she's his girlfriend."

"Skeeter better be a stand up stud. I don't want my Stella running around with just any old stallion who's going to break her heart."

"Don't you worry. He's been a gentleman. I made sure."

I glanced over at her for a second, then looked back at the road. "Your strength seems to be coming back."

"Yeah, it's been slow, but it gets better every day."

"Have you gone riding yet?"

"No."

"Riding would be good rehab for your leg muscles."

She looked out the window. "I'm not ready."

"You're scared?"

"Yes, I am."

"The quicker you get back in the saddle the better."

She snapped her head to glare at me. "You did not seriously just say that?"

"Yeah, why not? It's true."

She reached across the cab and backhanded my shoulder. "You are such a hypocrite."

"What are you talking about? I didn't quit after a wreck."

"Yes, you did. Just because it wasn't your wreck doesn't make a difference."

"I can get back in the saddle any time."

"Prove it."

"All right." I pointed at her to accept the challenge. "Let's go for a ride after I show Stella."

"I can't ride Harley. He acts weird and rears up if he senses that a rider is scared."

"Has he been ridden since the accident?"

"No."

"I'll ride him. You can ride Stella."

She studied my face to see if I was joking. I was serious, so she said, "Fine."

"Fine." I laughed.

"What's so funny?"

"I just talked you into getting back in the saddle."

She tilted her head and looked at me with a sympathetic smile. "No, stupid." She patted my knee. "I just talked *you* into getting back in the saddle. It was really easy, actually. I wonder what else I could convince you to do."

I smiled at the possibilities of that. "I'm pretty sure you could convince me to do almost anything."

Her eyebrows angled together, then her cheeks turned pink again. "What makes you say that?"

"You get an expression on your face when you're disappointed in me and I honestly don't ever want to see it again. I'd rather just do whatever you ask me to do."

"Really? Good to know." She leaned over and turned the volume up on the radio because a Carrie Underwood song had come on. She sang and tried to encourage me to sing the next line, but I shook my head. "Come on. You don't want to see my disappointed expression, do you?"

"I can't sing."

She started into the chorus. We both laughed when she got to the line about the guy singing off key. As we drove back to the ranch, she sang along to a couple other songs and she tried again, unsuccessfully, to get me to join her on an Eric Church song.

When we arrived, I rolled up their driveway, parked, and stared at her.

"What?"

"You have a beautiful voice. I really like listening to it."

Although she must have known she was a good singer, she seemed flattered that I thought so. "Thank you."

I leaned closer with the intention of stealing a kiss, and she didn't move away, which I took as a good sign. A truck drove up the driveway behind us and distracted her.

She sat back so we weren't within kissing distance and said, "That must be the guy who wants to see Stella. I'm going to get cleaned up while you show her."

Disappointed that I'd missed my chance, I said, "Okay. Hold on. I'll get your crutches out of the back." I helped her out, then grabbed the grocery bags and followed her up onto the porch. After holding the door open for her, I put the bags on the floor inside the door. Lee-Anne had already brought Stella out of the barn tacked up with Shae-Lynn's saddle and she was shaking hands with the guy. I went over and shook hands with him too. "Billy Ryan."

"Paul Delorme." He ran his hand down Stella's front legs. "I'm looking for a good match for my daughter."

"How old is she?"

"Twelve."

I hooked my thumbs in my pockets and glanced at Lee-Anne. She shot me a look as if she was warning me not to say anything. I had to say something though. "She might be too fast for a green rider."

"She's not green. She's been riding since she was four years old and barrel racing since she was eight." He put his fingers in Stella's mouth. "You said you want twenty thousand for her?"

"Yes, Sir."

"Do you normally ride her?" he asked Lee-Anne.

"No, Sir. I'm a trick rider."

"Do you mind riding her around the ring a couple times? I want to see how she moves."

Lee-Anne took Stella through a series of figure eights at a lope and then breezed her for a while before making her way back over to us.

"That's a nice horse," Paul said. "Do you mind if I bring my daughter by tomorrow morning? I'd like to have her ride Stella before I make my final decision."

I looked up at Lee-Anne. "Is that all right with you?"

"Yeah, that's fine. I'll be around."

"Okay, I'll come by around eight."

I shook his hand and walked him back to his truck. Lee-Anne hopped off Stella and was walking towards the barn when I hollered at her, "Keep her tacked up. Shae-Lynn and I are going for a ride."

"Really? How'd you talk her into that?"

"I'm charming."

She laughed, not convinced. "I guess that's one name for it. You want to ride Misty?"

"No. I told her I'd ride Harley to shake the cobwebs off him."

She nodded even though she didn't seem to agree it was the best idea. After Paul drove away, I went into the house and picked up the groceries from the floor. The kitchen was at the back of the house, so I took my boots off at the front door, and crossed through the living room. There was a picture of Shae-Lynn and Lee-Anne riding together on a pony in a frame on the mantle. They were probably only about four and five years old in the shot. There was also a series of black and white photos. One was of their dad hollering and snapping the reins during a chuck race; one of Lee-Anne hanging upside down off Misty in a suicide drag; and one of Shae-Lynn coming around a barrel tight on Harley.

Once I made my way to the kitchen, I heard a door open down the hall. A blow dryer started humming. The pie needed to chill for three hours, so I washed up and mixed the ingredients for that first, slid it into the fridge, and started on the lasagne.

I was working on the third layer when Shae-Lynn rested her shoulder on the archway that led from the living room and said, "Hey."

I turned my head to look over my shoulder. She was wearing tight jeans and a cotton blouse with skinny straps. The fabric was sweet with tiny flowers on it like something a little girl would wear, but the fit was sexy. It made me think thoughts that her dad would have definitely not appreciated. Her hair was curled into loose waves and her cheeks were powdered with something light pink and sparkly. Her eyes were lined with a charcoal colour that made the green of her irises seem as if they were backlit. I was about to say, "Holy shit," but I stopped myself and it came out more like, "Ho."

She frowned and then laughed nervously as if she wasn't sure how to take it. After scanning the countertop she said, "You've been busy." She leaned on her crutches and made her way over to stand next to me to dip her finger in the tomato meat sauce. When she touched her fingertip to her tongue to taste my creation, I was hit by another urge to kiss her. "Not bad," she said and moved away as if she knew what I was thinking. She reached over and grabbed a handful of grated cheese to sprinkle it on top of the row I just made. "How long did it take you to find the cheese grater?"

"A long time." I looked up at the big farmhouse clock above the table. It was seven-fifteen. I smiled because, although she didn't need to, I liked the fact that she put that much effort into getting ready. "You were in there for a long time. Did you fall asleep in the bath or something?"

"No. I just took my time. I thought it was going to take you longer to show Stella."

"He wants to come back tomorrow with his daughter so she can ride her."

"Oh." She paused to let the information sink in. "Does that mean you're staying in Calgary?"

"Yeah, I guess so. I'll crash at a hotel and come back in the morning."

To my surprise, she said, "You can stay here."

I glanced over to check her expression. I knew she didn't mean to suggest that anything was going to happen, but I wanted to make sure she wasn't just being polite. "I don't want to put you out."

"We have three guest rooms. It's fine."

Spending as much time as possible with her sounded good to me. I pretended to be focused on the cheese so she wouldn't see the grin on my face. I wanted to be clear in my head about what was going on, though, so I didn't end up getting crushed. Without looking up I said, "You look nice. Do you have plans with Nate tonight, or something?"

She opened a drawer to take out a box of tinfoil, then covered the lasagne. "No. I don't have plans with anybody tonight. Except, you did say something about going for a ride."

Relieved that the effort she put into getting ready wasn't for someone else, I opened the oven door and slid the dish in. "Okay, we have forty-five minutes. You ready, scaredy cat?"

"Oh. I'm ready. Are you ready?" she challenged.

"I just need to get my boots on, which might take the entire forty-five minutes since someone convinced me to wear boots that aren't broken in."

"You don't have to do everything I say."

I chuckled, not sure I could stop myself.

She smiled, maybe from the confirmation that she had me by the reins. Or, maybe from the visual of me wrestling my boots on. "I'll meet you outside." She pushed her shoulder into the back door and manoeuvred the crutches to step out onto the back porch. Feeling like I'd done three shots of whiskey, I walked back through the living room and sat on the bench near the front door. As I was bent over fighting with the leather, my heart rate sped up to an alarming rate. I took a deep breath before I went outside.

Lee-Anne had tied both horses to a hitching post at the side of the house. Shae-Lynn's crutches were leaning against the fence and she was standing next to Stella holding onto the horn. I walked over and gave her a leg up. She had to use her arms to lift her body weight until she was centred in the saddle. I slid her left foot into the stirrup then walked around the other side to do her right foot. "How's that feel?"

"A little bit weird. It kind of feels as if I'm going to slide off."

"You look good. I'll let you know if you're leaning." I adjusted the stirrups on the saddle that was on Harley and checked the cinch. My hands were sweating, so I wiped them on my jeans before I grabbed the horn and put my foot in the stirrup. As soon as I was seated, Harley reared up.

"Harley, whoa," Shae-Lynn said sternly.

His front hooves pounded down on the ground and he dropped his head trying to throw me. I clenched the reins and pulled back. He side walked, then spun to his left, which made me lose my seat a little. "Whoa," I shouted and pulled back hard on his mouth. He bucked, spun again, and reared up. "Easy, easy easy," I repeated, not at all easy myself. He reared up again and I considered jumping off.

"Relax, Billy," Shae-Lynn yelled. "He's reacting to your nervousness."

His hooves pounded down again and made my weight lurch forward. I released the tension in the reins and exhaled, trying to make my body relax. Harley shook his head a bunch of times and then tried to bolt, so I had to pull back on him again. I sat softer in the saddle. Eventually, after circling him a bunch of times, he settled down. "Whoa, easy." I exhaled and trotted him in a wider circle around Shae-Lynn and Stella.

Once I had control, I looked over at Shae-Lynn and winked. She grinned. "You all right?"

"He's squirrelly. The wreck must have traumatized him."

"No. He's just responding to having a scared rider on him."

I smiled to dismiss that theory. "That can't be it since I'm not scared."

She laughed at me. "You can lie to yourself and to me, but Harley knows the real reason you stopped bull riding."

"He's squirrelly."

"Whatever you say. Let's go before you get worked up again." She clicked her tongue to make Stella walk on then she turned to look back over her shoulder. "Be good, Harley. Billy's a little nervous."

"I'm not nervous. He's squirrelly," I shouted. I exhaled heavily one more time and gave Harley a gentle leg squeeze. "Come on, buddy, don't make me look bad." He flipped his head around a couple more times and then trotted to catch up to Stella and Shae-Lynn.

Chapter 18

Shae-Lynn and I rode along a stream for a while, then cut across to a trail that led through a stand of trees. The terrain got steeper and rockier as we made our way up to a ridge. The trail widened as we crossed a grassy pasture, so I moved Harley up next to Stella. Shae-Lynn glanced over and smiled, relaxed.

"How do your legs feel?"

"Good."

"We should turn back or the lasagne will burn."

She pulled out her phone and called Lee-Anne to ask her to take it out of the oven for us. She hung up and smiled again as if she had a plan. "I want to show you something. It's just a little farther."

She squeezed her legs and Stella transitioned into a gallop. I kicked Harley and blew past them, so Shae-Lynn took it up a notch. We raced each other over a series of rolling hills before she veered off and headed towards another ridge. I chased after her until she stopped on the crest of a hill. Harley slowed to a walk and stopped next to Stella. The view was of a lake framed by a mountain range on one side and expansive grasslands that stretched as far as the eye could see on the other side.

"Wow," I said. Harley exhaled heavily and shook his entire body to release tension. "Good boy, Harley." I patted his neck.

"Good boy, Billy." Shae-Lynn leaned over to pat my knee.

I smiled. "The horse was tense, not me."

"Mmm hmm," she said to mock me.

"It's nice here."

She nodded, not that anyone would dispute it.

The glow of the setting sun illuminated the profile of her face and the curve of her lips, which made me say "I bet sitting by this lake is where you had your first kiss."

"Uh, no." She readjusted her position in the saddle. "I don't invite boys to my house."

"Why?"

"My dad would scare them away."

"Who was your first kiss?"

She seemed embarrassed at first, but told me, "A boy named Miles. I was at an ice-skating party for one of my friend's birthdays. He was her brother. It was sloppy and tasted like Doritos."

I laughed. "What happened after that?"

"He ended up going out with one of my other friends and we never mentioned it again. Who was your first kiss?"

"A girl named Cassie. I had a crush on her all through grade six and seven, but I had trouble talking to girls back then."

Shae-Lynn smiled as if she was picturing me back then. "I remember that. It was cute how your face went all red and you tripped over your words. How did you finally make your move?"

"On the last day of elementary school, our class went on a field trip to the waterslides. My plan was to ask her if it would be all right if I kissed her. Eventually, I worked up the nerve because I figured if things went badly I could avoid her over the summer and she'd forget all about it. She said yes, and right afterwards she said, 'You should have done that a long time ago'. To be honest it's still to this day the best kiss I've ever had."

"Really?" She shifted in the saddle again as if her back was stiffening, but she didn't want to leave yet. "What made it so good?"

I thought about it for a while then shrugged. "How she made me feel."

172

"And how was that?"

"Peaceful."

She nodded, agreeing that would define a good kiss to her too. "Where is she now?"

"I don't know. She moved away that summer and I never saw her again." I stared out at the scenery for a while. When I glanced over at Shae-Lynn, she was looking at me. I smiled and asked, "What?"

She shook her head. "Nothing. I was just thinking." She pulled the reins and turned Stella around. "We should get going if we want to make it back before it gets too dark."

I turned Harley around and galloped to catch up to her. She smiled as the horses walked side-by-side. "Race you back, Shae Lynn."

"Shae." She smiled and squeezed her legs and took off.

She beat me by almost a hundred metres and stopped in front of the barn. I got off Harley and walked over to help her dismount. She rested her hands on my shoulders and let her body slide down mine. I carried her a few steps away from Stella and eased her down until her feet were touching the ground. Her arms were still wrapped around my neck. We both looked up at the same time and our faces ended up only a centimetre apart. I gazed into the green of her eyes before glancing down at the flesh of her lips. If Harley could have sensed how fast my heart was beating, he would have gone berserk.

"That felt good," she whispered.

"Definitely."

She seemed to be searching my face to figure out if I was referring to the riding or the body contact. She closed her eyes and inhaled slowly. "I know you need the money, but I kind of hope the sale doesn't go through. I would love to keep riding her until I'm ready to get back on Harley."

I licked my lips trying to figure out what to do next. Part of me wanted to kiss her. Part of me wanted to tell her to run as fast as her weak little legs could take her. She seemed to be waiting for me to make a move. When I didn't, her arms slid down off my shoulders and she stepped back.

"Do you mind getting my crutches, please?"

I jogged over and brought them to her. "I'll take care of the horses and meet you inside."

"Okay. Thanks." She smiled, but it seemed sad before she turned on the crutches to make her way back to the house.

I watched her for a while, still unsure whether it was a good or bad idea to become more than friends. What I did know for sure was I wanted to take the next step. I led both horses into the barn. I had no trouble finding where the tack should go because everything was labelled and organized. When I was hanging the reins, I noticed framed pictures on the wall outside an office near the feed box. The first one was a picture of Shae-Lynn being hugged by four children. Her T-shirt had *The Africa Project* written on it. There was another picture of her with a group of kids standing in front of what looked like a brand new school. The third picture was of her with a bunch of kids playing soccer on a dirt field. Her T-shirt in that photo had *Right To Play Cambodia* written across the front.

Skeeter poked his head around the end of the stall trying to nuzzle noses with Stella. "Hey, stud. Watch yourself. She's a good girl and I'd like to keep her that way. Got it?" Stella leaned against the wall and stretched her neck over to get closer to him. "You two better say your goodbyes. Stella's going to be moving on tomorrow." Skeeter looked up at me almost as if he understood what I said. "Sorry, buddy. I need the money." I patted Stella, then left the barn.

When I walked into the house, Shae-Lynn had already set the table for three. She looked wobbly trying to carry the heavy lasagne dish with one hand and manoeuvre a crutch under the other armpit. I took the dish from her and placed it on the table. Lee-Anne stood in the doorway that led to the living room. She was putting on a leather jacket.

"Aren't you staying for dinner?" Shae-Lynn asked. "Billy made enough for all of us."

Lee-Anne smiled the same way she had earlier when she sent me into town to pick Shae-Lynn up. "No, I'm going over to TJ's place."

"I thought you said he was working tonight."

"Did I?" She raised her eyebrows at me. "Have fun. Don't wait up for me." She turned and left out the front door.

"All right, so it's just the two of us." Shae-Lynn picked up one place setting and hobbled back into the kitchen. It was hard to tell how she felt about Lee-Anne leaving us alone. I didn't want her to feel like I had come over with the intention of staying the night.

When she came back and sat down across from me, I said, "After we eat, I'll leave and get a hotel room. I don't want your dad to get the wrong idea."

She looked at me for a while, then blew on a forkful of pasta. "My dad doesn't need to know."

It was sassy, and I liked it. My blood rushed through my body. I took a deep breath and changed the subject to try to settle down. "I noticed those pictures of you in the barn. It looks like you've travelled a lot doing charity work."

She nodded. "I try to do two trips a year if I can manage it. Sometimes I go with a church group and sometimes with a charitable organization."

"Damn. I waste most of my time at rodeos and bars while you're off making the world a better place. You make me look bad."

She glanced across the table. "What are you waiting for?"

"I wouldn't know the first thing about helping kids in third world countries."

"Not that. What are you waiting for with your dinner? Aren't you hungry?"

I stared at her and my thoughts kept derailing to wonder what it might feel like to kiss her. The image I created in my mind made me feel insanely nervous and excited at the same time. My fork was suspended over my plate and I was having trouble focusing enough to make it move.

Her eyebrows angled together and she tilted her head to the side. "Are you feeling sick?"

"No." I ate a few forkfuls so she wouldn't figure out why I was acting weird.

"Charity work isn't just about helping kids. They also do things like build houses, dig wells, and teach farmers how to use modern technology. You'd be good at that."

"Are you trying to recruit me?"

"Maybe." She scooped another helping onto her plate and ate. "You're a good cook, too."

"Thanks. Don't forget to leave room for the Key Lime pie."

"Don't worry about that." She patted her flat stomach. "I can pack it in."

"I don't believe that. You're so tiny."

"Is that a compliment or an insult?"

"It's an observation."

She sat back in her chair and watched as I finished what was on my plate. "Do you remember what you said to me after I fell off Harley in the finals of my first pro event?"

I frowned and thought back. "Uh, I think I told you to stop crying."

"And?"

I laughed when I remembered. "I called you a runt and I said if you ever wanted to make it on the circuit you were going to have to cowgirl up."

She nodded and smiled. "I wanted to punch you in the face so badly."

"You should have. At least I would have known you were tough enough."

"All right. Next time I will."

"Good." I stood to clear the table. "I'll do the dishes. You go sit down in the living room. I'll bring dessert out to you."

"Wow. I could get used to this. It's like having a personal servant around." She stood and handed me her plate. I piled it on top of

176

mine and then picked up the lasagne dish with my other hand. "Thanks for dinner," she said as she put her hand on my chest. She definitely would have been able to feel how hard my heart was beating. She smiled before she let her hand slide away. "Do you want to watch a movie?"

I grinned and teased her, "Isn't that code for something else?"

"Ha ha. You know that a movie means a movie."

"I was just checking. You did invite me to stay at your house when nobody else is home, and we had a nice dinner, and—"

"Easy there, cowboy." She smiled and leaned her shoulder against the archway to the living room. "You showed up uninvited, brought the groceries with you, and made my favourite dinner without asking. I don't know why you did all that since you already know I'm not that kind of girl."

"Maybe I just wanted to."

Instead of responding, she tucked her hair behind her ears and dipped her head in an attempt to hide the blush that spread across her face. After she spun around and disappeared into the living room, I went into the kitchen to clean up. I quickly put everything in the dishwasher and turned it on. Then I took two pieces of pie into the living room. She was on the couch with her feet rested on the leather ottoman. A movie was queued up, frozen on the opening title, waiting for her to press play. I handed her the plate and read the French title.

"What did you choose?"

"It's a foreign film with subtitles."

"Great," I mumbled.

She laughed at my lack of sophistication. "Just sit down and turn that lamp out." I leaned over and turned it off. She threw a blanket over both of our laps, pressed play, and broke off a piece of pie with her fork. Before she took the bite, she said, "Thank you for everything."

"Don't mention it," I said and dug into my pie.

Once we'd finished dessert, she reached her hand over and

rested it palm up on my leg. I chuckled a little as I wrapped my fingers around hers.

"What are you laughing at?" she asked, a bit offended.

"I haven't watched a movie while holding hands with a girl since I was about fourteen."

"You think it's lame?" she attempted to pull her hand away.

I squeezed her fingers tighter to stop her. "No, I think it's sweet."

She smiled before she rested her head on my shoulder.

"So, does this mean we're on a date?" I asked.

"You're the one who showed up in shiny new boots. You tell me."

"I'd be okay calling it a date if you're okay with it."

She sat up. "What about Tawnie?"

"I was only putting an effort in with her because you asked me to."

Her expression contorted into confusion. "I didn't ask you to date Tawnie."

"Yes, you did. You said I needed to have a relationship with someone that lasted more than two nights to prove I was a stand-up guy."

"I didn't mean with *her*, dummy."

When I realized what she meant, my heart bucked and a big grin stretched across my face.

She returned the smile for a while before she said, "I'm okay with calling this a date, but you still have a lot to prove."

With more seriousness than I had ever promised anything in my life, I said, "I'll do whatever it takes."

She seemed to know that I meant it because she relaxed and rested her head back on my shoulder peacefully as the movie started.

Chapter 19

The movie was surprisingly good considering I had to read everything they said. When the couple kissed at the end, Shae-Lynn sat up and looked at me. She shoved my chest. "You liked it, didn't you?"

I laughed, not wanting to admit it. "It was all right."

"Maybe you're not as hick as I thought you were." She stared at me for a while, then asked, "Do you want a drink?" She used the arm of the couch to help herself stand and carefully stepped over to a hutch. "There's beer and wine in the fridge, or there's this." She opened the cupboard door to show that the hutch was full of hard liquor.

"That's a lot of booze."

"My dad's friends like to party. What do you like?"

"I like everything. What do you like?"

"I don't know. I've only ever had beer." She spun each bottle to read the labels.

"God. You're a parent's dream child. Try the whiskey. It will burn, but you'll like how it makes you feel."

She grabbed a bottle and two glasses, then sat down beside me. She poured them full to the top.

"Whoa, that's enough to kill you."

She laughed and handed me a glass. "So, it should be just

enough to give you a buzz."

"Yeah, that sounds about right."

She took a sip and winced. "Wow. It does burn." Her body bolted up straight and her eyes clenched shut.

I took a shot size gulp and got up to grab the guitar that was leaning on a stand next to the piano. I brought it back over to the couch and sat down next to her. "Will you sing for me?"

"Sure, but I don't think I know any Bruce Springsteen songs."

"Well, I don't know any Carrie Underwood songs. Can you sing Jason Aldean's *Dirt Road Anthem*?"

"Yeah." She smiled as I started to play. "Do you always play upside down?"

"Yup."

"They make left-handed guitars, you know?"

"This is how I learned. I can't switch now. If I try to do things the right way, I get messed up."

"That's not true. You learned how to ride bulls right-handed and then switched over to left."

"That's different. I learned on my weaker hand. Switching over to use my stronger hand made more sense."

She laughed, already sounding a bit tipsy. "It's not different. It's exactly the same. Either that liquor went straight to your brain or you've taken too many blows to the head."

"It's different." I held up my left hand. "I'm already using my strong hand. The guitar's just upside down."

"Okay. Let's see what you can do with your backwards hick methods."

I started from the beginning again.

She closed her eyes and moved her shoulders in a sexy way as she sang the first two slow verses. Then I picked up the tempo and she sat forward to rap the next four verses. We transitioned back into the slow groove and I couldn't take my eyes off her. After I strummed the last note, she looked at me and tucked her hair behind her ears. "You're pretty good, hick."

"You're better than pretty good. You just made that my new favourite song."

She reached her arm over so I would pass her the guitar. "I wonder if my strength is good enough to play yet." She rested it on her leg and positioned her fingers. She strummed a few notes and smiled. "You have to sing."

"Nope. That's never going to happen." I leaned back and took another swig from my drink. "I'll just listen."

"What if I play this?" She played the first verse of *Glory Days* by Bruce Springsteen and raised her eyebrows as if she was waiting for me to jump in with the lyrics.

I shook my head. "That's tempting, but no."

"Oh, come on. Why not? I won't laugh."

"I'm not worried about you laughing. I'm worried about making your ears bleed."

She chuckled and reached for her drink. Her mouth pressed against the glass and she winced again. She giggled, then said, "I feel tingly already."

"You're a lightweight. Please tell me that you've done at least one bad thing in your life."

"Well, there is one thing I wish I hadn't done."

"I hope it was illegal, or a tattoo or something."

"My best friend's boyfriend was cheating on her and I caught him with the other girl. I told my friend and she hasn't talked to me since."

"That's not a bad thing. That's a good thing."

"I lost a friend over it. That's bad. I should have just minded my own business and let her find out for herself."

"No. That's what friends are for. You did the right thing. It's not your fault she doesn't know what a real friend is."

After a long silence, she swallowed a big gulp of whiskey and said, "I stole something once."

I pointed at her, impressed. "Now we're talking. What did you steal?"

"There was this group of really popular girls at my school. They asked me to hang out with them, but they said I had to steal a pair of diamond earrings to be initiated. I asked the sales lady at a department store to see a pair and when the other girls distracted her, I switched the earrings for some cheap cubic zirconia ones that we got at a drugstore. How's that?"

"It's pretty respectable deviance."

"Except I went back to the store an hour later and switched them back. Then I confessed everything to my parents and I never hung out with those girls again."

I shook my head in mock disappointment and laughed. "You're horrible at being bad."

"What's on the list of bad things you've done?"

"Oh, darling, that list is so long. I wouldn't even know where to start."

"Tell me the worst thing you've ever done."

My smile disappeared as I thought about it. I wanted to be honest with her, so I shot back more liquor to get the nerve. "Thanks to Rochelle you already know a pretty good sample of the bad things I've done. You probably don't know that I was arrested for stealing a truck."

She shook her head and took another sip from her glass. "That's the worst thing you ever did?"

"No. I haven't told anybody the worst thing I ever did."

Her eyes darted to glance at me before she stared down at her drink. "You can tell me if you want."

I tilted my head back and drank as much as I could before it made me cough. I could feel her watching me as I ran my hand through my hair. "The day my dad died I was hanging out with some girl I didn't even know in her camper. I lost track of time and when I heard them announce on the loud speaker that the bulls were coming up, I got dressed and ran over to the arena. I was too late though. They'd already pulled the chute gate for my dad." I exhaled and finished what was left in the glass.

"I don't understand. How is that the worst thing you ever did?"

"I was supposed to slap his back three times for good luck and I wasn't there."

She didn't say anything and I didn't want to know what her expression meant, so I stood and cleared the dessert dishes. It was dark in the kitchen, but I didn't bother to turn the light on. After I stacked the dishes in the sink, I sat on a chair and leaned my elbows on my knees. A few minutes later, Shae-Lynn came in and rested the crutches against the table. I could see her feet right in front of me. "It wasn't your fault."

I looked up at her.

"It wasn't your fault." She stared at me for a long time as if she was waiting for me to show some sort of emotion. When I didn't, she moved to sit on my knee and wrapped her arms around me for a hug. She whispered in my ear, "It wasn't your fault, Billy."

"He was superstitious for a reason."

"Could anyone slap his back for good luck or did it have to be you?"

"Anybody could have done it, but it was supposed to be me that day."

"Hand me your phone."

I reached around to my pocket and gave it to her.

"What's the password?"

"Rank."

She smiled and typed it in to unlock the screen. I watched as she searched the web. "Here. Watch this." She held the screen up and pressed play.

As soon as I saw what it was, I said, "No. I don't want to see that ever again."

"Just the beginning."

"No."

"Billy, do you trust me?"

I studied her expression, then closed my eyes for a while. "Yeah, I trust you."

She pressed play and held the screen out for me to watch. The video clip began with a female news anchor announcing that a bull rider had been killed by injuries he sustained at the rodeo. The footage rolled and showed my dad loading into the chute. Ron Miller pulled his rope and slapped his back three times. My dad nodded, then the chute gate opened. Shae-Lynn pressed stop and hugged me again. "It wasn't your fault, Billy. It wasn't anybody's fault. It was a freak accident." I hugged her back and we sat that way for a long time. Her breathing was so slow and peaceful. Her hair smelled like strawberries and her skin smelled like coconut. "You can talk about it with me," she whispered.

I nodded because I knew I could tell her anything, and closed my eyes because I knew I was going to. It scared the shit out of me to be so vulnerable in front of anyone.

"What did it feel like to be there and see it happen?"

"It was a helpless feeling, but that wasn't the worst part."

"Was it when the doctors told you that he passed?"

"No." I reached up to rub my eyes. "Cole and I decided that it would be best not to tell our mom over the phone, so we drove back to the ranch to tell her in person. When we walked in the house together, the look on her face made it seem like she already knew something was wrong. She asked, 'Where's your daddy?' Cole and I both stood there staring at her, speechless. She studied the expressions on our faces then she asked again, 'Where is he?' Cole said, 'He was in a wreck, Ma.' She looked out the window at the truck and asked, 'Does he need help getting out of the truck or something?' Eventually I said, 'He was in a bad wreck.' She shook her head as if she was trying to make it not true. She asked which hospital he was in and she fumbled around to get her purse and coat. I said, 'He's not in the hospital.' She screamed, 'Where is he?' It took a long time to work up the courage, but eventually I said, 'He's dead.' She collapsed to the floor — not like someone who fainted and puddled down. She blew back and crashed against the table as if I'd shot her in the chest with a shotgun. Cole rushed

184

over to help her and she wailed on him. She punched and scratched him, screaming that we were liars and that Dad wasn't dead. Cole didn't even try to stop her. He just let her beat on him until she had no fight left in her. When she started crying, he hugged her. She looked over his shoulder at me."

I squeezed my eyes tightly to try to erase the image of my mom's expression. Shae-Lynn placed her hand on mine. "What was the worst part?" she asked with the same gentle and patient tone she used on the kids at the daycare.

"My mom was disappointed in me for letting it happen. That was the worst part."

Shae-Lynn hugged me, and the warmth of her slow breath felt good on my neck.

"I'm trying to be a better person now. I swear."

"I don't blame you. Your mom doesn't blame you. Even if she does, she shouldn't. It couldn't have been prevented."

"If he wasn't a bull rider it could have been prevented."

"His profession didn't have anything to do with it. He could have died in a tractor accident or an oilrig fire. When it's your time, it's your time."

"Do you honestly believe that?"

"Yes. That's why we need to appreciate the moments we have. No regrets about the past. No worries about the future." Her hand slid over my chest and up to my neck. Her fingers were so soft it felt as if she was touching me with silk. "Ow. Shit." She abruptly arched her back and dug her fingers into my shoulder. "Ouch."

I repositioned my arms to support her. "What's wrong?"

"Ow. My back's in spasm. Ouch. Jesus."

I scooped her up.

"Sorry," she said as I carried her into the living room.

"Don't be sorry."

She groaned. "But we were having a moment and I ruined it."

"It wasn't ruined. Do you have pain killers or something?"

"No, I stopped taking them so I wouldn't get hooked."

I laughed because she was such a good girl. "Grab the whiskey."

I bent over the coffee table. She reached her arm out and picked up the bottle.

"Which one is your room?"

"Uh, having a moment wasn't code for anything."

"I know. I was going to give you a massage. I won't if you don't want me to."

She paused for a second to consider it. "Last door on the left."

I carried her down the hall and kicked the door to swing it open. She squeaked in pain when I eased her down on the bed. "Do you have massage oil or lotion?"

"There's a tube on top of the dresser."

I reached over to get it and tossed it on the bedspread. "Raise your arms up." I lifted the bottom hem of her shirt and pulled it over her head. She was wearing a strapless pink satin bra underneath. She looked a bit self-conscious when she noticed that I was checking her out. When I smiled, her cheeks blushed. "Unbutton your fly."

She frowned and looked at me suspiciously. "I realize that your other first dates all end the same way, but this one is not going to."

"I'm not trying to get in your pants. If you want a proper massage, I'll need to work on your legs too."

"How about you just do your best with my jeans on?"

"I can't believe you don't trust me. The quality of this massage is going to be compromised."

"I'll take that into consideration when I evaluate it."

I smiled and tickled her ribs. "Roll over."

She took a swig of whiskey straight from the bottle, then rolled onto her stomach. I knelt on the bed and straddled one knee on either side of her hips. The massage lotion was cold, so I warmed it between my palms before sliding my hands across her back. The spasm felt like a tight ball of iron cables. She groaned and buried her face in her pillow.

"Sorry."

"Do you even know what you're doing?" she mumbled into the pillow.

"Not really, but as long as you don't have a serious back injury you probably won't end up paralyzed."

Her body shook as she laughed at my stupid joke.

"Stop moving. How am I supposed to work my magic if you keep bouncing around?"

She laughed some more, then said, "I just thought of something bad to put on my naughty list."

"Yeah? What's that?"

"I'm letting a cowboy with an awful reputation get me drunk and put his hands all over me."

I smiled, but didn't agree. "That's his bad, not yours." I moved my hands up her back and dug my thumbs into her shoulders for a while. She relaxed and I kneaded my way back down to where the spasm was. She groaned again, so I lightened the pressure. Eventually, the knot worked itself out, but I kept massaging her. "You threw that competition so Tawnie would win and I would have to buy Stella. That was bad."

"Mmm. Who says I did that?"

"Did you?"

"Maybe. Sorry."

"It's all right. I kind of like that you were jealous."

She lifted her head and glanced at me. "Who says I was jealous?"

"Why else would you be mad enough to do that?"

She smiled and buried her face back in the pillow. "Why did you steal a truck?"

"Technically I borrowed it without permission."

"That's still stealing."

"Yeah. That's how the cops felt about it too." I moved my hands over her jeans and massaged the back of her legs. "Cole was on his last strike with my dad and he was going to get sent to reform school if he screwed up one more time. I borrowed the truck one night after a party to make sure we got home before curfew."

"Aw, that's sweet. You broke the law to make sure your brother didn't get shipped off."

"My dad didn't think it was sweet. He sent me to the reform school instead, but I got myself kicked out after six months and got to come home."

"I don't even want to know what you had to do to get kicked out of a reform school."

"No, you probably don't want to know that."

She made a quiet moan, then asked, "Where did you learn how to massage like that?"

"I used to hang out with Amy, the massage therapist who tours on the circuit sometimes."

"Oh, my God. Are there any girls at the rodeo you haven't slept with?"

"There are a few. I try to avoid the girls my brother has already slept with, although we've had a few miscommunications in that department. I definitely haven't slept with your sister." I slapped her ass. "Roll over."

She rolled over and grabbed the whiskey bottle off the nightstand. I massaged her thigh as she took a sip. "Do you want to sleep with my sister?" She handed me the whiskey.

I took a swig and gave it back to her. "That's kind of a trick question because of course I want to sleep with her, but I wouldn't."

"Why?"

"Well, for one reason, she has a boyfriend."

"And?"

"I don't think her sister would appreciate it."

She smiled and watched as I bent her knee to massage her hamstring.

"Plus, Cole already slept with her."

She made a funny gasping sound and opened her eyes and mouth in complete shock. "No. He. Did. Not."

I mimicked her stunned expression and said, "Yes. He. Did. Too."

"I don't believe you. She would have told me."

I shrugged, not sure why Lee-Anne hadn't told her. "I think they actually liked each other, but it didn't work out because of the long distance thing."

"Oh." She watched my hand as I ran my thumbs along her muscles.

"Did you take all those photographs?" I pointed at the framed black and white pictures hung on her wall. They were all powerful close up portraits — a little girl with a tear running down her cheek, an old woman who looked as if she was praying, a man who looked as if he had just finished an Iron Man, and a bull rider who looked as if he had just nodded for them to open the chute gate. I frowned and got off the bed to look at it more closely. "Is that me?"

"Yeah, it's from a couple years back. Do you like it?"

I stared at it for a while, then turned to look at her. "Yeah, I like it a lot."

She drank another sip before handing me the bottle. "You were happier when you were riding."

I glanced at the photo again before I wandered around to look at the other things in her room. The bunny she'd won at the midway was propped on the bookshelf looking dopey. I picked up one of her pink good luck armbands off the dresser. She wore one on her left arm when she competed and had ever since she was a kid. Instead of acknowledging that she was right about me being happier back then, I said, "I guess this didn't really work on your last run."

"Yes it did."

"How do you figure that? You were nearly paralyzed."

"A thousand pound horse landed on me and I'm going to be fine. I call that lucky."

"It would be luckier if you didn't fall in the first place."

"Lucky charms can't prevent bad things from happening. They keep you as safe as possible until it's your time to go." She held her hand out so I would pass the armband to her. "Come here." She

189

slid the armband over my wrist and pushed it up to just below my elbow. "This one is yours now — for the next time you ride."

"I'm not going to ride again."

"If you do, it will keep you safe. I promise."

I smiled because I believed her. "Thanks." I sat behind her on the bed and massaged her shoulders.

"How long is this massage going to last?"

"Sixty minutes, and I charge by the minute."

"How much do you charge?"

"It's negotiable and I might be persuaded to take a trade."

"Is that code for something?"

I laughed. "Maybe."

She drank some more and exhaled like someone who was nervous.

I pointed at a picture of her on a pony. "You were cute back then."

"I'm not cute anymore?"

I shook my head. "Nope."

She looked down and watched as my hands moved along her arms. "That's not very nice of you to say."

"You're not cute anymore. You're like snow."

"That doesn't make any sense. You're definitely drunk."

I leaned over her shoulder so my lips were nearly touching her ear. "You know that period of time after it has just stopped snowing, but nobody has gone out yet? You kind of want to run out on the fresh snow because it is so pure, but you don't want to run out on it because you know that if you do, your own footsteps will ruin how perfect it is."

"Yeah."

I slid my palm along her ribs. "You're so beautiful, like that snow."

Her eyelids blinked rapidly and for a long time it seemed as if she was holding her breath. I leaned in to press my chest against her back and tilted my head down to kiss her shoulder. She inhaled and whispered, "Thank you."

She placed her hands over mine as I moved them over her abs. My fingertips caressed the soft curve of her cleavage as I continued over the satiny surface of her bra. I kissed her neck. She turned and sat up on her knees to face me. I clutched my fist around silky chunks of her hair and pulled her head toward me. She gasped a little and her lips parted as she waited for mine to touch them. My breathing sounded as if I'd just gone a round. Every single cell of my body wanted to throw her down and make love to her. I wanted it so badly that my arms started to shake from the strain of resisting her. An anxious feeling crept in and filled my body as I realized I had no idea what to do next. I knew what I would do if she were any other girl, but she wasn't. I didn't have a clue how to be the guy she wanted me to be, the guy she deserved. Her bottom lip quivered and her eyes widened like a startled deer as she waited for me to do something. The drunk feeling immediately left my body and was replaced with panic.

"What's wrong?" she whispered.

"I want to kiss you so bad it hurts."

She leaned her forehead against mine. "Then do it."

I swallowed and closed my eyes, but didn't make a move because I knew what would happen if I did. She was so innocent. So perfect. I was definitely going to mess everything up if I slept with her.

Her phone rang on the bedside table. She didn't seem to notice. She didn't even blink. I sat back on my heels and tried to force air into my lungs to slow the body rush that was surging through me. She slid her hands up my neck and cradled my face. Her eyebrows angled together as she searched my expression.

The ringing was not helping the alarming feeling that was tearing through my body. "You should answer the phone."

"I don't want to. Are you okay?"

The phone stopped ringing and she still hadn't taken her eyes off me. "I feel like I'm going to throw up," I admitted.

The phone buzzed with a text message that lit up the screen.

It was from Nate, so I picked it up and read it. *Confirming that we're still on for tomorrow. Pick you up at 1pm.*

I handed her the phone and stepped off the bed.

She read the text. "This isn't what you think. It's not a date or anything. There is a reception at his country club tomorrow. A couple of the members of the committee who are deciding on the music scholarship I applied for are going to be there. He thought it might be a good opportunity for me to network."

"It is a good opportunity. I should let you get your rest now."

She blinked a few times and her hurt was obvious, but she didn't say anything.

I ran my fingers through my hair, feeling guilty as hell. "Which drawer do you keep your nighties in?"

"The top middle one."

I opened the drawer and pulled out a tank top and boxer shorts. She sat back against the pillows as I tossed them to her. "Good night, Shae-Lynn." I leaned over and kissed her forehead. Then I took the whiskey with me and left.

After puking three times in the bathroom, I sat on the couch and tipped the bottle back. I thought that if I drank enough I would forget about how badly I wanted to go back into her room. The alcohol wasn't working. It was only making me feel like throwing up again. I stopped drinking and stumbled out onto the front porch for some fresh air and to keep myself away from her bedroom door. I paced with a wobble back and forth and hit my forehead repeatedly with the heel of my hand, hoping that the pounding would somehow help my brain figure out what the right thing to do was. No matter how I reasoned it, the right thing was walking away from her so she could have a better life with a guy like Nate. A guy who wouldn't eventually do something selfish to break her heart.

At three in the morning, Lee-Anne came home. I was slouched over on the front porch steps. She got out of her car and walked over to stand in front of me.

"You should probably get that heart condition of yours checked out by a doctor."

My fist was clutching my chest as if I'd been shot.

She frowned. "What are you doing out here?"

"Trying to sober up enough to drive."

"Drive where?"

"Home."

She swung her purse and hit me across the side of the head four times. "Asshole."

I didn't even put my arms up to protect myself because I wanted it to hurt.

"You can't just use her and leave, you son of a bitch."

"I didn't use her. Nothing happened. I swear."

She smacked my face and the sting made my eyes water. "If nothing happened, why are you trying to sneak out of here in the middle of the night?"

"I just have to go."

"What about the buyer for Stella?"

"Uh, he backed out."

She glared at me. "Why are you leaving?"

"Shae-Lynn's better off without a guy like me. I'd rather she figure that out now before it's too late."

"When's too late? Because if it's after she's fallen for you, it's already too late. She's liked you since she was old enough to know what a boy was."

"Don't make this harder than it already is. I like her so much it's killing me, but I don't know how to be the guy she wants me to be."

"Yes, you do. Real relationships are just like bull riding. You have to be willing to risk getting hurt, and you have to hang it all out, and never give up no matter how scary or hard it gets. You know how to do it. You're just too much of a coward to try."

"I can't compete with a guy like Nate."

"You're right. A quality, well respected man who retired from the

193

rodeo to open a successful and lucrative business is no match for an emotionally stunted adolescent who quit, scared because he didn't want to end up like his dad, but still hasn't actually moved on."

The build up of emotion crept up my throat. I shook my head wishing what she said wasn't true, but it was.

"Fine. If you want to break her heart, go ahead. I'm not going to stop you."

I blinked hard. "She deserves someone better than me."

"Well, yeah, obviously. But she wants you."

"I'm no good for her. You and I both know that."

"But she is good for you. You and I both know that too." She hit me one more time, then stomped up onto the porch and disappeared into the house.

It wasn't until six in the morning that I felt sober enough to drive, although I probably still wasn't. I got in my truck and called Paul Delorme. He didn't answer, so I left a message, "Hi. This Billy Ryan. I'm calling to let you know that I changed my mind and I won't be selling Stella right now. Sorry to have wasted your time and I apologize if your daughter is disappointed." I hung up, started the truck, and drove away.

Chapter 20

As soon as I got back to Saskatoon, I felt like complete shit for leaving without saying goodbye to Shae-Lynn. I wanted to call to apologize, but I forced myself not to because I thought it would be easier for her to forget about me if she thought I was an asshole. The problem was I couldn't stop thinking about her. It was torture not to talk to her and it was killing me to live with the guilt of hurting her.

I called Tawnie intending to tell her that it was over, but the day I called, her grandpa had had a minor heart attack. She was stressed and already crying when we talked, so I didn't do it. Instead, I just stopped calling.

On the Thursday before the High River rodeo, I was sitting in my mom's kitchen holding my phone fighting the urge to call Shae-Lynn. Mom stood at the counter in her work clothes making coffee. Cole sat down across the table from me with two slices of toast on a plate. "What's wrong?" he asked me.

"Nothing."

"Why do you look like someone just ran over your dog?"

Mom turned to glance over her shoulder at me.

"It's nothing," I mumbled.

Unconvinced, she turned back to fill three travel mugs with coffee. She reached over to turn the garburator on. It made the horrific grinding sound and then clunked to a complete stop. I shot Cole a look that made it clear I wanted to rip his face off and shove it down his throat.

"Sorry. I'll get to it," he mumbled.

Mom sighed and faced me. "You have seemed a little down lately, honey." She walked over and put two of the mugs on the table before returning to get hers from the counter.

"It's just stress." I stood and picked up the mug to take it with me. "Do you need me to give you a ride to work?" I offered.

"No, thanks. Linda's going to swing by."

"Should I get your wheelchair?"

"No, today's a good day. I feel great." She picked up a package from the counter and handed it to me. "This was delivered for you yesterday."

It was the custom-made belt I had ordered for Shae-Lynn's birthday. The sight of it gave me a pain in the chest that made me wince, and my breath caught in my throat for a second.

Mom frowned in a concerned motherly way, so I avoided looking at her.

Cole took a bite of toast and said, "I'm leaving for High River tomorrow at noon if you want to come with me."

"Are you planning on riding?" Mom asked.

"No, I was just going to hang out with everyone. Maybe I'll play some pool." He raised his eyebrows and grinned because he meant he wanted to hustle.

I checked Mom's expression to see if she knew what he meant by playing pool. She obviously had no clue because she picked up her purse and said, "You should go, Billy. I don't like seeing you look so sad. It will be good for you to just have fun. High River is only forty-five minutes from Calgary. Maybe you two could go by the Roberts' ranch to check on Stella and say hi to the Roberts. Oh, there's my ride." She kissed us both on the cheek. "Love you."

"Love you," we both said then watched her leave out the back door.

"Are you in?" Cole asked.

"You don't have any money."

"I sold the quad. I got thirty-five hundred for it. I don't have much more time before they come to collect."

"I haven't hustled in a long time. What if we lose it all?"

"We won't."

"We can't make enough in one night to cover the entire debt."

"Don't worry about it. I'm going to enter the hundred thousand dollar stock contractor event."

"Entering and winning are two separate things."

"I'm going to win." He grinned with inflated confidence.

I shook my head and walked towards the door. "You're delusional. You should mention that to your psychiatrist at your next meeting."

"It's not delusional if it's true. Are you coming this weekend?"

"Only if you don't screw up the hustle. And you better fix the God damn garburator or I'll fix it and shove you down it." I stepped out onto the porch and let the screen door slam behind me.

In High River, we checked into a room at the hotel where the rodeo participants were staying. Then we headed out to a bar that had pool tables. We chose the bar that was having a karaoke night because we figured there would be a lot of suckers there. We lost the first five games we played. The first two were for beers and the other three were for twenty bucks each. There were two club boys at one of the other tables checking us out, so we started to act as if we'd had too much to drink. Cole was better at the acting drunk because he was good at getting loud and obnoxious. I was better at duffing shots and acting as if I was an inexperienced player. Eventually, the club boys walked over and challenged us to a one hundred dollar game. We pretended to try our hardest. When it got down to the game winning shot, Cole took his time lining it up and then missed it by the narrowest margin possible.

"Come on!" I yelled and shoved his shoulder. "How'd you miss that?"

One of the club boys sunk the eight ball for the win and they both grinned at us waiting to get paid.

"God damn it," I whined. "You just lost us a hundred bucks."

Cole opened his wallet and flipped through a stack of hundred dollar bills. "Do you guys want to go double or nothing?"

The club boys both nodded and racked them up.

"What are you doing?" I got off my stool and pretended to stumble a little. I did the loud whisper that drunk people do, "Are you crazy? We can't beat them. We're going to lose another hundred."

"I almost had it. Just one more game."

"All right fine. One more, but if we lose, you can't bet any more. That's our rent money."

"Yeah, yeah." He tipped the bottle as if he was taking a sip of his beer.

We lost two more double or nothing games by just one shot before Cole started acting frustrated and competitive. He bet them everything he had in his wallet. I argued with him to make it look like I wasn't okay with him betting that much on one game of pool. I shoved him and sulked while nursing my beer. As I was waiting for my turn, I recognized the voice of the karaoke singer who just started her song. I stood and walked around the corner so I could see the stage. She was wearing a tank top and a denim mini skirt with boots. The song she was singing was Carrie Underwood's *Good Girl*. After she finished the last note, the entire bar erupted into cheers. She glared at me, then put the mic down and gingerly walked without crutches down the steps of the stage.

"Billy, it's your turn," Cole said.

I turned around and ran the table. After I sunk the eight ball, I hung the cue stick on the rack. Cole pretended to be shocked and ecstatic about my dumb luck. He was going to be pissed that I didn't play it more casually, but I wanted to go find Shae-Lynn. The club boys handed the money to Cole and I walked away.

Shae-Lynn was sitting at a table near the stage with her sister, Nate, and one other bronc rider. I walked right up to her. "May I speak with you, please?"

"This isn't a good time," she said without even looking up at me.

I glanced at everyone else at the table. Nate smiled. "Hi Billy."

"Hi." It was impossible not to like the guy, so I turned my back on him and focused on Shae-Lynn. "Do you want me to say what I have to say in front of everyone?"

Her cheeks turned pink and she stood. I pulled her hand and led her out to the patio.

She crossed her arms. "You have eight seconds."

"I'm sorry."

"All right. Bye." She turned to leave, so I reached for her elbow. "Shae-Lynn."

"*Shae.*"

I exhaled and pushed my hat back. "You don't... I've been, uh. Ever since... This. Shit." I exhaled again and wiped the sweat that was dripping down the side of my face. "I don't know how to say what I want to say."

She frowned and studied my eyes. "You're not drunk."

"No."

"Why were you acting like you were?"

I looked around to see if anyone was close enough to hear us, then I lowered my voice, "We were hustling those guys."

She shook her head, unimpressed, and obviously not surprised.

"I want to make things right with you."

"You don't have to. You were right. We wouldn't have worked. I'm just glad you left before anything happened. Don't worry about it." She turned again, but I still had a hold of her elbow, so I tugged her back towards me. "Let me go, Billy. I'm here with Nate."

It felt like she slapped me and it took me a second to get over the sting. "But I want to tell you how I feel about you."

"I know how you feel about me. You like me enough to sleep with me, but you don't like me enough to make me your girlfriend.

Since we've known each other forever you decided to take off before you used me instead of taking off after you used me. It's kind of sweet in a really pathetic way."

"That's not why I left. I like you enough to make you my girl-friend — more than enough."

She blinked slowly and her eyes were watery when she opened them again. "I don't want to be your girlfriend, Billy. You'll only break my heart." She yanked her arm out of my grasp and walked back into the bar.

I had to sit on one of the plastic patio chairs because the wind was knocked out of my chest. It felt worse than the time the bull sat down on me in the chute and collapsed my lung. I was still gasping to force oxygen back in when Cole walked up. "We have to go. Those guys are pretty pissed that we hustled them."

"Go ahead. I have to work things out with Shae-Lynn."

"I'm not leaving you here by yourself. Work what things out? Since when do you and Shae Roberts have things to work out? Is that why you blew the hustle?"

I stood and stormed back into the bar on a mission.

Cole was right behind me. "What exactly are you planning to do?"

I approached the stage and wiped my palms on my jeans. My heart was racing like a thoroughbred. I exhaled and leaned over to ask the girl who was organizing the karaoke to show me the binder of songs. I flipped through the pages until I found one that I knew how to play on the guitar.

"That one's got some tricky parts," she said.

"Yeah, I know. I'm going to butcher it, but I've got something to prove."

Since it would be entertaining, she smiled, loaded it up on the computer, and handed me a microphone. "What's your name?"

"Billy." I adjusted the microphone in the stand and picked up a guitar that was out for the house band. It was a right-handed guitar, so I turned it upside down to hold it left-handed, pulled the front of my hat down, and took a bunch of deep breaths.

The girl spoke into her microphone to introduce me. "Everybody put your hands together for Billy. He's going to attempt *I Will Wait* by Mumford and Sons because apparently he's got something to prove."

About three people clapped. Cole cheered, but then checked over his shoulder to keep track of where the club boys were lurking.

I stepped up to the mic and said, "I can't sing, so I apologize in advance." The music started and I played the guitar with the intro. When the lyrics came up on the screen, I read the first couple of words in my head before I realized I was supposed to be singing. I didn't jump in and sing until the third line. I was having trouble keeping up with the notes on the guitar at the same time as reading the lyrics, so there was a half-second delay until I found the rhythm. Eventually, I stopped reading and sang from memory. It probably sounded like a bullfrog getting violated.

Even though I hadn't looked up, I could feel every single person in the bar gawking at me. Quite a few people were laughing. Cole yeehawed when I hit the chorus again. I finally looked up. Shae-Lynn's hands were covering her mouth in a horrified expression. Lee-Anne was grinning. I skipped the singing for one verse and just focused on the guitar. The last couple of *I will waits* were more like talking than singing. When I finished, Cole gave me a standing ovation. Everyone else cheered, except for Shae-Lynn. Lee-Anne bounced up and down. Shae-Lynn was still frozen in the same position with her hands clamped to her mouth. I leaned the guitar back on the stand, then hopped down from the stage and stood in front of her. Lee-Anne pulled her up by the elbow to make her stand. "Shae-Lynn —"

"Shae," she corrected me.

"Yeah, about that, I ain't never going to stop calling you Shae-Lynn."

"Why?"

"Because Shae-Lynn is the prettiest name I've ever heard and

I like how it sounds when I say it."

She pressed her lips together.

"Shae-Lynn, I know I'm not good enough for you, but I want to be. I'll do right by you. Please give me a chance to prove it."

She stared at me for a long time. It felt as if everyone was holding their breath, waiting for her to answer. She grabbed my hand and pulled me. I let her drag me out the back exit into an alley. "Are you nuts?" she hissed.

"It's a distinct possibility."

"That was so embarrassing."

"Sorry."

"Not embarrassing for me; embarrassing for you."

I laughed, just glad it was over. "Hopefully it was worth it."

She shook her head to indicate it wasn't.

"Shae-Lynn, I know I screwed up when I left, but the reason I did it is because you deserve someone better than me. But the thing is: I don't want you to be with someone better than me. It might sound selfish, but I want you to be with me because the only time I ever feel at ease is when I'm with you. Based on how terrified I am of hurting you and on how much my chest hurts when I'm not with you, I'm pretty sure that I love you."

She blinked slowly, stunned, then her gaze locked onto mine. "You what?"

"I love you."

She turned her head and looked somewhere off in the distance to process what I said.

I reached over and wove my fingers between hers. "Say something. Please."

Her eyelids dropped and her lashes rested like butterflies on her cheek before she met my gaze again. "Do you remember when I told you that I was in love with someone once?"

"Yeah."

"What I didn't mention is that I'm still in love with him."

I stepped back and took my hat off. I couldn't breathe and

a pressure behind my eyes made them sting. I swallowed hard. "Nate?"

She exhaled slowly, then whispered, "No."

"Who is it?"

Her fingers tightened around mine. "You, stupid."

I lunged forward, pushed her up against the brick wall, and kissed her. Her hands slid up and held my face as she kissed me back. Her tongue touched mine and it tasted like her cherry lipgloss. I pulled her even closer and felt her chest rise with each breath. It felt like my first kiss, only better. The same jolt I had felt when we first touched at the hospital zinged through every nerve in my body and made my skin tingle. The world around us faded away as her peaceful easiness washed over me. When she made a strange sound, I opened my eyes.

She was crying.

I leaned my head back and ran my thumbs over her cheeks. "Hey. What's wrong?"

She blinked a couple times and inhaled. "Nothing's wrong. I've been dreaming about this moment for a long time. It feels really good when a dream comes true."

I smiled then kissed her again. Her right hand slid down my chest and she let it rest over my heart. We made out for a while before she leaned her head back and stared at me with those big green eyes. I put my hat on her head and tilted it back. "So, does this mean I get to call you my girlfriend?"

"You tell me."

"I'd be okay calling you my girlfriend if you're okay with it."

She was quiet for a while before she said, "I'm okay with it. Just don't break my heart."

"I won't. I promise."

I kissed her again, but we were interrupted by the sound of a throat clearing. I turned around. Tawnie stood about six feet away with tears running down her face. She wiped her hand across her cheek before she said, "I'm honestly not surprised you would do something like this, Billy. I am shocked at you though, Shae."

Neither one of us responded.

"I guess the perfect Shae Roberts isn't as perfect as everyone thinks. Before you give it away to Billy you should probably know that I'm pregnant and he's the daddy." She turned on her heel and ran down the alley.

My brain felt like it slammed against the inside of my skull and paralyzed the rest of my body.

Shae-Lynn lunged out from behind me and rushed back to the bar, still wearing my hat. She pounded on the door until a bouncer opened it and let her in. I couldn't move.

Before the door swung shut, Lee-Anne poked her head out, frantic. "Billy, they're beating up Cole. Hurry."

Tawnie had made it to the end of the alley and was about to turn the corner when Lee-Anne lunged over and dug her fingers into my arm. She tugged me so violently that I stumbled and had to put my hand down on the pavement to break my fall. When I looked up, Tawnie was gone. Lee-Anne pulled me again, so I followed her back inside.

Chapter 21

I ran through the bar and burst out the front doors. There was a crowd gathered in the parking lot. Cole was on the ground getting stomped by the two guys we'd hustled. Before I could reach him, Blake and Tyson pulled up in a truck and jumped out. They took a club boy each. I rushed over and crouched down next to Cole. He was curled up in the fetal position, protecting his neck with his hands. "You okay?"

He looked up and smiled as if he found it amusing.

I shook my head, but it was my own damn fault for agreeing to come with him in the first place. Blake was getting his ass kicked, so I grabbed the club boy's shirt and threw him against the hood of a car. When he came at me, I punched him square on the jaw and he dropped to the pavement, twitching. The guy Tyson was beating on ran away once he saw that his friend was out cold. Cole chased him, but he was wearing dress boots, so he gave up after about twenty metres. The guy got away.

I held my hand out to help Blake off the ground. He stared at my offer for a few seconds before taking it.

"Thanks, boys," Cole said after he jogged back to where we were standing.

Blake wiped the blood from his lip with the back of his hand. "That offer is still on the table, Billy. Have you reconsidered?"

I glanced at Cole and then scanned the crowd of faces searching for Shae-Lynn. "No."

"They're only taking the top ten Canadian guys who throw their hat in the ring — in case you come to your senses and realize it's your only option." He turned his head and spit out a mouthful of blood on the pavement. "You only have until the end of the month and then Cole's going to have to pay up in some other way. If he comes up short or takes off, they'll pay your mom or Shae a little visit."

I lunged at him and crushed his throat with my grip. He sucked in a gasp and fell silent as I tightened my fingers. "If your dad's goons go anywhere near anybody I know, I'll be coming after you. You understand?"

Blake's fingers clawed at my hand, attempting to release the strangle hold.

I shoved him and he stumbled. "Ty, you better get your cousin out of here before I break his riding arm," I mumbled.

Tyson pulled Blake by the collar of his shirt and pushed him towards his truck. The crowd dispersed. Shae-Lynn was standing near the front door holding my hat. She walked over and handed it to me, then turned back.

"Shae-Lynn."

"Don't bother," she said and kept walking.

"Come on, Billy. We need to get out of here," Cole shouted. He climbed into the driver's side of the truck. Tyson and Blake were already backing out in Blake's truck. Police sirens approached from down the street, so I ran and jumped in the truck as Cole put it in gear. "Wooeee!" he hollered and gunned it out of the parking lot.

"I'm going to guess that the guy who got away has the money."

"Yup, but it was fun, wasn't it?"

"No. It wasn't fun. You lost all your money and got your ass kicked."

"I didn't get my ass kicked. I was turtling to conserve energy."

"Oh, is that what that was?"

"How did it go with Shae?"

"Awesome until Tawnie showed up and told me that I'm the father of her baby."

"What?" His head snapped to look at me and he almost drove off the road. "She's pregnant?"

"That's what she said."

"Holy shit."

I rubbed my face with my palm. "What am I going to do? I don't want to have a kid with Tawnie. I barely know her."

He stared out at the road ahead of us. "She's probably lying. Chicks say crazy things when they're jealous."

"I don't know. She left a message yesterday that said she needed to talk to me about something."

"You used protection, didn't you?"

I winced.

"Damn it, Billy. How many times have I told you to be careful?"

I shook my head, angry at myself.

"Maybe it's not yours. You should ask for a paternity test."

"Pull over."

"Why?"

"I'm going to puke. Pull over."

He drove onto the gravel shoulder and stopped. I jumped out and stumbled into the grass ditch. I puked liquid for three heaves. Once my stomach was empty, I dry heaved a bunch of times. Eventually, the contractions stopped and I rolled onto the grass to stare up at the stars. Cole hopped the ditch and sat down beside me. I heard him light a cigarette, then I smelled the smoke. "Do you remember that Lisa girl from Regina that I dated for a while?"

"Yeah, sort of."

"I got her pregnant."

I sat up and looked at him. "What happened?"

"She was only seventeen and she said she wasn't ready to have a kid. She decided to have an abortion and I didn't try to stop her."

"Does Mom know?"

"No. Nobody does." He took a long drag from his cigarette. "If I could go back in time, I would try to stop her. I know it was her body and her choice and everything, but there is not a day that goes by that I don't think about that little baby."

I exhaled and leaned my elbows on my knees. "I don't want Tawnie to have an abortion."

"You better tell her that you're willing to cowboy up before she makes up her mind."

I pulled out my phone and dialled Tawnie's number. She didn't answer, so I left a message, "We need to talk. Call me back." I hung up and glanced at Cole. He wasn't looking at me. He was staring at the cars driving by. "Let's go get drunk," I suggested.

Cole laughed. "I think you've got enough problems without another of my nude rooftop flagpole shows to deal with."

We both stood and got back in the truck. "Fine. I'll get wasted. You can take care of me for once."

"For once? Who do you think took care of you on the circuit all those years when Dad was off getting drunk and sleeping with whores?" He shoulder checked and pulled out onto the road.

I glanced at him, then stared out the windshield, completely depressed. "I'm going to be a shitty father."

A Carrie Underwood song came on the radio and I got too choked up to talk, so I just leaned against the window and stared at the buildings flashing past.

When we arrived back at the hotel, Cole got out and headed towards the lobby bar. "I changed my mind," I called after him.

"About what?"

"Getting drunk. I'm just going to go to bed."

He frowned, trying to work out what to do. Obviously he determined that I needed to be alone because he said, "I'm going to try to pick up." He glanced over his shoulder towards the bar where a crowd of girls loitered near the door. "Looks like I shouldn't have any trouble finding somewhere to crash."

"Yeah, all right. I'll see you in the morning."

I shuffled towards the elevator and pushed the button. The hall seemed a mile long. Once I was in the room, I didn't bother to turn on the lights or even take off my boots. I brushed my teeth and splashed water on my face, but I still felt rank. My phone was in my pocket, so I took it out and flopped down on the bed to call Shae-Lynn.

The call connected and I could hear music and people in the background, but she didn't say anything. I listened to her breathing. It was calming. Eventually she spoke in a very quiet voice, "Billy, I don't want you to call me anymore."

"I know you hate me right now, but I'm freaking out and I could really use a friend to talk to."

"Talk to Tawnie."

"You're the only person who knows how to make me feel better."

I could hear the air exiting her lungs as she exhaled. "Hold on a second." The sound muffled as she spoke to someone away from the phone. Then the noise of the music and people faded as if she went through a door to somewhere quieter. "Maybe once you talk to Tawnie, you'll feel better."

"I don't see how."

"Maybe she doesn't want to keep the baby."

I rubbed my face with my palm hoping it would somehow erase reality. "I don't want her to have an abortion, but I don't want to have a baby either. I don't know what to do." My voice cracked and I had to inhale to prevent myself from losing it. "I'm going to end up just like my dad."

She mumbled something to herself, then said, "It's going to be okay, Billy."

"How is it going to be okay? I don't know how to be a dad."

"Nobody does the first time. I think it will be cute to have a little Billy Ray running around. You can take him fishing and on trail rides. I can picture him wearing a little black cowboy hat to match yours and he'll probably have a skinny little butt like you."

"It might be a girl."

"Yeah, that would be sweet. She'll be so beautiful. I can picture her calling you *daddy* and climbing up on your lap so you'll read her a story. That would be nice, right?"

"I'm not ready for it — at least not now, and definitely not with Tawnie."

Shae-Lynn was silent for a while. "You can't plan out everything in life. Sometimes things just happen. Whether you're ready or not, you have to make the best of it. When you look back later, you'll be grateful for how things worked out."

"Having a kid with Tawnie is going to screw things up with you and me, and I really don't want that."

"I guess it wasn't meant to be. Everything happens for a reason even if we don't know what that reason is at first."

"Do you really believe that?"

She didn't say anything for a long time, then she whispered, "We can always be friends."

"Promise?" There was a knock at the door of the hotel room. "Hold on. Cole must have lost his key." I got off the bed and stumbled in the dark to open the door.

Shae-Lynn was standing in the hall. "I promise," she said as she stepped forward and wrapped her arms around my neck. I hugged her back tightly and dropped my head down to rest my chin on her shoulder. Her body relaxed against mine and the rise and fall of her breathing made me feel like everything was going to be okay. We stood for a long time, then she reached down and held my hand. She led me back into the room and let the door close behind us. She climbed onto the bed and tugged my hand so I would lie down next to her. "Everything will seem better in the morning," she whispered.

I squeezed her hand and moved closer to kiss her forehead. "Thanks for being here."

"Don't mention it."

Chapter 22

In the morning, there was a knock at the hotel room door that woke me up. Shae-Lynn was still next to me holding my hand. Her eyes opened when I moved. The sun was already up and angling through the crack in the drapes. There was another knock, then I heard a key card slide. "Are you two decent?" Cole asked as he opened the door.

"Yeah." I rubbed my face to try to wake up.

Shae-Lynn sat up and looked at the clock on the bedside table. It was eight o'clock.

Cole stepped into the room. His eye was black and his lip was swollen. He stood, grinning at us. "Fully clothed and sleeping on top of the covers. Disappointing, but since your dad's here looking for you, that's probably a good thing."

"What?" she shrieked and hopped off the bed. "Lee-Anne promised she would cover for me."

Cole shrugged, loving the drama. "All I know is that he's down in the restaurant asking everyone if they've seen you."

"What did you tell him?"

"I avoided him, but I made Tyson tell him that he saw you leave with Lee-Anne around midnight. Rochelle told him you were with Nate, so he's probably going to get a Trent Roberts whupping."

I chuckled at the thought of Nate catching shit from Trent, and

Shae-Lynn threw a pillow at my head. Her phone rang and when she checked the call display her expression turned to panic. "It's my dad. What should I say?"

"Tell him the truth. You're an adult," I said.

"I can't. He'll stop respecting you."

"I don't care."

"I do."

I smiled, glad that she cared. "So, lie."

She answered, "Hi, Dad." She turned around to face the window and Cole went into the bathroom. "I'm sitting at the lake, why?" She glanced over her shoulder at me. It looked like it was killing her to lie. "I did sleep in my bed. I just woke up early and went for a walk to watch the sunrise. I'll head back to the house now. Do you want me to make breakfast?" She closed her eyes and tilted her face towards the ceiling as if she was praying for him to believe her. "Oh, when are you going to be back?" She smiled. "Okay, I'll see you when you get home. Love you." She hung up and pointed at me in a threat. "You have to get me back to the ranch before he gets there."

"No problem. How does it feel to be a grown up?"

"Lying to my dad doesn't make me a grown up. It makes me a liar."

"It makes you a bad girl. Exciting, right?"

"No. Let's go." She knocked on the bathroom door. "Hurry up, Cole. My dad will whup your ass too if I don't make it home before him."

Cole opened the door with a toothbrush hanging out of his mouth. "All right. Let's go then."

She grabbed his toothbrush. "Do you mind if I borrow this?"

"Yeah, that's kind of gross," he said and laughed.

He searched his bag for his pill bottle and took his medication. I stood and unpacked the box that had Shae-Lynn's belt in it. When she came out of the bathroom, I gave it to her.

She smiled, surprised. "What's this?"

"Happy birthday."

"My birthday isn't for almost two weeks."

"Yeah, I know, but just in case your dad kills me before then."

She opened the lid and her mouth dropped open. She didn't move. Cole stepped in to look over her shoulder. He whistled. "Damn. That's fancy. Looks like someone might have a little crush on you."

The expression in her eyes made my heart flip over in my chest. "Billy, this is too expensive. I can't accept it."

"Well, we can't return it. It's got your name on it."

She placed the box on the table and slowly unrolled the belt as if it would shatter if she moved too quickly. She examined the pink and lilac crystal bead design that included green clovers, bluebells, the number thirteen, a palomino horse running the barrels, and a bucking bull with a rider who had his right arm up in the air. The letters that spelled *Shae* were encrusted in sparkling rhinestones and the *Lynn* was stitched in smaller scrolling letters across a tiny heart. She ran her fingertips over the sparkling beads. "It's beautiful."

"Try it on."

"I don't want to wreck it."

"It's for wearing. Put it on or you'll hurt my feelings."

She removed the buckle from her leather belt and fastened it to the crystal belt. She adjusted it to sit on her hips and then wrapped her arms around my neck. "Thank you. I love it." She clutched my hair between her fingers and pulled my head forward for a kiss. I hugged her body tight against mine and kissed her good in case it was the last one I ever got from her.

"Yeah, okay, that's enough of that," Cole said. "I'm still standing right here."

"Sorry," Shae-Lynn said and stepped back.

"You've had sex with a girl when I was in the same room," I said and pulled her back in to me.

"You could have left."

"So can you. Get out."

"Her dad's hunting her down and there is a rumour that Lyle might be out there looking for me too. We need to leave."

"Jesus, Cole."

He picked up his bag and opened the door. "I'm driving away in five minutes whether you two are in the truck or not."

"We'll be there," Shae-Lynn said.

The door closed behind him and I looked at her. "I really don't want this to be it."

"I don't either, but you need to sort things out with Tawnie. Thank you for my belt."

I hugged her into my chest and rested my chin on the top of her head. We stood like that until Cole texted to tell us Trent was in the lobby and we should go out the side exit. We took the emergency staircase down and ran out of the side door into the parking lot. I reached down and held her hand as we rushed towards the truck. Cole was already sitting in the driver's seat with the engine running. She slid in next to him. I hopped in and closed the door.

"Oh my God, that's his truck in front of us," she said and flopped down onto my lap. Cole looked at me and laughed because if her dad saw her with her head in my crotch it would have made everything worse. I laughed too, but then my smile faded when I spotted Lyle talking to a group of guys in the parking lot.

"This is not funny," she hissed.

"Calm down," Cole said. "He went to the drive-thru across the street. He'll be a good ten minutes there. I drive fast." Cole turned out of the parking lot onto the main street. "If you're so concerned about your dad knowing that you spent the night with a guy, why did you ask me for Billy's room number last night?"

She sat up and glanced at me. I waited for her to answer, but she didn't say anything. Cole turned his head to look at us for a second before he focused back on the road. She pulled out her phone and called Lee-Anne. She'd obviously woken her sister up. They argued for a while and got their stories straight, then she hung up and sighed. I squeezed her hand, which made her relax.

Forty five minutes later, we cruised down the gravel road that led to their ranch. A truck came into view behind us. She peeked out the back window. "Shit. That's him."

"Jesus, the old man hauls ass," Cole said and pushed the accelerator.

We literally skidded into their driveway surrounded by a cloud of dust. Before the truck even stopped, Shae-Lynn crawled over my lap and opened the door. When Cole parked, she jumped out and was standing near the hood when her dad pulled up beside us. She smiled and waved at him.

He got out of his truck and walked around the front of ours. "Hey, what are you boys doing here?" He studied Shae to watch her reaction and that's when I realized he was going to notice that she was wearing the same mini skirt and dress boots from the night before. She avoided making eye contact with him. I made a mental note to teach her how to be a better liar.

"We were in High River," Cole said without missing a beat. "Billy wanted to come by and visit Stella since we were so close." He hopped out of the truck and hugged Shae-Lynn as if they were just meeting up. "You and Lee-Anne missed a good party last night. It got crazy after you left."

"Really?" she said quietly and hugged him back. "What happened?"

"A bunch of shit that your dad probably doesn't want to hear about."

"What happened to your face?" Trent asked.

"Oh, I just had a little disagreement with someone over who won a bet. It was nothing." He turned back to Shae-Lynn. "How's Billy's horse doing?"

"Good." She looked like she wanted to crawl into a hole. "She's in the barn if you want to see her."

"Actually, I turned her out while you were at the lake," Lee-Anne called from the porch.

I got out of the truck and put my hat on. Trent stared me down. "Did you have a good time last night, Billy?"

"Um, yeah, it was all right. I went to bed not long after Lee-Anne and Shae-Lynn left. Cole's more of a partier than I am."

He nodded and continued staring at me. "Paul Delorme told me that you backed out of the sale. He said he offered you twenty-five and you still turned him down. I thought you needed the money."

"I, uh."

Shae-Lynn frowned. "You told Lee-Anne that Paul backed out of the sale."

I cleared my throat. "No, I meant to say I backed out."

"Why did you do that?"

Cole piped in, "Yeah, bro, why would you turn down twenty-five thousand dollars for a horse you don't even want?"

"Shae-Lynn needed a horse to rehab on until she's recovered enough to get back on Harley."

"We've got plenty of horses here," Trent said.

"Yeah, well, Stella's kind of special though."

Shae-Lynn blinked, about to cry. "Billy, you guys need the money. Don't keep her on my account."

Her dad stared me down for a long time, and when I didn't respond, he looked at Shae-Lynn. "That's quite the belt you've got there."

"Oh, yeah." She readjusted it on her hips and glanced up at his face. "Haven't you seen me wear it before?"

"No. I think I would have remembered it." He smiled, maybe because the sweat was dripping down the side of my face. "You boys should come on in for some breakfast. Shae made something, didn't you, sweetheart?"

She blinked slowly and pressed her lips together. It seemed like she was about to crumble under the weight of the lies that were piling up when Lee-Anne said, "She's got pancakes and bacon on the griddle. I hope you guys are hungry."

Shae-Lynn smiled. "Yeah, I made lots. There's enough for

216

everyone." She turned and gave me a wide-eyed look that made me want to laugh. I had to bite my lip to keep a straight face.

"Sounds good," Cole said. "Maybe we should eat first and visit Stella later."

I nodded and followed him towards the house.

Trent was behind me and when I held the door open for him, he said, "Watch yourself, cowboy."

I lifted my eyes to meet his. Swallowing wasn't possible — I tried, but my throat was too tight. "Yes, Sir," I finally said.

We stood in silence for a long time before he said, "Shae's damn near perfect, and I'm not just saying that because she's my daughter."

"Yes, Sir. I know."

"She doesn't make very many mistakes. When she does, she learns from them and she leaves them in the past. The fact that she has loved you since she was old enough to talk, and kept loving you all this time through all your bullshit, makes me think that maybe loving you isn't a mistake. But you need to know she's not like your mama. If you turn out to be a mistake, she will learn from it and leave you in the dust. I will make sure she always has the financial means to kick your no good ass out of the truck and leave you on the curb. Don't you ever forget that."

"Yes, Sir." I smiled, but I wasn't sure if I should.

"I'm not joking. If you're not serious about her, you might as well just move on to the next girl now."

My heart did a series of double kicks, then went into a spin. "I'm serious about her."

"All right then. Prove it."

"I plan to."

"Good. Do it right." He stepped into the house.

Elated, I followed him.

217

Chapter 23

As we drove away from the Roberts' ranch Cole said, "You and Shae were out in the pasture visiting Stella for a long time. Did you have a good time?" He raised his eyebrows expecting to hear some juicy details.

"Yeah, it was probably the best time of my life."

"Nice. What'd you do?"

"Walked, held hands, and kissed."

He laughed, but then he looked at my face and realized I wasn't joking. "Holy shit you're serious, aren't you?"

"Yeah." I rubbed my face with the palm of my right hand and tried to massage the tension out of my chest with my left. "I don't think I can live without her."

He punched me really hard in the shoulder. "Are you listening to yourself? You're getting soft over a girl."

"She does something to me."

"She obviously doesn't do something *something* to you."

"No, it's not like that. It's way better than that. Have you ever been in love?"

"No, and I'm going to avoid it if it makes me act like you're acting right now. I can't believe you're not going to help me pay off my debt because you decided to fall in love with some goody-two-shoes girl you never even used to notice."

"I noticed her."

"You didn't even know what colour her hair used to be."

"Yeah, well I know her now."

"I hope so, since despite the fact that I'm going to get murdered, you gave her a twenty-five thousand dollar horse, a belt that probably set you back another thousand, and you dropped at least five hundred dollars on those boots because she said your other ones looked old. And that's just the stuff I know about."

"My boots were old."

"Have fun planning my funeral and moving Mom into a dinky welfare apartment."

"I don't see why I have to be on the hook for your debt anyway."

"You're not on the hook for it. I'll pay you back. All I'm asking is that you temporarily stop throwing away all your money on romantic gestures so I can at least borrow something to stave off my impending death."

"Blake's dad isn't going kill you. He's all talk."

Cole glanced at me seriously, then focused back on the road.

"Jesus Christ. They're going to kill you?"

"Let's just say it's not in my best interest to test them."

"God damn it, Cole."

We drove the rest of the way to Saskatoon in silence. We arrived home just after six o'clock. A hunting knife was stabbed in the door frame with a note. *Time's up. Don't make me come back here.*

Cole read it and his Adam's apple bobbed. I rushed into the house. It was quiet. Mom's purse and keys were on the table next to a new pile of bills. "Mom!" Her bedroom door was open. She wasn't in it. "Mom. We're home. Are you okay?" I called through the bathroom door.

"Billy," she said. She sounded like she was crying.

"What's wrong?"

Her voice trembled as she said, "My legs went weak while I was in the bath. Can you go get Mrs. Spooner from next door and ask her to come over to help me?"

"I'll help."

"No. Can you just get Mrs. Spooner, please?" Her voice cracked.

I ran to the neighbour's house and knocked on the door. She followed me back over to the house and called to my mom through the bathroom door.

"Janice, I need a little help getting out of the bath," Mom called back.

Mrs. Spooner tried the door, but it was locked, so I got one of Mom's hairpins and jimmied it. Mrs. Spooner went in and closed the door behind her.

"What's going on?" Cole asked as he joined me in the hall.

"Mom was stuck in the bath and wanted me to call Mrs. Spooner over to help her."

"How long has she been in there?"

"I don't know."

"Hopefully not since yesterday."

I glanced at him and frowned as the thought sunk in that she might have been in there since we left. "We need to hire a nurse."

"I know. I've been telling you that for months." He glanced down at a text on his phone. "Shit," he mumbled.

"What?"

"Lyle's just making sure I got his note."

I shook my head and leaned against the wall. I was so tired of everything.

"Maybe it's about time you came out of retirement," he said. "If we both ride, we'll have a better chance of taking home the hundred thousand dollars."

While I was thinking about it, Mrs. Spooner opened the bathroom door and popped her head out into the hall. "I've got her all wrapped up in her robe. Can one of you get her chair and one of you help me lift her out of the bathtub?" Cole went to get the chair from the living room. I followed Mrs. Spooner into the bathroom. Mom was shivering and hugging her knees into her chest.

"How long have you been in here?"

She looked up at me. Her eyes were red and puffy from crying and she had dark circles below them. "Not too long," she said, weakly.

I bent over to slide one hand under her legs and the other one around her back. I lifted her out of the bathtub and carried her out into the hall. Cole was waiting with the chair. Mrs. Spooner touched my back and whispered, "Let me know if you need anything else."

"Thank you."

She left quietly and Mom rolled herself towards her room.

"Mom. We're getting you a nurse."

"I don't need one, Billy."

"Really? How long were you in there?" I shouted down the hall.

"I told you; not long." She turned the chair to face us. "It's humiliating enough that I needed to ask my children and the neighbour to get me out of the bath. Please don't make it worse by hiring a stranger to make me feel like I'm a complete invalid."

"It's obviously not safe for you to be here by yourself."

"Can we not over-react, please? I just had a bad day. It doesn't happen very often."

"It happens all the time," I shouted because my frustration about everything was coming to the surface.

She started crying again. "We can't afford a nurse." She wiped her eyes with the sleeve of her robe.

Cole walked down the hall and bent over to hug her. "Don't cry, Ma. Billy is working two jobs and I'll find one eventually. We can afford it."

"Billy can't work two jobs once he's back at school."

Cole looked at me, but kept hugging her.

My phone buzzed, so I checked to see if it was Tawnie. It was a text from Shae-Lynn. *Video call me when you have a minute. I need to talk to you about something and I think it's better if we are sort of face to face.*

Cole rolled Mom into her room. I went into my room and

picked up my iPad to call her. She was sitting in her room and she looked like she'd been crying as much as my mom. After wiping her cheeks and inhaling to compose herself, she said, "Your stress wrinkle is showing."

"We came home and found Mom stranded in the bath. She won't tell us for how long, but she may have been there since yesterday."

"Oh my God. That's awful." She leaned her elbows on her desk and covered her face with her hands. Eventually she looked up. Her lip was trembling. "Billy, I need to tell you something. It's really hard and I wish I didn't have to, but—" She started crying and wiped the tears from her eyes.

My heart seized up. "Just say it."

"My dad heard that Tawnie's pregnant with your baby."

"How did he find out? I never told anyone except Cole." I glanced through my open door at Cole's bedroom door across the hall.

She could obviously tell I was considering murdering him to get rid of the majority of my problems with one simple act. "It's not Cole's fault. Everyone would have found out eventually anyway."

"Your dad can't tell you what to do. You're an adult. You can make your own decisions."

"This is me making my own decisions. I just happen to agree with my dad that it's better if we don't date."

It felt like a two-by-four smashed across my shoulders. I had to brace my hands on the desk. I couldn't talk because I couldn't breathe.

"I'm sorry, but after you left, I came to my senses."

"Please don't. At least give me a chance."

"No. Your life is a mess and you have a baby on the way with a girl who lives in Edmonton. I don't fit into that equation, and honestly I don't want to."

I closed my eyes and rubbed my temples. "Don't quit now, Shae-Lynn."

"I'm sorry to hurt you, but I deserve more than what you can give me."

I stared at her, desperate to think of something to say that would change her mind. "I love you."

"I love you, too." She blinked and the tears rolled down her cheeks. "I always have, but I can't anymore. I'm sorry, Billy." She reached forward and, although it seemed to pain her, she ended the call.

I stood up and threw my iPad across the room. It slammed against the wall and the screen shattered. Rage flared inside me and I pushed the entire bookcase over. Everything dumped off it as it toppled to the floor with a crash. I threw a bunch of shit against the wall in a crazy rampage. Then I stood in the middle of my room staring at the mess.

"What the hell?" Cole asked as he stood in my doorway assessing the damage.

An impulse to beat the hell out of him tore through my muscles, but I knew it would upset Mom, so I exhaled to control my fury. "Get out of my way." I shoved past him, ran down the hall, and burst out the front door. I sprinted down the street for about a block before slowing to a jog. Eventually, I ran out of steam and had to walk. I pulled out my phone and called Tawnie. "Listen, I'm tired of whatever game you think you're playing. Call me back or I'm going to hire a lawyer. I have rights as a father and you can't dick me around. Stop being a bitch and do the right thing."

Chapter 24

The following Wednesday, I took half a day off from Hank's to interview home-care candidates. It was just after noon when I got home. Cole's truck was in the driveway, but he wasn't around, so I thought he hadn't gotten out of bed. I pounded on his bedroom door. "Get up. The first interview is in ten minutes." There was no answer, so I knocked again. "Jesus, Cole. Could you please act like an adult instead of a fifteen-year-old stoner for just one day?" I opened the door. He wasn't in his room and the bed was made. I texted him as the doorbell rang.

After the last interview was over, I leaned on Mom's bedroom door. "The person I hired is going to start on Friday."

Mom nodded so I would know she heard me, but she wasn't happy about it.

"I have to run an errand, but I won't be gone long. Will you be okay alone for about an hour?"

"Yes. Please don't baby me." She glanced out the window at Cole's truck. "Where's your brother?"

I shrugged and ran my hands through my hair. "Is it all right if I ask you a question?"

She nodded.

"If you could have changed Dad, what would you have wanted

him to be like?"

She smiled in a nostalgic way, but it faded. "Why do you ask?"

"I just don't want to be like him."

"You're not like him. You got his good looks and bull riding talent, but you never were like him in any of the ways that matter. You were more of a man by the time you were thirteen than he ever was. Just be yourself, baby."

I crossed the room and hugged her.

She pressed her lips together as if she was trying to force her mouth into a smile. She wasn't quite successful. "Try to track your brother down and make sure he's all right."

I nodded, closed her door, and called Ron Miller as I walked out to my truck. "Hey, is it too late to sign up for the stock contractor event?"

"You'd be bumping one guy out, but it's your choice since you're ranked higher."

"Would I be bumping Cole, Tyson or Blake?"

"No, it's a young kid named Mikey."

"Good. Count me in."

I hung up and called Cole again, but he still wasn't answering, so I left another message, "Thanks for your help with the interviews, shit head. I'm leaving for Calgary Friday morning at eight. If you're not here, I'm leaving without you." I hung up and drove to the bank. I took out all the money I had in my tuition account, then headed over to the Palomino.

Stephanie opened a bottle of beer and put it on the bar for me as I sat down on a barstool. "What are you doing here on a night off?"

"Is your brother still a bookie?" I asked her.

"Yeah."

I slid the envelope of money across the bar. "Will you place this bet for the stock contractor event this weekend in Calgary for me?" I handed her a piece of paper with all the details.

She read what I wanted to bet on, then opened the envelope

and fanned through the stack of hundreds. "How much is this?"

"Ten thousand."

"It's a lot of money to throw away if you're wrong."

"Let's not think about that, all right?"

She nodded and tucked the envelope in the till. "How's that girl you're sweet on?"

"She doesn't want anything to do with me."

"Why?"

"Because she's smart."

Stephanie laughed and walked away to serve some middle aged guys at the other end of the bar. When she came back, she leaned her elbows on the bar and smiled at me in a way that felt a lot like pity. "Don't give up, darling. My husband chased me for two years before I finally gave in."

"It's not that simple. I got another girl pregnant."

"Jesus, Billy." She straightened and shook her head in disappointment. "Why'd you go and do that?"

"I'm an idiot." I tilted the beer bottle back and drank all of it. "See you next week." I stood up.

"Good luck."

I couldn't tell by the look on her face whether she was referring to the bet or the mess my life was in.

When I got home, I sat in my truck staring at my phone. Every day since Shae-Lynn had broken it off, I had resisted the urge to call her, but the longer I sat there staring at my phone the more trouble I had convincing myself that avoiding her was for the best, especially since it was her birthday. Eventually, I texted her *two lines from a Lady Antebellum song that expressed how much I missed her.*

She wrote: *We Owned The Night.*

I miss you so bad I can barely breathe.

There was a pause before she wrote back: *I don't know that one.*

I'm Dying Without You by Billy Ray Ryan.

Sounds like a sad song.

Heartbreaking.

After a long delay, my phone buzzed again: *Show them how it's done Saturday night.*

Are you going to be there?

There was no response.

By Friday, Cole still hadn't come home or called. The home care nurse showed up as I was packing my gear into my truck. Right after I hung up from leaving another message with Cole, a friend of his from high school walked up the driveway. "Hey, Billy."

"Hey, Al. What's up?"

"Just came by to pick up my new truck."

Confused, I frowned and stared at his goofy grin. "What are you talking about?"

"Cole sold me his truck and a bunch of his other shit. He said he'd leave the keys on the kitchen counter because he wasn't going to be here."

"Where did he say he was going to be?"

"He didn't. He just said he would leave all the other stuff in the truck."

"What other stuff?"

"His fishing gear, tool kit, hockey equipment, flat screen, and his buckles." He handed me a piece of paper. It was a bill of sale that had Cole's signature on it. "He told me to give you the money."

"The truck's worth more than this." I pointed to the amount written on the paper. "The damn thing is only three years old."

Al shrugged. "I didn't expect him to take my first offer." He handed over a wad of cash and a cheque. "I had to post date some of it until I get paid. Is that all right?"

I rubbed my eyes. "It's not enough anyway, so it doesn't matter when you pay it."

"That's what Cole and I agreed on. I already transferred the insurance over."

"I mean it's not enough to cover his debt. Never mind. I'll get the keys." I found the keys on the counter and opened the back door to toss them out to Al.

"Thanks, man."

"Yeah. Enjoy."

I didn't want to watch him drive away, so I closed the door and leaned on it. When Cole was eighteen, he gave away everything he owned and then went out to the barn with Dad's shotgun. He sat on a chair with the gun on the floor between his feet. The stick he used to push the trigger slipped and caused the gun to tilt, so he ended up blowing a hole through the roof instead of his head. Grandpa stopped him before he was able to set up for a second try. Then he was hospitalized and diagnosed. None of us ever talked about it afterwards.

I walked down the hall to the den where we kept the gun cabinet. The firearms were all accounted for and the lock was in place, which didn't mean too much since he had enough medication to off himself in a much less messy way.

He didn't leave a suicide note the first time, but I checked his room to see if he had this time. Nothing initially looked out of the ordinary in his room and there was no note lying around. The wooden box of my dad's rodeo and childhood mementos was open on the floor. The photos were spread out and some of the letters were unfolded. On the top of the pile was a picture of Dad and Cole at Cole's first professional rodeo. Cole had won, and Dad had his arm across his shoulders, which was as close to a hug as either one of us ever got. They were sitting on the tailgate of Dad's truck.

That's when I realized where Cole probably was.

I made my way down the hall and stepped into the kitchen. I shut my eyes and slowly opened the door to the garage. A faint smell of engine oil and exhaust fumes wafted towards the open door. My eyelids clenched tighter, waiting for another odour to hit me. I really didn't want to be the one to find his dead body, but Mom finding it would have been worse. It took every bit of strength I had to open my eyes. My racing heart stopped. Then

I exhaled the breath I'd been holding. Dad's truck was gone and the only thing left was a giant oil spot on the concrete.

I phoned Blake and woke him up, again.

"What the fuck, Ryan? Don't you sleep?"

"Cole has until Saturday to pay up, right?"

"Yeah."

"So, they wouldn't do anything to him before that, right?"

"I don't know what you're talking about."

"Yes, you do and if I find out that they touched one hair on his body before then, I'll come after you. You understand?"

"Whatever. I'm not scared of you, Billy, and what those guys do to Cole has nothing to do with me."

"It will have something to do with you if I go to the cops."

"Go ahead. I don't care if my dad goes to prison. You'd be doing me a favour."

"Just make sure they don't hurt him. I'll get the money."

"Have you fucked Shae yet? Because I was thinking about giving it another go with her — whether she wants to or not."

My jaw muscles clenched and my left hand curled into a fist. "I'm going to assume that was your attempt at some sort of asshole sense of humour, but in case you're serious, I should probably warn you that I would gladly rot in jail next to your dad if it came to that. Don't go anywhere near her."

"We'll see. She might choose me when I beat you this weekend."

"Too bad you're not going to beat me."

He laughed. "We'll see about that too."

I hung up and turned around. Mom was leaning on the archway that led to the dining room. "Was that about Cole?"

I shook my head and wiped my mouth with the back of my hand, so she wouldn't see the lie.

"Did you get a hold of him?"

"He said he's going to meet me in Calgary." I looked down at the ground and ran my finger across my eyebrow.

"Billy. Don't lie to me."

I made eye contact. "He said he was going to be there."

"Where's he been?"

"He didn't tell me."

She frowned and studied my expression for a long time before she crossed the floor and turned the tap on. "If I find out you're lying and he's dead in a ditch somewhere or has his mouth wrapped around a shotgun, I'll whup your ass."

"You mean you'll get your nurse to whup my ass."

She smiled and turned the garburator on. It worked. I watched the water swirl down the drain and considered telling her the truth. It would only stress her out though, so I decided not to.

"Come here, hon." She put her arms out so I would step in for a hug. She squeezed me tightly and kissed my cheek. "I take that back. It's not your responsibility to make sure your brother is all right. Have a good ride this weekend. Make your daddy proud."

"I'd rather make you proud."

"I already couldn't be more proud of you."

I closed my eyes and squeezed her one more time. "I'm not perfect, Ma."

"I know, honey."

"Love you." I put my hat on and left.

Chapter 25

Rochelle pulled into the hotel parking lot in Calgary the same time as I did, so I carried her bag inside for her.

"Has Tawnie talked to you yet?" she asked as we checked in at the lobby desk.

"No. Why? What has she said to you?"

She shrugged and handed the girl her credit card. "Nothing. She didn't want to talk about it. Lee-Anne was the one who told me." She sighed and leaned against the desk as the girl processed my card and handed me a key card.

"Do you think Tawnie would lie about something like that?"

"I don't know. She did say she needed to talk to you. That's why we went to the Lemongrass that night. She said you had stopped calling, and she was hoping you'd be there so she could talk to you."

"Did she seem upset or excited?"

"Neither. She just seemed eager to find you. We got there right before you went up on stage and sang that song for Shae. That was so adorable, by the way. Tawnie didn't think so, obviously. When Shae pulled you outside, Tawnie downed her shot and mine before going after you. I felt bad for Tawnie, but honestly, I was secretly so excited that Shae was getting what she has wanted for so long. I guess this baby kind of puts a wrench in that."

"She drank two shots?"

"Yeah."

"You're positive?"

"Yeah."

My phone buzzed with a text from Lyle asking where my brother was. "Thanks Rochelle," I said distracted. "I need to go. I'll see you around." I walked over to the fairgrounds and crossed the lot to where the participants were parked. I was hoping to see the Roberts' motorhome, but it wasn't there. I asked a few people I knew if they'd seen Cole — nobody had. Mutt and all the other guys were sitting around a campfire drinking beer when I walked up.

"Hey, Billy. Welcome back from retirement." Mutt tossed a can of beer at me.

"Thanks." I sat down on a fold up chair and opened the pull-tab.

"We heard that you and Tawnie are going to be proud parents."

"We'll see," I mumbled.

They all laughed, probably because they were glad it was my problem and not theirs.

"Have you been training a lot?" Mutt asked.

"Nope. I haven't trained at all."

They all laughed again. Mutt almost snorted beer out his nose. "So, I'm going to need to be on my toes when you get tossed."

"I'd appreciate that, thank you."

He clapped his hands and then rubbed them together. "This is going to be a great event. Both Ryan boys. Both Wiese boys. And every other cowboy with try and rocks for brains. All in one arena with a bunch of rank bulls. I live for this shit."

We all toasted to that.

"Where the hell is your brother?"

I shrugged. "Well, if he doesn't show up by tomorrow, my top three guesses will be murdered, committed suicide, or run off to Mexico with some chick he just met."

They all thought I was joking.

Three beers in, Mutt was in the middle of telling a story when he stopped mid-sentence and said, "Man, this weekend keeps getting better."

I turned to look over my shoulder at what he was already looking at. Tawnie walked up and stood in front of the campfire. "Hey, Billy. Can we go for a walk?"

"I'm kind of busy right now."

She frowned and looked around at each of the guys who were all staring at her. "I thought you wanted to talk."

"That was before I figured out you were lying. Now I couldn't care less."

She tucked her hair behind her ears. "Can we please talk privately?"

"You had your chance to talk privately. You didn't return any of my calls. Now I'm busy. You can say what you need to say in front of these guys."

"I would rather not."

"Admit to them that you lied and I'll talk to you privately."

She looked around again and shifted her weight to her other foot. "I lied, okay? I was never pregnant and the only reason I said it is because I'm jealous that you chose Shae instead of me. Are you satisfied?"

"Yeah." I got up and walked with her to the back of the lot where the horses were penned.

"I'm sorry, Billy. I never should have lied about being pregnant."

"Well, you did and now everything with Shae-Lynn is ruined."

"I'll talk to her and explain everything."

"She's not the problem. She's the most forgiving person on the planet. It's her dad who's never going to let me near her. He thinks I'm a major douche bag who knocked you up and tried to move on to his daughter."

"I'll talk to him and tell him the truth."

"It won't make a difference."

"How did you know it wasn't true?"

"I heard that you were drinking at the bar. I know you would never drink alcohol if you knew you were pregnant."

233

"I'm sorry, Billy. I saw you and Shae together and you both looked so happy. It just blurted out of my mouth. I don't even know why."

I hooked my thumbs in my back pockets and kicked at the fence post. "You really messed me up."

"I'm sorry."

"Sorry isn't good enough. I was ready to step up to the plate to support you. I even started to look forward to the idea of being a dad."

"Oh, Billy, I'm sorry. I know you would have been a good daddy and I honestly would have been happy if I was pregnant with your child. What do I have to do to get you to forgive me?"

"Well, if Shae-Lynn were here she would convince me to forgive you just because it's the decent thing to do, but thanks to you she's not here. I don't think I'll ever be able to forgive you for that."

"You really love her, don't you?"

"Yes."

She laughed in an unimpressed way. "She must be quite something in bed to rope you up the way she has."

"Not that it's any of your business, but we haven't slept together."

She frowned. "Then what makes her so special?"

"The way she makes me feel when I'm with her."

She glared at me, jealous as hell, then turned and walked away.

A gate swung open behind me. Trent was on the other side of the pen. He reached up to toss hay in for his chuck horses. He made eye contact with me before he walked away. I stood by myself with the stock for a while before heading back towards Mutt's camper.

When I rounded the corner by a supply shed, someone called my name. It was difficult to see in the dark, but a guy I didn't recognize was standing behind Tawnie. His left arm was clamped around her neck and his right arm was holding a gun to her temple.

"Billy," she whimpered.

The guy who was holding the gun to her head stepped back into the shadows. Three other thugs were leaning against the wall of the shed. I looked over my shoulder to see if anybody else was around who might be able to help me. "Whatever it is you want, the gun isn't necessary."

"Shut up."

"Let her go."

"No, I think we'll hold on to her until we're finished our business with you."

"I don't know you. I don't have any business with you."

"Oh, but you do." The tallest guy who was standing closest to me grabbed the collar of my shirt and dragged me into the shadows.

I struggled with him, so a second, muscular guy stepped in and they both pinned me to the side of the shed. "What do you want?" I choked out as the tall guy's fingers tightened around my throat.

"Shut up," the tall guy grumbled. "If you make a sound, I'll hurt blondie here in a way that I will thoroughly enjoy."

I glanced at Tawnie. She was shaking.

He grabbed my face and forced me to look at him. "Lyle wants to make sure you understand how the deal is going to work. I'm going to break your finger — not so bad that you can't ride — just bad enough that you can't win. If you drop out of the competition, we'll break every bone in your body and hurt your other girlfriend in a way that I will also enjoy. Understood?" He pushed me to the ground and twisted my right arm behind my back.

I coughed to recover from the chokehold. "When I ride, my brother's debt is completely erased, right?"

"As long as you get out of the chute." He wrapped his hand around my pinkie finger and positioned it, ready to snap it sideways.

"All right. Do what you gotta do, but let her go first," I said.

The guy who had Tawnie shoved her and pointed the gun at her. "Get."

Her eyes locked with mine, so I nodded and she ran.

"He's left-handed, Mike." Blake stepped out from the shadows.

"What the hell, Blake?" I muttered through the pain.

235

"Shut up."

I glared at him. "Can't beat me fair and square?"

"I can. This has nothing to do with me. You screwed Mike out of a spot and he's pissed."

The tall guy, who was apparently Mike, twisted my left arm and pulled my finger sideways. It cracked loudly and the pain shot down the side of my hand. I groaned, then spit out, "Fuck you, Blake."

Blake stomped on my left hand. It made me shout in pain and he laughed. "See you tomorrow." He kicked me in the left shoulder before he walked away. The other guys followed him into the darkness and left me lying in the dirt.

Tawnie showed up with Mutt and all the other guys sprinting behind her. She knelt beside me. "Oh, my God. Are you okay?"

"Who did it?" Mutt asked, ready for a fight. He frowned and looked around. "It was Blake, wasn't it?"

I didn't answer. Tawnie turned my hand to look at the damage. The pinkie was sticking outwards at an unnatural angle.

"We should tip off the cops and take Wiese down," Mutt said.

"We can't. I need to ride tomorrow to get rid of Cole's debt."

"How are you going to ride with a broken riding hand?"

I looked at the ninety-degree angle of my finger. "Just push it back in. It'll be fine."

"I'm not pushing it back in. That's nasty," Mutt said.

"Tawnie. Push it back in for me."

She shook her head, still traumatized. "I can't. It's going to hurt you."

"I'll do it," a guy named Dewey said. He rushed over and without even hesitating, snapped it back into place.

I cursed so loud, the entire participants' area probably heard. "God damn. That hurt." My eyes watered from the pain.

"You should get some ice on it." Tawnie helped me up. "I'll take you back to the hotel."

Lee-Anne was walking back from the pens and paused when

236

she noticed us all crowded together. She glanced back and forth between Tawnie and me.

I stepped forward. "Where's Shae-Lynn?"

"She thought it would be better if she didn't come." She eyeballed Tawnie with a bit of a sneer. "Apparently that was a good decision."

"It's not what it looks like."

"I don't care, Billy Ray. You're free to do whatever you want," she shouted over her shoulder as she walked away.

"Wait." I jogged after her and pulled on her elbow to make her stop. "Tawnie's not pregnant. We're not together."

She crossed her arms and stared me down. "I don't think that changes anything. You're still a chicken shit asshole who ran away when things got serious."

I blinked hard, not sure how I could prove to her that I had changed.

She sighed and her voice softened. "What happened to your hand?"

I shook my head, not wanting to explain, since it only proved that nothing had changed. "Please tell Shae-Lynn that I'd like her to be here tomorrow."

"No." She strutted away.

When I turned around, I almost bumped into Tawnie. I forgot she was even there. "Bye Tawnie," I mumbled. I left her standing there and made my way back to the hotel.

Room service brought me a bucket of ice, but my hand swelled up like a bullfrog's chest. I taped the fingers together and took some painkillers and anti-inflammatories. Unfortunately, it just kept ballooning as the night progressed. I phoned Cole. He didn't answer. Shae-Lynn didn't answer either, so I closed my eyes and tried, unsuccessfully, to sleep.

Chapter 26

The only thing that had changed by the morning was that the swelling in my hand had turned bright red and my left shoulder was so stiff, I could barely put my shirt on. The event wasn't for six hours and without Cole there to pass the time, I got really nervous. I called Shae-Lynn. She didn't answer, so I texted her.

Tawnie was lying. I hired a nurse to take care of my mom. I can transfer to the University of Calgary and get a job here. I'll do whatever it takes to earn your dad's respect. I ain't never going to quit proving how much I love you, no matter how long it takes.

She didn't respond.

When I arrived at the arena, Ron Miller took one look at my hand and shook his head. "You're going to have to withdraw."

"No. I can do it. It's just a little swollen. It doesn't hurt."

"You can't even stretch your glove over that watermelon. You'll get hurt."

"I'm riding even if you have to duct tape me to the bull."

"Don't be an idiot. The reason your dad got tossed the day he was killed was because he tried to ride when he was injured. You know that, right?"

The information sunk in, and although I hadn't known that, it didn't change anything. I shook my head and attempted to curl my fingers around the rope.

"I don't want you riding."

I pushed my hat back and stared out over the arena. I thought about it for a while, then mumbled, "I have to do it."

He put his hands up in surrender. "All right. Your brother's up third and you're sixth."

"Have you seen Cole?"

"No, why? Is he more banged up than you?"

"He's fine." I pulled my hat back down over my eyes. "When's Blake up?"

"Last."

The crowd gathered in the grandstand. I searched the face of every girl. Lee-Anne and Rochelle sat in the first row, but Shae-Lynn wasn't with them. Lyle and a posse of goons stood behind the chutes. He tipped his hat when he noticed me, and grinned as if he was looking forward to repayment of the loan in whichever form it came in.

The first two riders were PBR guys. One was thrown, and the other guy scored a ninety. When the announcer said that Cole was the next rider up, everyone behind the chutes shifted their attention to me. I scanned the arena, hoping to spot Cole. The bull was loaded, and Ron stood on the rail staring at me.

"Where is he?" he shouted.

I shrugged and swallowed down the acid that crept up my throat. Lee-Anne stood and shaded her eyes with her hand looking for him in the participants' field. She made eye contact with me and shook her head to let me know she couldn't see him.

"He has sixty seconds or we're going to turn out," Ron shouted.

I nodded and looked around again. They piped music through the speakers to entertain the crowd while we waited. Images of him dead in a ravine, under a rail bridge, splattered in a shed somewhere, drowned in Dad's truck at the bottom of a lake, and lying on a motel bed with white foam bubbling out of his mouth all flashed through my mind.

Equal parts of panic, grief, rage, and relief swarmed around in my stomach and made me light-headed. Lyle pointed at me and winked. I leaned over and propped my hands on my knees to keep from falling down.

With about two seconds left, the crowd erupted. Cole came running from behind the grandstand with his chaps flapping. He was carrying his rope in one hand and his hat in the other. "Sorry I'm late." He grinned at Ron and pointed at me. "Let's get 'er done."

The tension in my neck and jaw released as I climbed up on the rail and he eased into the chute. I wanted to hug him, but I punched his shoulder instead. "Where the hell have you been?"

"Preparing." I pulled his rope and he noticed my purple hand. "What happened?"

"Nothing." I reached over and slapped his back three times with my right hand.

He jammed his mouthguard in, tucked his chin and then nodded. Ron pulled the flank strap and the bull shot out as if someone fired a cannon. The crowd stood to watch. It was the best bull I'd ever seen. He swapped ends twice, dropped his shoulder, then belly rolled.

"Yeah, baby!" I hollered.

It was a strong bull and when he launched himself off the dirt, he caught major air. When he landed, the ground actually shuddered. Cole rode perfectly and held on for an extra second after the buzzer. He tugged the rope to free his hand and flew about twenty feet in the air as he dismounted. Mutt took a shot to the ass to protect Cole as he ran to safety.

"Yeah, baby! That's how it's done." I high-fived Ron and then ran down to meet Cole where he'd climbed over the fence. I tackled him to the ground and trapped him in a headlock. "Where'd you learn how to ride like that, you son of a bitch? God damn that was good."

He shoved me off and stood up to watch the board for his

240

score. It took a while and when it finally flashed up, the crowd moaned. Cole's jaw dropped. "Ninety-one? That's bullshit." He turned to look at me. "That was better than a ninety-one, right?"

"Yeah." I leaned on the railing and cranked my head towards the judges. The crowd booed. Lee-Anne and Rochelle threw their drink cups at the booth.

The other competitors came over to congratulate Cole and shake his hand. "You were robbed, man. That should have been closer to ninety-five if you ask me."

Blake sauntered up and swatted Cole's back. "Nice effort, buddy." He winked at me. "What happened to your hand, Billy? It looks pretty sore. I hope you can still ride since Cole's ninety-one probably isn't going to be enough to take home the prize money."

"Who cares about the prize money? All I care about is beating you. And since I can ride better than you with my right hand, that ought to be easy," I said.

He laughed, so I stuck up the puffy middle finger of my left hand and flipped him the bird.

"Does your mom know that you're so disrespectful?"

"Your mom doesn't think I'm disrespectful. In fact, she was begging me to give her the finger. Over and over again. She couldn't get enough."

He lunged at me and tried to tackle me to the ground, but I threw him against the fence. "Hey, hey, hey," one of the PBR guys from the States jumped in and held Blake back. "Settle it in the arena." Blake tried to swing at me, but they held him back and pushed him behind the grandstand.

"I need to borrow your bull rope and glove," I said to Cole. Then I leaned over to puke in a garbage can, but I hadn't eaten anything, so I dry heaved.

"You can't ride right-handed."

I stood upright and inhaled to fight the nausea. "Why not? I did it for the first two years."

"You were a kid."

241

"I don't need a score. I just need to get out of the chute."

"Why?"

"They're going to erase your debt if I do."

"Why would they do that?"

"I don't know. They must have the betting rigged. They said I just need to ride."

"You believed them?"

I glanced at Lyle and his lynch men. "Why not?"

"Even if they did say that, they're not exactly men of their word. Blake probably only told you that so you would enter and he could beat you. He can't get them to erase the debt."

I bent over and dry heaved into the garbage can again. After I stood, I said, "All right, then I guess I'll have to win."

Cole looked down at my left hand, but didn't say anything. We watched the fourth rider score an eighty-seven. The fifth guy got tossed. As my turn approached, I loaded a tobacco sized wad of bubble gum into my cheek and scanned the massive audience searching for Shae-Lynn. When I couldn't find her, I glanced at the exit and considered making a run for it. As they loaded the bull, I had to hold the rail so my chicken shit legs wouldn't get a mind of their own. The bull I drew was a young one named Tommy that had a reputation of never doing the same thing twice. Watching them load him into the chute made me panic more.

Cole grabbed my arm. "You don't need to do this. I got myself into this mess. I'll live with the consequences."

I exhaled and slid Shae-Lynn's pink armband over my forearm. I kissed it and then said a prayer before climbing into the chute. "This isn't about you anymore. I got something to prove."

Cole climbed up and let me get set. "You sure you want to do this?"

"Yeah, I'm tired of being a pussy."

"That a boy." He pulled his rope for me.

I adjusted my legs and exhaled to make my heart slow down. Tommy lurched in the chute and threw me forward. By the time they got him standing straight again, my arm was shaking so bad I couldn't control it. "Wait. I can't do it."

"Yes, you can."

"No. I changed my mind."

"Shae's going to hook up with Blake if he beats you." He slapped my back three times.

"Fuck that."

I nodded and the gate swung open.

All I could see at first was a hairy mound of flesh jerking around and the dirt spinning beneath us. The cowbell clanked and it seemed like the crowd had disappeared. It was just the bull and me. He ducked off and double-kicked before I got my rhythm. All of the muscles in my right arm strained to the point of tearing with each jolt. The chesty breath of the bull increased in intensity as he grunted and snorted with the effort of trying to kill me. He spun, stopped abruptly, and dropped his shoulder. My head shot forward and it felt like my brain collided with the inside of my skull before rebounding back and wrenching the muscles in my neck. Glittery stars floated around in my double vision for a second, then my arm went tingly. I blinked and sensed Tommy's back end above my head. I leaned back and spurred him a couple times. Then the buzzer went.

My hand was stuck. I tried to loosen the rope with my left hand, but my puffy fingers were useless. The bull bucked and threw me over his shoulders. His front hooves trampled my leg and he stumbled a little, which gave Dewey a chance to stand in his sight to distract him. Mutt jumped on the bull's back and released my hand. I fell to the ground and the bull stomped my thigh with his back hoof before he strutted to the exit gate.

"You're my bitch," I mumbled as I flopped back on the dirt and admired the way the clouds were streaked across the sky.

Mutt stood over me. "You okay?"

"Yeah. I just can't move."

"That's not okay."

243

"What's my score?"

He turned his head and watched the board. "Ninety." He nodded his approval. "Not bad for someone who was using his wrong hand and hasn't been on a bull in like a year."

"Not good enough to win, though."

"Depends on your definition of winning. Are you going to lie there all night?"

I rolled over and rested on all fours until I was able to muster the strength to stand. Mutt held my left armpit and Dewey held my right. They escorted me to a gate because I couldn't climb the fence.

Cole ran over and met me. "Are you hurt?"

"No. I just forgot how hard it is." I sat down on a platform because my leg muscles were too exhausted to carry my weight. I drank one bottle of water and dumped a second one over my head. "Do you feel sorry for me?"

"No. You did good."

"That's not what I mean. Did you pretend you needed my help so I would have an excuse to keep touring on the circuit even though I quit?"

He glanced at me and tipped his hat back before leaning his elbows on the rail. "I don't feel sorry for you, Billy, but I wasn't going to let you run away because you got spooked."

"So, you're not as useless as you act?"

He laughed. "I didn't say that, but I can take care of my own shit."

I smiled and watched as they loaded the next bull. Tyson rode eighth. He got tossed. The ninth rider scored an eighty-five. Blake was the tenth and final rider. He drew a good bull that had scored high in its other outs. I looked up at the judges' booth again. Lyle and his crew of misfits had moved and were standing near the exit to the grandstand.

"Blake's lucky he drew a good bull. Do you think he can beat ninety-one?" Cole asked.

"If his dad bribed or threatened the judges, your only chance of winning might be if he gets a no score." I leaned forward and rested my elbows on my knees as Blake loaded into the chute.

Cole paced around without taking his eyes off the ring. "If his dad was in the business of fixing the judging, Blake would have won more buckles in his career."

"What's the plan if he beats you?"

"Run," he mumbled, made eye contact with Lyle, and started pacing again.

"Where were you?" I asked.

He glanced over his shoulder, but kept pacing. "Who cares?"

"I was just wondering. Mom thought you were dead."

"I told you. I was preparing."

"How?"

"I went to visit Grandpa. He trained me for a couple days. I also interviewed for a job with a friend of his from the oil company while I was there. I start next week."

"That's great. Why didn't you just tell me where you were going?"

He shrugged. "I visited Dad's gravesite too. It was something I needed to do by myself."

Completely understanding and so proud of him, I nodded. Lee-Anne whistled to catch my attention. She tilted her head up and to the side so I would see who was sitting in the top row of the grandstand all by herself. She was wearing a white dress and her strawberry coloured hair was glowing in the sun ray. The gate opened and Blake's bull bucked out. Without breaking eye contact with Shae-Lynn, I held my breath and counted off each second. "Eight," I said. Then the buzzer went.

"Shit," Cole said. "That was a great ride."

The crowd got to its feet and I lost view of Shae-Lynn. I climbed the fence, but couldn't spot her in the sea of heads.

"What's his score?" Cole shouted. "I can't look."

I spun around to check the scoreboard. The crowd fell silent waiting for the numbers to light up. When they did, I blinked to make sure I was seeing them right. "Holy shit." I threw my hands in the air. "God damn it. Eighty-nine. Yeah, baby! You won!"

Cole dropped to his knees and tilted his head back as if he was thanking God. He grinned and pumped his fists. "Yes. A hundred thousand dollars."

"Actually, it's three hundred thousand dollars." I smiled at him.

"What do you mean?"

"I put ten thousand on you to win and the odds were twenty to one."

"You bet on me to win?"

"Yup."

He sprung to his feet. "You're crazy."

"Well, sometimes that pays."

"Idiot! Why would you bet on me to win?"

"'Cause I knew you could do it." I hopped down from the fence, ran over, and gave him a hug.

He squeezed back so tightly I couldn't breathe. After a while he choked up and said, "I wish he could have been here."

"He's here. He's watching over us and he's proud of you."

"I miss him."

"I know, man." I slapped his back three times. "I do too."

Cole's hands clenched the material of my Kevlar vest for another second before he stepped back. He wiped his eyes with the back of his sleeve. Then he turned to the crowd and let out a loud, long, "Yahoo!"

Tyson and all the other guys, except Blake, swarmed us. They lifted Cole onto their shoulders. He waved his hat at the crowd and pointed at me. I smiled and tipped my hat. He'd never looked happier. That's what Shae-Lynn was talking about when she said it made her happier to see the people she cared about happy than to get what she wanted. I climbed over the railing onto the grandstand and wove through the spectators making my way up to the back row. The crowd thinned as I neared the top. I searched for strawberry hair.

She wasn't there.

I leaned over the back to see if she was already out on the grass. "Shae-Lynn!"

"Shae," her voice said behind me.

I spun around. The crowd parted. She was five rows down, leaning her back against the side railing.

"Sorry. Shae."

Her cherry glossed lips stretched into a grin. "Aw, you're not going to give up now, are you? I secretly like that you're the only person on the planet who calls me Shae-Lynn."

I smiled and pushed my hat back. "I'll never give up on anything that has to do with you unless you ask me to."

"Good to know."

"Did you get my text about moving here?"

"Yes, but that won't be necessary."

"I want to."

She shook her head. "No. I mean, it won't be necessary because I was offered a music scholarship to the University of Saskatchewan and I'm going to accept it."

"What? You're moving to Saskatoon?" I couldn't contain my excitement.

"Is that all right?" she joked.

"Yes." I scrambled down the five rows to get to her. She squealed as I eased my good hand across the small of her back, circled her waist to lift her, and swung her around. Her arms tightened around my shoulders and her cheek rested against mine, giving me that peaceful feeling. When I finally put her down, I slid my hands up to cradle her face and leaned forward to rest my forehead on hers. "You do realize that being with me makes you hick."

"What can I say? You do it for me. You always have." She tugged at my belt buckle to pull my hips closer. "If that makes me hick, then I guess I'm pretty much as hick as it gets." She winked and touched her lips to mine with an easiness that shot more adrenaline through my blood than riding bulls ever did. It was the best

247

kiss of my life.

"Yeah, baby!" Cole shouted at us from the fence.

He made both of us laugh, but we didn't break the kiss. I held my right arm in the air and gave Cole a thumbs up, then swept Shae-Lynn off her feet to a chorus of cheers from everybody else who'd been watching us.

Acknowledgements

I would like to thank my parents, whose steadfast faith in my ability has always instilled the belief in me that I could achieve whatever I set my mind to; my brother and sister for having my back my entire life; and my husband Sean for his patience and unconditional love.

Thank you to Rasadi, Kamaljit, and my critique partner Denise Jaden who were kind enough to read the early drafts of *Rank*.

Thanks to Scotty, who spooked when I didn't have the reins, and left me no choice but to cowgirl up when I was only five.

A very special thanks to Charlotte Ledger for falling in love with *Rank*, and to everyone behind the scenes at HarperImpulse – Harper Fiction and HarperCollins Publishers.

Finally, thanks to the readers.